ODO'S HANGING

ALMA BOOKS LTD
London House
243–253 Lower Mortlake Road
Richmond
Surrey TW9 2LL
United Kingdom
www.almabooks.com

First published by Hodder and Stoughton in 1993
This edition published by Alma Books Limited in 2012
Copyright © Peter Benson, 1993, 2012

Peter Benson asserts his moral right to be identified as the author of
this work in accordance with the Copyright, Designs and Patents Act
1988
Printed in Great Britain

Typeset by Tetragon

ISBN: 978-1-84688-194-7

ODO'S HANGING

PETER BENSON

ALMA BOOKS

Them hath he filled with wisdom of heart, to work all manner of work, of the engraver, and of the cunning workman, and of the embroiderer, in blue, and in purple, in scarlet, and in fine linen, and of the weaver, even of them that do any work, and of those that devise cunning work.

Exodus 35:35

1

There is no one like Turold. I have seen him in every way. I have seen him drunk, lurching from the workshop to the cloisters, past the long entry to the gates, and he has howled at the moon from the watchtower. I have never been more frightened than at that sound. It cuts, shreds, melts and pierces, for he is in pain, the pain of art. He is a bigger man than any I have seen, his beard is longer and thicker, his eyes are set back in his head, deep and brown, like they've been pushed back by thumbs. His lips are pink and his cheeks are red. Hair covers his forehead, his forehead is creased and high, there is a scar that runs from his temple to the bridge of his nose.

I have seen Turold asleep. He sleeps only four hours a night. He lies on his back with his mouth open, and as he breathes out, his lips flutter. His tongue rests in his cheek, he is thinking, removing scenes from the day and replacing them with new. More colour, more movement, more men, ships and horses. His beard lies like a pet on his chest, his eyes are still, moonlight does not disturb him.

I have seen Turold work. I am his mixer, fetcher, carrier, messenger and watchman. I sleep under planks behind the workshop. He is the greatest designer. I am proud to be his boy. Clergy pay silver for his cloaks, stoles and maniples, knights pay gold for embroidered cloaks and banners, and murals for their halls, Bishop Odo pays gold and favour for the best work. I have seen this fat man dressed in the finest chasuble Turold designed, embroidered by the most cunning nuns; as he moved to his altar, God's glory radiated from the Bishop and through the vestments, so the abbey filled with light and the song of colour.

Art.

Sleep.

Design.

Turold thinks deeply about his work, then, when he is at his table, he sketches quickly. I have learnt that at this time, it is my job to be still and keep others quiet. I was never told to do this, I worked it out for myself. I am Turold's perfect shadow. I know what it must be to have his mind.

I cannot speak, I do not know who my parents were, I am too small, my hair is black. When I was four, the monks took me in and I worked as their boy. I fetched and carried, I skulked in corridors outside their cells, and I hid in the abbey roof to watch their prayers. They prayed towards me but did not know I was there; I listened to everything they said. They thought I was a stupid boy, they never knew that dumbness breeds the ideas speech deafens.

When I was seven, I had only grown an inch, I was treated as I had been three years before, I was not allowed to grow. I was bored, I was not allowed to learn things other children were taught. I was fed and given a bed in the corner of the kitchen, a warmer place than any in the house, but that was my only comfort. I could do more than carry a bucket, so when I was eight and passed to Turold, I felt like a pigeon, released from hands. Now I am fourteen, and his education meets theirs in confusion. He is not the believer he could be, and not always likely to hold his tongue in his head.

I have seen Turold eat, three times a day for six years. No man puts so much in his mouth at once, and no man makes so much noise as he chews. He talks with his mouth full, and drinks before swallowing his food. His beard dribbles, his lips shine, and his eyes come out of their deep holes, like snails poking out. His tongue is fat, his cheeks are round, his nose is the size of a small pie and the colour of blood.

I have seen Turold fight. His fists are the size of horses' hoofs, hard as stone and quick. Only strangers bother him, only men who hope to prove their strength or show their courage. If courage means stupidity, these men are brave, but how can they be so stupid? Life goes in circles, the monks taught me this, and Turold has painted it and drawn it on linen. He has stitched, he has proved it; from heaven to hell and back again, from life to death and into new life, from the clouds to the rivers to the sea, from the flight of a single pigeon over the towers and cloisters, and in the four seasons.

Thinks.

Eats.

Fights.

I have heard Turold argue. The monks wanted to increase the rent. I followed him to Rainald. I can stand behind him and not be seen. I think he does not know I am beside him any more, though he would notice if I was not; I was there when he met the monk.

'You take,' he said, 'but what do you give?'

'Succour,' said the monk, 'through and in Christ.' He sat low in his chair, as if the world was on his head. He stretched his hands, weakly, and muttered, ' "For in that He Himself hath suffered being tempted, He is able to succour them that are tempted." '

'I enjoy temptation.'

The monk smiled, as if he had seen and done everything in the world. 'We are old friends.'

'And that gives you the right to rob me?'

'Please. We are robbing no one. We raise sufficient for our needs, that is all. More brothers join us all the time, each day it becomes harder to keep the house.'

'The house should keep itself!'

'Turold.' Rainald leant towards him. 'I think you have the best workshop you could wish for, and you could not find cheaper.'

'I could.'

'But quieter? Cloistered?'

Turold shrugged. He picked at dried paint on his hands.

Rainald spread his hands. 'Forgive me,' he said, 'but the case is out of my hands. Your workshop could be let ten times over at double the price; you must believe when I say that you are as honoured as we are honoured to have you working under our roof. But as we favour you, so must you, in return.'

'I thought forgiveness could only come from God, but you ask me to forgive you? Please,' said Turold, 'do not place such a burden upon me. My shoulders are not so wide.'

'There is temporal forgiveness as there is divine. I do not need to remind you of that.'

'You,' said Turold, 'should have been at court. Your answers could please anyone.'

'I am,' said the monk, 'of another's court.'

Turold slapped his forehead. 'Of course,' he said, 'what are religion and politics if not unsubtle...'

Rainald held his finger to his lips. 'And what is Turold if not so unsubtle himself?' He shook his head, and took on a grave, worried face. 'One day your mouth will lead you into trouble.'

Turold could not argue with this. He has a river of good in his heart, the only thing that floods his anger when the anger should not be shown, but the good is only drawn out by the patient. Rainald is a patient man, as devoted as a saint, as willing to help as a dog, as gentle as a pigeon.

Pigeons are my friends. I keep three pairs in a box in the orchard, fancy birds will bill and coo. I scrounge corn from the mill, and keep this dry in a sack hung from the wall.

Pigeons are the sweetest things. They trust me completely, though it is not in their nature. I have thought dangerous thoughts about them and me, imagining that I am their God and they are my flock. I can pick one up and hold it to my chest, stroke its head, slip two fingers around its neck and kill it. I have this power, but I do not use it. I love my birds, even when they fail to return. Or they might return but refuse to come down from perches on the abbey, from where they can look down and gloat. Then, of course, they think they have free will, but they are never out of my reach. I have the bag of corn and I have a sling-shot, and I can use it.

Rainald said, 'I think, however, that you will not need to worry about your rent for much longer.'

'Why not?'

'That is not for me to say. My lips are sealed, by order.'

'Temporal or divine?'

The monk looked away. 'Temporal.'

'Odo?'

'Bishop Odo's willingness to show favour is the least of his virtues.'

'He has never shown me favour.'

'Maybe, maybe not, but he is about to. Your prayers are to be answered.'

'Meaning?'

Rainald put a finger to his lips.

'You cannot know what my prayers are.'

'I hope that you say them, but I would not presume to know them.'

'Of course,' said Turold, 'not.'

Turold rose from boy to the painter Master Bertin of Rouen to this place; now Bishop Odo will send men on horseback to bring him to his hall. I followed, and was allowed to be present in the glamour of that hour.

Odo, the warrior Bishop of Bayeux, son of Herluin of Conteville and Herleve the tanner's daughter, brother of Robert, Count of Mortain, half-brother of William, Duke of Normandy and King of England, is a great and powerful man. Ordained bishop at nineteen, father of a dozen bastards, at Hastings he rallied the young men in their panic, in meditation he holds the attention of martyrs. Chastiser of Northumberland, his preaching is famous for its brevity, his politics are tactless. As William's vice-regent and Earl of Kent, he owns four hundred and thirty-nine English manors. As patron, he is respected for his work in the cathedral school of Bayeux, and loved for his indulgence of the many scholars he has sent to

Liège and Rennes. His cathedral is decorated with the finest ornaments, his hall is richly decorated. Shields and banners, flags of command, gonfalons, murals and hangings cover the walls, the furniture is carved, his salt is fashioned from walrus ivory. At our visit, tables were laid for a feast, the smell of food filled the place. I kept close to Turold, who was seated beside the Bishop.

The Bishop also inspires fear in men. This fear has no limits. People do not relax around him, no one laughs unless he laughs first, no one eats before him, no one argues with him. Two great men must recognise each other's greatness, only then can they be like brothers; Odo considers Turold's work the finest in the world, Turold is pleased to have the ear of a man who knows what he wants and pays for it.

Gold.

Silver.

Women.

'A question,' said Bishop Odo. 'What does my hall lack?'

The company was quiet. No one wished to give the wrong answer, for Odo's displeasure could echo through the rest of their lives. Paths could be blocked, positions denied, a future blighted. Only Turold spoke, in a whisper, in the Bishop's ear.

Others leant towards the two men, but no one heard what was said. Some resented Turold's presence. He was an indulgence, the producer of useless goods. Real men fight in battle, Turold did not. Real men work land, Turold did not, real men keep the company of women for one reason, Turold did not. Real men draw the fear of arms in their wake, Turold only fought with his fists. If Odo had a weakness, it was for useless goods. He stood up, banged the table and spoke.

The following morning, Turold found Rainald in contemplation in the vegetable gardens. The monk did not need to look up to know who it was that disturbed his peace. 'Bishop Odo has provided you with an answer?'

'You know what he wants?'

'Yes.' The monk's voice was full of resignation, for he too had been summoned by Odo. 'You are to design his hanging, and I am to intercede between you and the nuns of Nunnaminster.'

'That,' said Turold, 'I do not understand.'

'And that,' said Rainald, 'is why I accompany you.' He folded his hands together and looked straight at his friend. His pale blue eyes were as soft as pools of rain water that lie on marshy ground, edged with fine hairs, big and wide and open. 'You are required to act with a greater care than you have ever done. The Bishop's order is the most important; you must treat it and behave with honour and reverence. Your work will be seen by William, your interpretation must strike a fine balance. Offence is not cheap, Turold.'

'Do not lecture me on the value of offence. I have offended...'

'But never the Duke of Normandy. King of England...'

'Never the Duke.'

'Then take care.'

'I am sure,' said Turold, 'that you will advise me if I do not.'

'I will advise against the thought and kill the deed.'

'How many times have you said that?'

'I have never meant it more,' said the monk. 'Yesterday's command is today's labour and tomorrow's pride.'

'And you preach against pride.'

'The pride of man is not of the Father. His pride is holy.'

'Bishop Odo's work is no more holy than his gonfalon.'

'His gonfalon is blessed by the Pope and sanctioned by William. However close you feel to him, never forget that you are as easily crushed as the English. You have been to England?'

'You know I have.'

'And has Canterbury forgotten you?'

'I don't know.'

'Winchester is not Canterbury, Turold.'

'If I have workshops, any place is the same as the next.'

'The great man speaks...'

'He speaks, he works; mostly, he works.'

'Do it well.'

'Well is the only way I know.'

'Well would be better if married to humility.'

'In whose eyes, Rainald? Yours? Odo's? William's?'

'Only in God's eyes, Turold. Only his are large enough to see you properly.'

'I am honoured?'

'Honour is a temporal thing. God is all powerful, all forgiving. He has no need of honour. Honour requires the threat of deceit in both parties. God is incapable of deceit.'

'As I am.'

'Be careful. All men are capable of deceit, as most men are born of it.'

'Rainald,' said Turold, 'sometimes I believe you have rejected your fellow men.'

The monk stretched his arms as if addressing a congregation, and said, 'God's world is my world, and His creatures reflect His love. I reject nothing that comes from Him, nothing that He has created. Only we create misery, it comes from free will.'

'God did not create misery?'

'It is how we use his gifts that gives us grace.'

'And sometimes,' said Turold, turning to walk away, 'I think you have confused the message.'

'And you have not?'

'Arts are the message and the reply,' said Turold.

'Earthly pleasures are...'

'Earthly! Temporal!' Turold took my sleeve and pulled me away. 'Give me strength!' he shouted; we left the vegetable gardens, passed through the cloisters to the workshop, and while I ran to fetch food from the refectory, Turold cleared his tables and sat down to work.

All work, the monks teach, should be for, in and of the glory of God. Men must struggle to live in Christ, and reflect their love for Him in their work. Thus arts are given breath. And thus I am taught, though not by Turold. He will listen patiently to his masters, but betray them in my company. He is a blasphemous man; only I am privy to his blasphemy. Because I cannot speak, he will forget that I can hear, or maybe he thinks I cannot tell, or maybe he forgets that I am there. That is most likely, for when he is working, he is not aware of anything but his arts, as while the monks labour in their gardens, they meditate on the Lord, His works and their reflection of Him.

2

Turold, Rainald and I sailed for England in April. They had sailed before, but I had never, and was sick. The swell lifted the ship slowly, up and down and sideways in long, evil heaves. First I was high and the ocean was below, then we were low and waves were curling above. Then we were level and the water met the sky at a misty horizon, gulls wheeled and cried over us. Their voices were like distant human screams, though they were close. I felt that I was inside an invisible ball, I clung to the side as if I was bolted there, and nothing could move me.

Beneath us, the deep swam with horrors. I concentrated my faith in the captain, who said that he had made the crossing hundreds of times, and would not get lost. He could find the way by considering the time of day and the position of the sun; even under cloud and rain he could see it, as if his eyes could pierce gloom and see wind.

Turold and Rainald engaged in conversation and argument. At that time they considered the fear of God. Turold believed that this fear was a terror to believers, Rainald rubbed his head, creased his brow and said that this was not true. 'The fear of God is shown in reverence,' he said. ' "The fear of the Lord, that is wisdom; and to depart from evil is understanding." I think if Job, though afflicted as no man has ever been, could utter these words, they must hold more truth than even you could dispute.'

'Affliction is a signpost on the road to truth?'

'I could not have said it better.'

'Out of the mouth of babes?'

'You quote David, I quote Moses.' Rainald smiled, satisfied. He has front teeth, and dimples in his cheeks. 'We are closer than either of us thinks.'

'To England or the Lord?' Turold looked out across the water.

'Both,' said the monk, 'and each other, I believe.'

I was allowed to carry my pigeons abroad, in a basket loaded with Turold's packs and Rainald's chest, lashed to the bottom of the boat with rope and sailor's knots. The cunning arts are endlessly different, and everywhere. The knots were quickly tied and fast, for as we rode the swells, and the basket threatened to slide across the deck, the ropes held, the pigeons cooed.

The knots could have been an art of their own; as carvers make rope from stone or wood, or illuminators twirl paint and ink into their knots, so here knots were doing what knots have to do. They have to hold fast, they do not have to prove a designer's skill or please another's eye. I would rather be lost at sea with a sailor than a designer, and when we were saved, he could tie his knots uselessly, and then they could be art.

Even if I could talk I would not say this to Turold. The sea began to anger him. He said it was impossible to think while being tossed. He could not concentrate on the thread of his argument, and he was not allowed to drink. The captain, following William's order, forbade cider and wine aboard; a man so skilled in navigation showed more interest in my pigeons than he did in Turold's work or the reason for our journey. Turold is not an arrogant man, but he can brood if people are not talking about him. I took a hen from the basket and showed the captain how to hold her. He gave the tiller to a crewman and said, 'How old is she?'

I held up eight fingers.

'Eight years?'

I smiled and shook my head.

'Eight months?'

I nodded.

'And they can return to their home from many miles away, as if they read the heavens?'

They do read the heavens.

'And you don't need to teach them to do this?'

I shook my head.

He held the bird to his mouth and said, 'You and I are cousins.' The hen blinked, he puckered his lips and kissed her lightly on the top of the head. His hands were huge and cut and grazed; the bird turned to look at me and her tail went up. He could have crushed her and not noticed, but when she struggled for a moment, his fingers were prised apart as if they had no strength, and she escaped his hold.

Freedom for this bird came as a surprise, the expanse of water that stretched below and beyond her, even more. She flew up, twisted away from the sail and then dropped towards the swell like a stone, tipping back and splaying her feet as she fell. Her wings were paralysed by shock, I ran to the side, the captain cried, 'She's away!' and 'I'm sorry,' I clicked my fingers, she looked towards me, I saw a look of horror on her face, we dipped in the water so I lost sight of her behind a wave. When I saw her again, her eyes were wide, I clicked again, she thrust her head forward and beat her wings furiously, twisting her body this way and that, fighting for height. Turold and Rainald joined me at the side; 'Back!' yelled the captain. 'Unless you want to swim!'

Turold was first back, then Rainald, who laid a hand on my shoulder before returning to his bench. The heat of his touch burned through my clothes to my skin, and when I turned to look at him, I saw my bird reflected in his eyes. Not a reflection of the bird over the sea, but of the bird sitting on its perch, waiting for me to feed.

The pigeon climbed into the sky, but she was confused and frightened by the ship. She saw it as a giant bird below her, flying with one wing across a solid sky, as a pair of gulls began to swoop and caw at her; she tumbled, as is her nature, and lost them.

Gulls are not the wisest of God's creatures. Their stomachs are closer to their heads than any other bird's; before they had a chance to approach the pigeon again, she found the confidence to approach the mast-head and alight there, balancing perfectly, as she could do on the abbey tower, as if to goad me. Ropes snapped against the mast below her, a pennant flew behind and the sail flapped at its top corner; I clicked my fingers again and then whistled, a high, long note I can hold.

I have wondered what my voice would sound like, and the more I wonder the more I think that I could speak as perfectly as Rainald, who knows beautiful words. Turold can use these words too, and the crudest. These he will deliver in the hope that they will shock, but from his lips they are expected.

She looked down at me, lowered her head and cooed back. I raised the note of my whistle so she could not resist, and with a hop, she jumped from the mast-head and dropped into my hands.

'The magic of it,' said the captain. 'She goes to the boy as if obeying his command.'

Of course she is.

'She is,' said Turold, smiling at me. She is my pet, I am his, he is Rainald's, Rainald is Bishop Odo's, Bishop Odo's is William's, William is God's. We are all God's, and though we are all the same in His eyes, we are not, and never will be, the same in each other's. We are the same in the eyes of a pigeon, so could a pigeon be God? This is blasphemy, but a luxury of dumbness is that idle thoughts are never given voice. Idle thoughts kill the men violence doesn't; the dumb live longer than any other.

England was, in that spring, blazed with flowers, high tree-covered downlands and the deepest forests. I recognised home in some of its places, though when we stood on the shore, and the sun dipped to our right, and I recalled the sun dipping to our left at home, I was bewildered.

Here along the way, the pigeons were anxious, flapping in their basket and bubbling. The tracks were well marked, and a week of warm weather had dried the ruts. Our carts and horses threw up dust, at our passage English people waited in forlorn groups on the verge, doing nothing, waiting for no one. Their faces had shown terror, then submission, now abjection, accepted now and expected to come. We were their masters though we did not stop to prove it; they had faith in us, proof was not needed.

On the way, we cracked a wheel, the carter refused to go further until it was repaired, and we would not leave our packs. We were in a valley, trees covered the sides of the hills that pressed down on all sides, and towered over the track so it appeared to be a tunnel. The daylight broke through the leaves and branches and settled on the ground like water; the horses were allowed to graze, the broken wheel was taken from its shaft, and laid on hard ground while the carter unpacked his tools.

I settled my pigeons then wandered through the trees, treading quietly, looking for birds. Here and there, wrens and tits flew away from me, and at one place, rooks were building their nests in the highest branches of ash trees. They called at my approach, then, when I was past them, returned to work.

A hanging Turold designed for the abbey church of St Pierre sur Dives, which hangs there now, shows Adam and Eve in the garden of Eden. They are standing beneath the tree of life, a single fruit is hanging from a branch, and a serpent is entwined about its trunk. The art makes the serpent appear one with the tree; its skin blends with the bark as if it were part of its growth, and its head appears as if twin to the fruit. Turold is saying something through his work, something more than

15

the story tells us, but only he and Rainald know exactly was this is. They argued about its meaning; they disturbed my pigeons and my pigeons disturbed me. 'I think,' Turold shouted, angrily, 'that if you believe I have made the serpent's head to resemble the fruit because I want to mean something...' he stopped here, and took a deep breath, then said, 'Think what you want! I painted a pear, I painted a serpent's head. Can I help it if they look alike?'

'And you call the fruit of the tree of life a pear! The Scriptures say nothing of pears!'

'The Scriptures say that Adam and Eve were naked before the fall, but I was required to clothe them!'

'You know the reason.'

'Flesh was created by God...'

'And lust by the Devil. We have argued this. There is no point disturbing old ground.'

'Unless it is fallow.'

'The best crops are grown on land that has lain fallow; there is a lesson in that.'

'A lesson or one of your sermons?'

Rainald laughed. 'You cannot,' he said, 'hurt me with your barbs.'

'My barbs are not for you,' said Turold. I imagined him patting the monk on the shoulder. I imagined Rainald smiling. 'They are for Philistines.'

'"For all the wells..."' said Rainald, ' "...the Philistines had stopped them..." '

'Exactly.'

The trees of England were more like Turold's tree of life than any tree in Normandy. I know this was not true, but as I stood beneath them and watched for birds in branches and holes, and the carter banged a peg into the split wheel, the trunks around me swirled and twisted with unnatural colour, and the leaves rustled with music. Strange, unholy music, enticing me and promising. Of course it did not, of course the English forests were no more dangerous than others. God protects forests as he protects man and beast. The carter's banging echoed through the trees, I saw a flash of colour as Turold stood and looked towards me. He called, 'Robert! We're away!' The wheel was hauled upright and trundled to its axle.

The rooks called again as I walked beneath them, one dropped from its perch as if to attack me, but alighted instead on a branch that overhung the track, and he watched us make our way up a hill and around bends on the way to Winchester.

3

Turold, Rainald and I lodged in rooms attached to a bakery. An alley passed our door; this led in a curve to a door set in a high wall. This door opened on to the precinct yard and buildings of the nunnery. Here, in a long, well-lit workshop, Turold was offered tables, trestles, pens, parchment and assistance. Here, in a high, freezing room, furnished with two chairs and a table, we met the Abbess Ermenburga, the stick-faced queen of Nunnaminster.

Turold sat in one of the chairs, Ermenburga sat in the other, with the table protecting her from the man. I stood behind him, so my head was level with his, and the only visible part of me.

'I would prefer to talk alone,' she said, the first thing she said. She had not welcomed us, or offered refreshment.

'You may,' said Turold.

'Please leave us,' she said to me, without looking at me. Her eyes were grey and fierce, her nose was long and straight, like an arrow's head, her body was thin.

'The boy stays,' said Turold. 'He cannot speak.'

Ermenburga looked at me. Her eyes narrowed, as if she was trying to spot dumbness in my face. She took a deep breath and clasped her hands in front of her. 'Your lodgings are comfortable?'

'They are, yes.'

'And the workshops? We have provided you with all you require?'

'You have, thank you.' Turold, polite as a fish on a line, and I am thinking — only men fish. They stick their rods out and wait for something to nibble their line. The fish's lips nudge, the fish's lips can smell, the fish's mouth has two sets of lips. They open and close and suck; the fisherman feels the bite, holds his rod upright and pulls his line in.

Before the interview, Rainald had reminded him that the nuns would resent his presence. Their embroidery was the finest in the world. Their designs did not lack cunning or imagination, the Norman's story of the events of the spring of 1064 to Christmas 1066 would be, could be, disrespectful to the English. The nuns had suffered rape, hunger, firing and the removal of their treasures, but nothing had dented their faith or reputation. Turold's presence could do more harm to them than an army; to be lorded over by a Norman designer was an insult, but there was little they could do. Compliance would, Ermenburga had been assured, result in the elevation of the nunnery to a position of importance previous abbesses had only dreamt of. Turold had Bishop Odo's ear, Bishop Odo — whose papal ambitions were as much common knowledge as his whoring — had his hands on many purse-strings.

'I am sorry,' she said, 'but I am sure your own workshops must be finely appointed. Your reputation preceded you, of course, so we made every effort to obtain the materials you required.'

'Please,' said Turold. 'Our lodgings are more comfortable than anything at home, the workshops are larger, lighter, altogether more suited to design.' He turned and put his hand on my shoulder. 'We will be very happy.'

Ermenburga narrowed her eyes again, turned away and slipped her hands into her sleeves. Men were God's creatures, but easier prey for devils than any woman. They were rarely allowed in the precincts, they were a disruption even when they did not try to be. 'I hope you will be,' she said.

'I know we will be,' said Turold, in his deepest voice.

Ermenburga held his stare for a moment, then she stood and the interview was over. Turold stood, walked towards the door, then he stopped and wiped his hands on his coat. It was freezing in that room, but I was not cold, and when I looked at Turold, there were beads of sweat on his forehead. They were dripping down his face and into his beard; 'Well...' he said, and with a soft boot he pushed me out, following slowly, then quickly, down the stairs to the yard.

In ways, Winchester reminded me of Bayeux, from the market to the merchants, from the abbey and clergy to the green fields and woods that surround both towns. From the busy streets to crowded houses, across the water meadows to the King's forest and back again, along the alley to our lodgings. I followed this way with Turold, as he began to prepare and sketch scenes for his work. Bishop Odo had given instructions about size and shape, and had suggested incidents, for which Turold was publicly grateful but which he resented privately. The patron could approve the work, the patron could reject the designer's sketches and employ another, but Turold would not dare to suggest to Odo that his sermons lacked bite, or his singing was flat. Do not make the mistakes children make. We are men at our work, and do not need advice. I know Turold's methods better than I know myself. Was I abandoned when I was three, four or five? Did my mother look back after she left me at the gate, or did she walk quickly away, dragging my brothers and sisters with her? Who was my father? Was he a bastard, is he dead, was it not my mother's fault? Why did Turold take me to help him, will I ever talk? I have a tongue, I can whistle, I can cough and splutter and form sentences in my head. I know the Litanies, the Psalms, Scenes from The Life; if I wasn't abandoned — as the monks told me — was I lost? Is my mother looking for me now, would Turold be accused of stealing me? I would not accuse him of anything, I would not leave him for anything.

Rainald spoke with Ermenburga. United in God, they prayed before they talked; he quickly, she long and hard, both kneeling, but apart. 'She,' he told Turold later, 'will cause you more trouble than you think. She lives in Christ but cannot rid herself of human failings.'

Turold laughed. 'And you have?'

'No one does, no one can. We are born to overcome vice, it is our duty to apply our minds to this task, in order that our spirits might draw closer to God; some are born with more resolve than others, but resolve cannot be learnt, however hard the suppliant tries. Abbess Ermenburga is abbess for more practical reasons than spiritual. Her abilities are envied by the abbesses of lesser houses. Do not underestimate her...'

'What abilities?'

'Please,' said the monk, 'if you do not know, simply imagine. Ermenburga is not the model of piety she would have us believe.'

'Show me a model of piety and I'll show you a liar.'

Rainald coughed, and did not take his eyes off his friend. 'Show me a designer who does as he speaks.'

'A designer,' said Turold, 'only has to do. Talk obscures his message.'

'And your message is?'

Turold scratched his head. 'Words are not enough. They will never have the power of an image.'

'Words create their own images, and each reader sees a different one.'

Turold sighed. 'I cannot explain, only work,' he said.

Rainald laughed. 'I am sorry,' he said. 'I do not mean to plague you.'

'You call your interest a plague? Am I the victim?'

'Only of your own truth.'

'My work is my truth.'

'Exactly. And if your truth had more meaning, you would have more meaning.'

'I should take that as an insult. You,' said Turold, patting the top of the monk's head, 'are forgiven.'

'Should I be grateful?'

'As Adam was made in the image of God, so was I.'

'The image, but not the essence.'

'You confuse me, and you confuse yourself.' Turold narrowed his eyes and dragged his fingers through his beard.

' "I am full of confusion; therefore see thou mine afflic-tion..." ', Rainald whispered, stood up and walked to the door.

'What?' said Turold.

'My mind is clear,' said the monk, but there was hesitation in his voice, and a chip of doubt in his eyes. He opened the door, turned and opened his mouth to say more, but nothing came. The sound of singing nuns drifted across the courtyard, and a bubble of noise from beyond the precinct walls. The spring was warm, and the sky was blue.

4

The baker, a shy, fat man, had a daughter called Martha. Every morning I saw her from my cot as she carried wood for the ovens. Her skin was pale, her hair was brown and fell in curls to her shoulders, her back was straight and her walk was stately, as if she had been taught to move by a lady.

Jesus said to Martha, 'I am the resurrection, and the life: he that believeth in me, though he were dead, yet shall he live.' From the foot of my cot, as I bent to watch her gather sticks, taking care to leave the stack as ordered as she found it, sweeping her hair out of her eyes, feeling weather on her skin, I believed, and I knew. She was mine when I smelt her as she brushed past me in the alley. My heart flew when I saw her, then it sank. I have had a woman, but have not loved, not in the way they do and want. I know what they want.

How can I approach Martha, take her face in my hands and ask? My eyes can speak, I can explain, I can tell a story, but only someone who wants to can understand what I mean. I pray a girl like her would desire, from the knot of hair that sits on top of her head to the soles of her feet. I listen to my own words in my head. She is proud, but this is not a pride that creates ugliness, it is something I do not understand. It is Turold's pride, not Bishop Odo's. She is sixteen years old.

Her breasts, God you have not seen any like them. She washes in the yard below. They are like apples swollen by a wet season. As water runs over them, they reflect the sun. Between them, flowers could bloom, and on their paps, dew balls form. Their flanks rise, their skin is like marble, cut from the newest quarry, shipped far and carved with cunning; I cannot compare them to any others, I would not look at others, they are all I need. She dries them carefully. She covers them with her shirt. I watch them disappear and think of them being rubbed by the rough cloth. I will steal a piece of white linen, sew it to her shape and give it to her. I will make a garment that holds and protects them, I will win her with this. She will wear it and never think of her breasts without thanking me. I will protect her even when I am not with her, I will be hers as she is mine, though we have not touched.

Turold worked a design in small scale on parchment. He followed a list of the events Bishop Odo wished to recall, and though the sketches were roughed, the sense was not. Here is Edward crowned, here are the folds of his clothes, here ships carry Harold to Guy of Ponthieu, here William's men demand that Guy surrender Harold to the Duke. The palace at Rouen, the men ride to fight Conan of Brittany — the figures, horses, trees, buildings and ships were drawn quickly but they never lacked life. Turold's mind was full. He worked long hours, he did not stop to eat or drink.

He was assisted by two nuns. He called them twin fowl. They rustled like birds, they flapped like birds, they moved from the paint table to Turold's trestles, they twittered among themselves like birds. When they bent over their work and their faces disappeared into their cowls, and their cowls fell down to appear as beaks, they looked as though they were pecking grain. Our grey pigeons, plain, old birds, too tough for the pot.

They kept distance between themselves and Turold, but they were closer, closer to me. Sometimes I caught some look of longing in their eyes as they looked at me, as if they wanted to fold me into their clothes and carry me to their cells. Other times they were anxious to explain what they were doing, and how carefully the ink should be worked. Confidence was the key to care; I learnt this from the nuns, and resolved to apply it to my own English design. Approach a task knowing that you will complete it successfully, and you will. Have faith in God and His willingness to watch over your endeavours, and you will be rewarded. If he could, Turold would argue with me, saying that all he needed was faith in himself, he would work and please with or without the greater powers, as if he did not owe his existence to any greater powers. He has no real faith, and though I have some, it is not as complete as Rainald's.

The nuns dressed in grey, Rainald dressed in black. Nothing deceived the nuns more, for they believed he was as dark as his habit, and did not possess the most forgiving nature. For a week, I never heard them exchange a word. Why do Christ's sisters and brothers live in different houses, why do they mistrust each other's reading of the Scriptures, why do they fail to understand that the eleventh commandment is the greatest? Turold will love anyone, though his lesser nature will obscure this true and honest feeling. He chided the nuns behind their backs out of affection, not malice. There was never malice in Turold, he was never anything but true to himself.

My dumbness excuses me; people believe I am dumb because I am stupid. 'His watchmen are blind: they are all ignorant, they are all dumb dogs...' I cannot tell them otherwise so I use their ignorance to my advantage. I could wander around the nunnery buildings, the cloisters and gardens, and I was never asked my business, or sent back to the workshop. Nuns would raise their hands to me, nod as if I was expected, or stare after me as if I was the ghost of their wombs. I became friendly with many and trusted by all; my imagined idiocy was my strength, for as I was allowed to wander, so I found the place where wools and linens were stored, in bolts on wooden shelves.

I was alone, and the linens rose above me. Their value was immense, I dared not touch them for fear of leaving a mark. White and clean in their rolled lengths. I stood back from them.

Many had already been cut and hemmed to the width and length Turold required; these were laid to one side, covered with a coarser cloth, ready for his use. To one side, in a basket, were oddments, scraps and short lengths. Nothing was wasted, everything was recorded, if not in ledgers, then in Ermenburga's head. Clerical matters kept her from many day-to-day affairs of the house, but she kept an interest in the linen store, as she had done before she was abbess, before she had the power and the power began to crack beneath her. The stick-faced queen sat in the store when her responsibilities were too much. It was less obvious than a chapel, quieter than her office, warmer than her cell. The bolts soothed her, they gave off the kindest smell.

I rummaged through the basket until I found a length to suit my design. I held it to my face. It was soft and clean, softer than any cloth that ever touched Martha's skin. I held it to my chest, imagining her size and the knot she would need to tie at her back. Thinking of her made me want her, wanting her made me wish. I folded the length, tucked it beneath my shirt and whistled my way out of the store, across the court, around the gardens, through the cloisters and down to the workshops.

I was not missed. When Turold saw me, he slapped his stomach and said, 'My horses will amaze you!'

He was happy with the design, happy with the twin fowl, English cider was a powerful brew, and he was reserved choice meals, at Odo's order. The designer had to be fed, if not he would not produce the finest work. Nothing was to be denied the man. Bishop Odo would use the hanging to stress his allegiance, to prove his taste and underline his wealth. The great use the great and become greater; I agreed with Turold, nodding and smiling. Sheets of parchment now covered the trestles, the air in the workshop was powerful and thick.

5

In the night, Turold left the lodgings and took the alley to the walls, and stood at a rise between towers to watch the dark flat across the river and the forests beyond. Here, above the roofs and streets, above the stench, he could take the day and turn it over his mind, look closely at its parts and release tensions that plagued him. The pain of art, the ache in his hands and the cunning of his mind. Sometimes, he believed his mind was working against himself. Certainly it was when he slept and dreamt, maybe when he was concentrating on design and all other thoughts were blocked. What was his mind planning? Did it envy his hands? Did it want to blind him? Could it ambush him when he was not expecting it, could it force him to say something he would regret? Arts were no defence, they could never win an argument. He put his hands together and held them over his head, half pointing, half praying. From a distance, he looked as though he might dive off the walls, and on to the piles of rubbish below.

Dumbness breeds stealth. As the night blew, I crept silently to a place close to him, close enough to hear him breathe. He did not hear me, I know he did not hear me, I have better ears than anyone and I did not hear myself, but I wanted to be near him. I do not want him to worry that he has no one in the world to stand between his art and himself and his patron and himself, or his mind and himself. I am here, and will repay him the kindness he has shown me. I am small enough to be hidden by a barrel.

I watched him for a minute. He did not move, he stared into the night. An owl called from the forest. Its voice carried an echo inside itself, the real echo drifted towards us, and as it died away, another hoot came. Turold turned his head to the sound, the sound was soft, a light, warm breeze ruffled his hair. He looked like a king, a second owl called from the north, and the moon came out from behind a cloud.

The young men are riding, and here Bishop Odo rallies them in their panic. William's thanks will cover the Bishop, the Bishop will repay his King's thanks. The Bishop will scheme and the Bishop will betray, the Bishop is a warrior and here he wields a mace. Turold said, 'Do you have a clean shirt?' He coughed. 'If you do not, I will give you one.'

I did not move. I was feeling my toes. I thought he was talking to himself. I did not have a clean shirt. The owls hooted together, and a dog barked in the town.

'Bishop Odo inspects the design tomorrow.'

The words come to me as if hung from a rope, showing themselves in front of me. Turold turned his head towards me. 'Robert?'

I stood up and showed myself. He looked away and said, 'Odo is a particular man.'

We stood side by side, and after a while, and after the moon had gone behind another cloud, and the owls called again and again, he laid his hand on my shoulder. I could feel his fingers' heat, he said, 'I love you.' He coughed. 'Fathers always hear their sons, however carefully they creep.'

I looked up at him and wished I could tell him how much I loved him, and how I would do anything for him in any place.

26

One place was the same as another, that was sure but did not matter. People work, eat, fight and love, that is all they do, and they do it everywhere. The only difference is no difference at all, people did it when Christ lived, people will do it when Christ is forgotten and Turold's work is dust. Any place; I wanted to prove myself, I did not want to stay the boy at his shoulder, the one ready to fetch a dry pen or another sheet. The little touches I do for him, filling in a leg here, tracing the outline of a horse, I do at his request. It was a quiet night, and it prayed for us.

Turold greeted Odo at the workshop door. The Bishop smiled and clapped the designer on his shoulders. In another time, the two men could have been equals; as it was, Turold stepped a fine dance around him, he knew his distance and he knew the Bishop's tune. This was power, and the voice was loud. Odo allowed himself a dash of envy at Turold's skill. He had said that the designer had been given greater gifts than he, and it hurt. Now, as he swept past me and led his train to the trestles, he said, 'I know you will please me.'

'I believe I will,' said Turold.

'Ah...' said the Bishop, as he bent over the first sheet and followed the early scenes.

Edward in state, instructs Harold.

Harold, five men, five horses, five dogs and one hawk. The hawk is unhooded.

The church at Bosham.

Harold feasts.

Harold's party take ship and leave England for his estates, carrying dogs and hawk.

Harold beaches in Guy's land.

Guy takes him. Harold rides. Both men carry hawks.

William's men are instructed to bring Harold from Guy.

William's palace at Rouen. It is a fine building; William sits on a cushion and listens to his men and Harold.

Bishop Odo hummed as he worked his way along, fingering figures here and there, tapping a horse and a ship, noticing the delicate twists of ink that made the trees. Turold followed, watching the Bishop's face, glancing down when he stopped to examine more closely; here Harold joins William against Conan, here the siege of Dinan, and here, in a scene Turold designed and planned to draw the eye as no other, Harold swears on the relics.

Odo stopped here and lingered, and wore a serious face. He had blotchy cheeks, winkly eyes, and three chins. 'Have you given this enough room?' he said.

'I have. Embroidered, it will appear larger, I will make sure of that.'

Odo turned now, and smiled at Turold. 'I am sure too, as sure as this…' and he slapped a hand on the sketches '…is what I want. Exactly what I want, except for one thing.' He looked back at the work and passed quickly along, past Harold's admonishment, Edward's death, Harold's coronation, the building of the ships, the loading and sailing. Turold kept up with him. 'What is missing?' he said, and as they stood over the beginning of the battle, he looked around the room to where the rest of the sketches were laid, all gently flapping in the draught that blew through. Sunlight fell here and there, I was a step behind Turold, Odo said, 'One thing.'

'What?'

'Guess.'

Turold shook his head. 'There is nothing I can think of.'

'Think.'

'I have.'

'Harder?'

'My Lord…'

Odo smiled as if he was smiling at a child, and said, 'Text?'

'Text?' The word leapt from Turold's mouth and surprised the Bishop, who lost his smile and snapped, 'Yes! Text! How are people to know what is happening?'

Turold shook his head. 'My design tells people what is happening! I have no need for words!'

'And if I say that I think you do, will you think that I am insulting you?'

'I would not say so...'

'But you would think so?'

Turold took a step back, and from where I stood, I saw his eyes. They were popping, and he was licking his lips. 'If the story cannot be interpreted without words, does it not reflect on my ability?'

Odo smiled again, moved towards the designer and put his hand upon his shoulder. He glanced at me, and winked. Bishop Odo, Earl of Kent, William's half-brother, winked at me in the spring of the year 1075, in Winchester, England. He looked back at Turold and said, 'Forgive me. I did not mean to insult you. Of course you make the story perfectly clear. Anyone can see that. It is the finest work.' He gestured towards it. 'But many of those who see the work are ignorant, and will not understand the...'

'And ignorant men can read?'

'Your idea of what makes a man ignorant is different from those of us who are required to treat with them.' Odo's face hardened, his blotches reddened. 'A text, Turold, or your gold will turn.'

'You cannot persuade me with gold.'

'I...' hissed Bishop Odo, and he moved so that his face was almost touching Turold's, '...do not need gold to persuade anyone.' His cheeks were blown out, he licked his lips, his eyes had sunk behind fat flaps of skin. The priests in his train shuddered at his hiss, I took a step back, Turold stood his ground.

'Text...'

'Yes.'

'But it will...'

'Turold!'

'It will make nonsense of my design.' He picked up two sheets. 'Here.' He showed where Harold swears on relics and said, 'I have balanced it: a group of men here, a group of men there. One in each group points to Harold who holds his hands thus. The reliquaries come between Harold and men, he stands alone, hemmed in by God. Only a fool could not understand what I have drawn, to what it refers…' he cleared his throat '…besides, there is no room.' Odo's priests were sweating, but Odo was smiling. Few men questioned him, he was grateful for the experience. He would temper the designer's tongue if he thought the man was insulting; now, he also enjoyed watching his priests squirm. He turned to them and showed his teeth. Turold said, 'What would you have me write? "Here William came to Bayeux, where Harold made an oath to him?" '

'That would do.'

'Ha.'

'But I have a scribe waiting. He will do as I require.'

'Waiting?' Turold turned away. 'Do I know him?'

'He is English.'

Now Turold exploded. 'English!' he yelled. 'And he will write Latin?'

'Naturally.'

'The English write Latin as they screw.' Turold did not smile, but Bishop Odo did. The priests hid their faces, the twin fowl, hovering in the background, turned away.

'Badly?' said Odo.

'Yes.'

Odo moved towards Turold and whispered, 'You are wrong. Twice.'

Turold tossed the sketches away and said, 'I am not.'

Odo's face turned again, hard and bright, and he said, 'You disagree with me?'

'On few things…'

'Disagree with me and you disagree with William…'

'I cannot work,' said Turold, without thinking, 'knowing that I must make room for text.' He turned and walked towards the door. 'It is impossible.'

'Turold!' Odo screamed, and his chins wobbled. 'Leave this workshop and you never work again.'

'I will always work.' Turold turned around and held up his hands. 'As long as I have these.'

'I could arrange for their removal.'

'And never see your hanging complete?'

'This?' said Odo, and he pointed to the sketches. 'I have all I need. The nuns do not lack imagination to finish the job.'

'You call it a job?'

'You overestimate your worth, Turold. You are thinking beyond your reach.' He walked towards the designer, and his face slackened. 'Look,' he said, stretching out a hand. 'Let us not fight.' Turold turned away again. 'Turold!' The face blackened again, and the voice was cruel. 'Never,' he said, 'never turn away from me again.'

Turold bowed his head now. I could see he was biting his lip, and his eyes were swivelling backwards and forward. 'My Lord,' he whispered. 'A text.'

'A text, yes. But we will discuss it in the morning. We like your designs, and that is what you are paid to produce. If I want a text, I will have one; it does not mean you will not be paid.'

'But the form of the work, the whole...'

'We will,' said Odo, and he clicked his fingers, 'talk again.' His priests stood behind him, anxious, all young and pale. 'Now I must meet Abbess Ermenburga, and I hope,' he said, leaning towards Turold, 'that she is less trouble than you.' He winked, I felt Turold flinch, and then he was gone, his priests following in his wake like ducklings, and the ducklings were in the sunshine.

Late, very late, late with the night, the stars, the moon and the angel of my dream; as dogs slept and the roofs glided with rats,

Turold woke me, and whispered in my ear, 'We are leaving.' He pointed at Rainald and shook his head. 'You and me, alone.'

The moon was full. He wanted his designs before we left. I was to climb the walls of Nunnaminster and steal them from the workshops. I was the thief, I could lose my hands. I would never be able to sew Martha's shirt.

I have my mouth open.

Turold stroked my hair.

There is a bird in every living tree.

I had been dreaming about Martha. We had been swimming in the river, and as we lay on the bank, I dried her body. Her legs were slim, and as I rubbed them with the cloth, it was as if I was polishing silver. The more I dried, the brighter she shone. I polished and she smiled, she turned over and I buffed her cheeks.

As I worked on them, they began to seep honey. I bent over her and began to lick it off, but the more I licked so the more came, and as more came she began to moan beneath me. One moment I had the cloth in my hand, and then it was gone. It had melted against her skin. I sat up, she turned over, leaned towards me and whispered in my ear. I could feel her lips against me, and a wisp of her hair on my cheek. She took my hand and pulled it towards her, and held it over her breasts. I could feel the heat coming from her body, and I saw a ring of tiny pimples around her paps. She tipped her head back and closed her eyes, her lashes fluttered and she whispered again.

Her stomach was like a patch of earth around the foot of a small apple tree. It is warm and clean and smells of fruit. I leant my head down and she thrust towards me. Her thighs came up, and then the rest of her body folded over me. She pulled my arms and I felt a rough hand on my shoulder. Turold whispered, 'Wake up. We are leaving.'

I sat up.

He pointed at Rainald. 'You and me, alone.'

He led me along the alley to a low part of the wall, hoisted me on to his shoulders, and I stood up to look down, across the precincts to the workshops.

I was on top of the wall.

Turold whispered, 'I will open the gate. Meet me there.'

I jumped down and stood in the yard. I was still with Martha, but I could not feel her, I do not think I knew what I was doing, only that I had to do what Turold asked. I could prove myself, I was working for his art's sake, I am his boy.

The nunnery slept. I crept across the precinct yard, using the walls as cover half the way, then counting to five before I slipped into the moonlight and ran to the corner of the linen store. I stood there for a moment and listened to my breathing, then I listened for other sounds. There were none. The walls kept out sounds of the town and sounds from the country beyond. I scratched my elbow, the sound echoed across the yard and into the towers of the abbey church. I looked over my shoulder, there was no one there. I looked in my heart and I looked in my soul; it was as quiet in these places as the precincts and my voice.

I followed the workshop walls slowly, feeling my way, smelling the stones, until I came to the door. It was not locked. I knew I had locked it. I was the last to leave the workshop in the evening, and that was one of my jobs: leave the key on a shelf above the little window. I felt the shelf, there was nothing there. The key was in the lock. I pushed the door, it swung back, I stepped into the workshop.

In the night it smelt of cold. Turold's sketches were as we had left them, and though I knew them well, they were changed by the moonlight as it cut through gaps in the shutters. Here the men appeared to actually mount their horses, and there they galloped into battle. Here, arrows flew between sheets, and I heard men scream. I took the first sheet, laid it carefully on the next, then moved slowly along the trestles. The night was solid.

I felt someone watching, someone had eyes on me. They had watched me come from the wall, across the yard, past the linen store and around the workshop. My footsteps had been heard, and my head seen as it bent to watch the horsemen move.

The horsemen moved. I gathered another sheet to the pile, then another, they all rustled together, and I came to the end of the first trestle. I was standing with a window in front of me. I had never seen it shuttered, it looked smaller, I turned around at the moment I heard a noise from a far corner of the workshop.

It was not a whisper and it was not a sigh, it was more as a creak, but not of a door. I dropped the sketches, the sound of them falling filled the shop. I bent down, pulled them across the floor towards me and whistled, softly.

The note hung but there was no answer. I heard a click, I folded the sheets together, stood up again, laid them on the trestle and took a deep breath. I was hot, I was cold, Turold's face came to my mind, and the sound of his voice in my ear.

'Be quick,' he said, 'and don't forget any.'

I looked at a sheet. It was the sketch of Harold saving William's men from the quicksands of the Couesnon; below, in the borders, eels swim.

Eel. I am tasting eel, and I pick up the next sheet, and the next. I had reached the end of the second trestle when I heard the creak again, this time closer, and just after it, the sound of rustling cloth. It was a faint noise, like a whispered word you do not quite hear, but it is there, in front of you.

The wind in the shutters, the wind through the branches of the trees in the precinct yard. Apples and pears.

My hands sweat, I was praying I would not smudge the sketches.

I could smell honey. The nuns keep bees. I thought about my pigeons. I would not have time to collect them, Turold will never let me take them, I will open their box so that they can fly, I will never see Martha again. Did I suck honey from her skin, or was it a dream? My mind is going like this as I pick the sketches up. I am holding so much cunning, I am doing something for him, I am proving that I am worth his time. I will do exactly what he wants, my pigeons will live. As I cross to a trestle that runs along the top of the workshop, I am full of pride.

'I will advise against the thought and kill the deed.' There is the breeze again, cooling the night and sending the leaves on the trees shivering again, and now there is another sound in the workshop, a whimper, as though someone is weeping on top of me. I froze, the weeping stopped, I turned to look over my shoulder and heard my name.

'Robert?'

It came as the breeze, disturbing the air as still water is disturbed, layering it with cold ripples that lay about me and tugged at my shirt. A sudden heat burst into my chest, then it dropped to my feet, a heat like cold that froze me, I could not tell.

'Robert?'

Hell.

Bishop Odo.

Rich food.

Martha's ankles.

I looked at the sketches. A Norman knight leant from his horse and struck an English footman with his sword. The horse was reined in, archers filled the border and their arrows had pierced the Englishman's shield. I heard his cry and the bellow of the horse as the reins cut, I saw spears and I saw the sword split the Englishman's head. Blood on the ground and blood in the air. I looked up as a cloaked figure slowly rose up in the workshop, six feet from where I stood, its head cowled and bowed, the arms folded in front, its legs slightly apart.

Devils.

Harold.

William.

My knees screamed at me, my mouth filled with salt, my head said, 'Run', Turold's words stopped me, I was fixed where I stood, the sheets of sketches felt no weight at all. To my right, there were twenty more sketches to collect. I could see the battle rage beyond me, Harold's death, William's coronation and the workshop door, half open. I moved to fetch the next sheet when the figure tipped its head back and the thin needly face appeared, and the eyes struck at me and collapsed my will. Ermenburga's mouth was open, her tongue flicked at me and she said, 'Robert. What are you doing?'

I shook my head.

I was thinking I might piss.

She stretched her hand out, it appeared from beneath her habit and I thought it had no skin. I thought it was all bones, it was white as snow and my mind was saying, 'Move back do not let her touch you it is devil's fingers' but she did, and held my shoulder. Her face drew closer, I saw tears on her cheeks and she whispered, 'I'm sorry. I forgot.'

I licked my lips.

'Don't be afraid,' she said.

No.

'If you are doing this for your master because he was insulted by Bishop Odo,' she said, 'then I support you.'

I nodded.

'You are?'

I nodded again.

She smiled now, I had never seen her smile. She had no teeth, her lips curled over her gums and I felt a blast of her breath. It came from her lungs and spread over my face, it smelt of cabbage, she said, 'Anything you do to impede the Bishop you do with my blessing.'

I narrowed my eyes and creased my brow.

'He is a beast.'

I looked at Turold's sketches. They lived in my hands. Bishop Odo.

Harold.

Guy.

Her face was close enough to kiss. Behind it, I could see pain, and I saw Odo bearing down on her. He was three times her weight. He would burst her, and I am thinking what do I do?

She said, 'You plan to leave?'

I nodded.

'Tonight?'

I nodded.

'And your master knows the consequences? He knows what the Bishop will do to him?'

I shrugged.

She took her hand from my shoulder and rubbed her forehead.

Here, at the siege of Dinan, Conan delivers the keys of the city to William. The keys hang from Conan's lance, William's lance almost touches them. The tips of their lances.

'You need a guide,' she said. 'You will go in circles without one.'

I shrugged at her.

She touched me again. 'I will fetch one. You collect the rest of the work; you are meeting Turold at the alley gate?'

I nodded.

'We will meet you there.' Her face was clean, like linen. Her nose, mouth and eyes were stitched on, and her ears.

I stared at her.

'What are you waiting for?' she said. 'Collect the rest.' She pointed to the sketches. 'Your master is waiting.'

My master is waiting.

'Finish here and go to him. Do not let him leave before we have come.'

Hold him.

Ermenburga's voice was loaded, all the words she said were nuts on a string, and I am picking them. 'Go,' she said, and I did. I rustled the sheets in my hands, and then I picked up the rest, all in a line along the trestles, as he had told me. I am praying for a voice, I am praying for success and when I have every sheet in my hand I am rolling them. Turold has a hide to cover them, I must get to the alley gate. I looked up, and I was about to nod at Ermenburga, but she had gone. She was quiet and she was thin, she was the stick-faced queen of Nunnaminster with the rustling sleeves and the boned hand, but she was born with Christ in her heart, and Christ lay all about her face.

I handed the roll to Turold. He said, 'This is all of them?'

I nodded.

'You are sure?'

I nodded.

'Then we leave.'

I grabbed his sleeve as he turned away, and shook my head. Spit flew from my mouth, and hit him in the eye.

'Let go!' he hissed.

I am shaking my head and pulling him, and as he tried to walk, my feet are dragged along. We are going to wake people and I tugged at him, I heard threads rip in his shirt, and he turned to hit me.

Please God. I am here. I must be able to speak. I must speak. Please give me the gift you gave everyone else. I have never met another like me. I am the only dumb boy in the world. I am tugging a strong man, all I have to do is tell him, a voice must be a lonely man's only friend. Is my voice living a life without me, lost as I am? Is it in a tree?

'Let go!'

I have two hands on him, and now he is going to hit me. His hand is raised, then as if in answer, the alley door opened and Ermenburga came from the precincts with a small nun.

Turold spun towards them, and I thought he would hit them but I jumped in front of him. I put my hands up, Ermenburga said, 'Quiet.'

'Abbess?'

Ermenburga said, 'Master Turold...'

'Do not,' he said, 'try to prevent us.'

She is going to laugh. 'No...'

'Abbess?'

'You should value your boy,' she said.

Yes.

Turold laughed. He was going to say something about me, but Ermenburga stopped him.

'This is sister Mildred.' Mildred bowed at us. She was a tiny nun, my size. Her face was small and old, her eyes were large. 'As I told Robert, you will go nowhere without a guide. She knows the way with her eyes closed. She...'

Turold held the roll of sketches under his arm. 'You will not prevent us leaving?'

'I am helping you.'

'Why?'

'No time,' she said, and she pushed Mildred towards us and then disappeared through the gate, the gate closed and we froze.

No time.

Locked gate.

Night.

Damp.

The night was a black ribbon above us, the wall that bounded the alley wept with damp, the voices stopped, started again and then moved away. Turold looked at us, shook his head, Mildred pushed between us and said, 'We must go now.' I heard a door close beyond the nunnery wall.

'We have packs to fetch,' said Turold.

'Hurry,' said Mildred. Her voice sounded like a crow's. 'I will wait at Southgate.' In the dark I could see her mouth.

'We will be there,' said Turold, and as he pulled me away, she disappeared ahead, around a bend in the alley, and all we could hear was her soft steps in the dirt.

We crept into the lodging, and as I tucked Martha's linen into my pack, Rainald stirred in his sleep, opened his eyes, saw us in the moonlight, closed them and opened them again. He sat up and said, 'What are you doing?'

'Leaving,' said Turold.

'Leaving?' Rainald rubbed his face. 'Why?'

'Odo.'

Rainald shook his head. 'Bishop Odo,' he said. 'And where are you going?'

'Home.'

Rainald laughed. 'Are you mad? You'll be in more trouble at home than here. That's if you get that far. You cannot run from the Bishop.'

'I'm not running,' said Turold.

'That is exactly what you are doing. Because of this afternoon's disagreement?'

'It was more than a disagreement. I will not have text in my work.'

'I heard.'

'You should have been there. You could have supported me. You are meant to intercede...'

'What is there to support?'

'You agree with Odo?'

'I agree with neither of you.'

'Of course.' Turold slapped his forehead. 'When have you ever taken sides?'

'I am on the Lord's side.'

'Why did I think you would say that?'

'Why tell me that I should have been with you? If I am so predictable, why do you bother with me at all?'

'Rainald.' Turold sat down, opposite the monk. 'If I am mad, why do you bother with me?'

'We were forced together a long time ago.'

'That is true...'

'It is too late for either of us. We will haunt each other to the grave.'

'Will we?'

'But we are friends too.' Rainald leant towards Turold. 'And that is why I must tell you to stay. If you leave, you are walking into more trouble than you have ever known. Bishop Odo's anger will descend upon you like rain.'

'I will take my chance.'

'You and the boy?'

I nodded.

'The boy is my only true friend,' said Turold.

I took a deep breath and pushed out my chest.

'You know that is not true,' said Rainald.

'Maybe not, maybe.'

The monk stood now and walked to the window. The forest was deep and dark. 'You will be lost within an hour,' he said.

'Ermenburga has provided a guide.'

'Ermenburga has what?'

'You heard.'

'She's with you?'

'She has her own reasons for despising Odo.'

'Has she?'

'The boy knows them.'

Rainald looked at me. I nodded.

'I thought you would know them.'

Rainald shook his head. 'I do not,' he said, and in the moonlight, I saw his face become long and grey, as if he had grown twenty years. 'No doubt I will hear.'

'I'm sure.'

The two men stared into each other's eyes. Rainald said, 'Even if you get to the coast, you will never get across the sea.'

'We'll take our chances.'

'Chance?'

'It's one faith...'

'And even if you did, if you reached home, his men would be waiting.'

'My faith,' said Turold, 'is in my art. I must take risks for what I believe in.'

41

'But to take such a risk because of a few words of text…'

Turold turned away and tied his pack. 'You want me to roll over at Odo's request? If I am to achieve nothing else, I will have proved the strength of my convictions.'

'Your convictions? You are selfish and mad, and a fool. A child.' The monk shook his head. 'Why does art choose children for its instruments?'

Turold stood up and glared at his friend. He knew there was truth in this, he looked like a big child. They had not spoken with raised voices, but I had never seen either angrier. There was a terrible air in the lodging. I did not know where to stand so I waited. Then, when he was ready, Turold went first, into the alley and towards Southgate. I felt Rainald's hand on my shoulder, and when I looked at him, he was crying. I broke away and followed my master, past Martha's, like a dog.

6

The forest was cold and dark, and stretched from coast to coast. I followed Mildred and Turold followed me. We trusted her, we did not question when she chose a path we would have missed, away from the main track. This climbed a hill, dipped down the other side, we avoided a village in the valley, crossed a river by a bridge and took a path that ran along the bank.

We walked quickly to keep up. When we dropped behind, she called for us to keep up. 'If you are in a hurry,' she said, 'why are you falling back?'

'We are with you,' said Turold.

The trees thickened the dark, they blocked out the sky, the only light came when the moon peeped from behind clouds and shone along ridges on the path. The ground was dry, we left no tracks, we disturbed no animals. Our footsteps echoed into the branches. I kicked a stick, it flicked against Turold's heel and flew into undergrowth. 'Ssh!' said Mildred. She stopped and we stood behind her. She stared through the trees towards a clearing that opened beyond us. 'Wait,' she said. 'Soldiers camp here.' She pointed to the right. 'I will go around this way and meet you back here.'

Turold did not argue.

I was there.

Mildred was a quiet woman, and though her silence was loaded with confidence, I thought, Is she guiding us for another reason? Whose soldiers is she protecting us from, or whose soldiers is she leading us towards? Had Ermenburga told her to make sure we were dead before the coast? Gangs of English haunted the forest, anxious to lay weapons on any Norman. I looked at Turold and I am praying for a voice. He was staring at patterns the branches of the trees made against the sky. His mind was occupied by the scene of night falling over the battlefield.

William camped amongst the dead and dying, the single apple tree is there, in the sketches. Turold had drawn its branches large and its twigs were fingers. It was the best tree in the work, it was the tree of death and here, as some of William's men amuse themselves by hacking the limbs and heads from the half-dead, and re-assembling the bodies so men with huge torsos have small legs and massive arms, and arms stick where the legs should be and legs poke from necks, and men have two heads or five heads, one in its proper place, four more at the empty limb sockets; it is a nightmare, and this is just the beginning. Suddenly, Turold turned to me and said, 'I am worried.'

I nodded.

'Can you hear her?'

I shook my head.

'I think,' he said, 'we might be betrayed.'

I looked into the clearing. It was quiet and cool, like a green pond. The grass was disturbed by a breeze. I thought I saw moonlight glint on armour; when I focused I saw it was a silvery leaf shivering.

'Betrayed,' said Turold. 'Betrayed by Odo and now we are betrayed by her.' He took my hand and led the way around the clearing. 'This country,' he said. 'I knew it would be like this.' I nodded.

'It is impossible to know who is on your side and who is not.' He flailed at a branch; it snapped back and caught him on the cheek. 'Even the trees are against us,' he said, wiping a streak of blood away. Then he put his hand up, crouched down and said, 'Ssh…'

I knelt at his side. Beyond us and beyond the clearing, three men were gathered around a tree stump. Mildred was talking to them. I could hear her voice but not the words. Turold said, 'What did I say?'

The men were English, armed with short swords, each carried a pack on his back. They were all big, but none bigger than Turold. He fingered the roll of sketches. 'Could I defend us with these?' he said.

I shrugged.

'Or this?' He took out a dagger. The blade was shorter than a man's hand, sharp and pointed. 'Could I?'

I do not know.

He asks me questions as if expecting an answer. Maybe he senses my thought, I am really his son.

'What did Rainald say?'

I remember everything Rainald said.

'If you leave, you walk into more trouble than you have ever known?'

I nodded.

'Was he talking about Odo, or does he know something we do not?'

I shrugged.

'Did Rainald betray us too?'

Turold is seeing enemies everywhere and now, as he laid his hand on my shoulder, I could feel him shake. He is afraid, and it is nothing to do with art. He thinks everyone is against him, the country is against him, all he has is his thoughts, the sketches, me and the desire for home. Familiarity is his hope, his eyes were shifting one way and another, and I knew he was thinking he was trapped. Mildred's voice crowed on, then it stopped, she turned from the men and walked towards us.

She took the quietest steps, her eyes were fixed to the ground, the three men waited where they were. One had his hand on the hilt of his sword, the second scratched his head, the third watched. An owl called above us, Mildred walked slowly and was almost upon us when Turold stood up, took her around the neck with one arm and clasped his hand over her mouth. He pulled her to the ground, laid her on her front, sat on her back and whispered, 'I am going to ask you questions. If you cry, I will break your neck. Do you understand? Nod if you do.'

She nodded.

I could see her thighs. Turold said, 'Who are those men?' He took the hand from her mouth.

'Friends.'

He put the hand back. 'Yours or ours?' He took the hand away.

'Yours and mine,' she said.

"Why should I believe you?"

'They can protect us,' she said. 'I have explained. I told them you are an English merchant and his boy. If you say nothing, if you do not give yourself away, you will be safe to the coast.'

'I believed that you were our guide.'

'I can be your guide but not your protector.'

Turold put his hand over Mildred's mouth and he thought. The men looked towards us but saw nothing. They waited patiently. Three people travelled faster and quieter than six, what use would three armed men be if we met twenty Norman soldiers? The English would provoke them. A nun, a merchant and his boy would attract less attention.

I went down on my knees and prayed. 'Our Father in heaven, give me the power of speech, a voice with which to praise thee and the words to warn my master.'

'Ermenburga said nothing about these men,' he said.

'She knows nothing about them,' she said, 'but believe me. We need them.'

So many people need so many people, and as the world lies beneath heaven, and as it tries to raise itself up, Turold shook his head, stood and offered his hand to Mildred. She took it and pulled herself up. I tugged at his sleeve, he shook his head. 'No,' he said.

Mildred came to me and put her hand to my face. Her hand was freezing, and her fingernails were long. 'You will follow your master?' she said.

I nodded.

Turold said, 'I can trust him.'

I had nowhere else to go.

Now six of us were stealing through the forest. We followed paths that did not appear to be there until we were on them, the armed men did not speak and made little noise. They noted things by trees we could not understand, and signs on the ground that meant we were safe. They could smell Normans at two hundred paces, they could see Normans through walls, each had killed more Normans than you could count on your fingers, each carried a price on his head. The one with the highest price led the others, we put our feet where he put his, the moonlight shadows followed us.

We had walked two hours when this man stopped and made us crouch behind undergrowth. A Norman patrol was approaching, marching the same path. 'Twelve men.'

'Twelve men.'

'Three mules.'

'Three mules.'

We waited before I heard them, then the rattle of their swords and the sound of their voices began to drift through the forest. They laughed about something, they were drinking. Their mules whinnied, their packs creaked, we crouched as low as we could.

I heard one say, 'How much longer?'

Another said, 'Why do you keep asking?'

'My feet are killing me.'

'We rest when I say.'

I peered through the bushes, and I saw them, twenty paces away. A third voice said, 'Mine are killing me too.'

The first soldier put his hand up and said, 'Enough! I have my orders, you have mine!' His voice was measured and slow. He was in command.

'I'm tired.'

'You're always tired.'

'No, I'm not.'

'You are.'

'You'll sleep before me.'

'I sleep when I need to.'

There was laughter here, and the patrol halted. I could hear them breathing. I looked to my right. Our three protectors were on their haunches, hands on their swords.

Seconds passed as hours do, slowly creeping over themselves. The Normans were relaxed and tired. One began to unbuckle his belt. The leader said, 'What are you doing?'

'I need to shit.'

'We all need to shit, but if you don't do it up, when we get to camp you'll be shitting out the wrong hole for the wrong reasons.'

More laughter here, except from the one who had unbuckled. He was doing up again and they moved towards us, passing so close to our hiding-place that I could have reached out and touched their boots. I smelt their boots and I smelt stale cheese. This reminded me of home, and I am thinking, what are we going to do when we are home? Does Turold know there will be nothing for us, we will not be welcome anywhere by anyone? Irritate Bishop Odo and you worry other people, anger him and those people pretend they never knew you. Turold jumps before he thinks, Turold's mind is on higher things, but he forgets that higher things must be supported by the every-day. I looked at him. His eyes followed the Normans, he licked his lips, we heard their rattling as they threaded their way through the trees. Turold stood up, one of the English pulled him back, put his finger to his mouth and held up five fingers. We waited for five fingers and then quickly, as rabbits in the path of dogs, we were away again, following the path towards the dawn and the coast, and the trees protected us along the way.

We reached the coast as the sun rose, walked on to dunes that banked the beach and sat to rest in a circle of sea-grass. The three men posted themselves where they could watch the approaches, Mildred passed bread and said, 'We are two hours from Bosham. We will lead you to the path, but then we must turn back. The men are anxious when they leave cover, and I must return quickly.'

The sea was blue and the sun glittered across it as silver thread. The sand was fine and yellow, a headland stood in the distance, and closer to us, other spits of land jutted out. A fresh breeze cooled the air, though the sea gave warning of heat to come. The bread was coarse, there was no cheese to eat with it, only a bottle of water, and two apples.

Turold and I approached Bosham at midday. The sun was hot, the quays were busy. Six ships were tied there, more lay at anchor in the bay. Sailors mingled with merchants, groups of soldiers were gathered in squatting groups, throwing dice and passing jugs. Turold bowed his head and I walked as close to him as I could, holding the corner of his coat.

'Why were you born dumb?' he said.

I do not know.

'Sometimes, I think your advice might be worth while.'

I nodded.

Bosham, where Harold embarked upon the journey that led him to Guy of Ponthieu, then to William and the relics of Bayeux. Bosham smelt of fish. I followed Turold to a stall above the quay where ale was served, and benches were crowded with drinkers, whores and whores' children. He collected two mugs, passed me one, drank his in one, collected another and told a sailor, 'We want passage.'

'Who doesn't?' said the sailor. 'But who can pay?'

Turold took out a bag and weighed it in his hands.

The sailor's ears filled with the sound of money, and his eyes widened.

'What's the rate?'

'That depends.'

'On what?'

'On who you are,' said the sailor. 'No one's going to carry anyone who comes along. If you're travelling, you must have a reason. And reasons cost money...'

'Do they?'

'Yes.' The sailor was as big as Turold, and had a beard. He had black teeth and a fish bone in his hair.

'I have good reason.' I moved from behind Turold's back, and he said, 'We have a good reason. Better than any.'

'I'm sure,' said the sailor, 'you do.' He narrowed his eyes, trying to place us in something he had heard, some warning or maybe a simple story.

It is a simple story, a tale everyone has heard, and everyone adds a chapter. Turold said, 'Are you sailing today?'

'Maybe.'

'Where?'

The sailor narrowed his eyes, as if he was trying to remember us. 'Where do you want to go?' he said. He looked over our heads, I turned around. A patrol was passing along the quay, two foot-soldiers and one on horseback. He gestured towards them and said, 'They worry you?'

'Should they?'

The sailor put his hand on Turold's arm, said, 'You tell me,' and squeezed. Turold tried to pull away, the sailor did not let go, Turold grabbed the man's hair. Immediately, two other sailors pounced, I ducked under the table, the table buckled under the men's weight as they toppled on to it, mugs and food spilt, and then they were on the ground.

As long as Turold had his hands on the first sailor, as long as he could kick, as long as he could spit curses and take blows he felt safe. His strength scared me, a splash of blood landed on my cheek and in a blink I saw the sailor's face. He had lost a tooth and his ear was torn, he yelled, the two other men pulled at Turold, Turold kicked at them and caught one in the balls. The other swerved and aimed a foot at Turold's head. Turold stood up quickly, clenched his fist and struck the man in the chest.

The fist disappeared into the man's chest, his mouth opened and a blast of breath left his body as a rabbit bolts from cover, the man's eyes bulged, then he dropped.

The first sailor touched his mouth, the second held his balls, the third put his hands on his chest. I put my head out from beneath the table in time to see a foot-soldier come from behind and strike Turold's neck with his mace. Turold's face popped with surprise, his legs straightened and then they buckled, he went down like a tree. He groaned, a chain was taken from a saddlebag, wrapped around his wrists and I heard a voice say, 'The man's as stupid as they say.'

I jumped out.

'And the mute!'

I was not afraid. I bent down and put my hand on the roll of sketches. The mace crashed on to the back of my hand. I did not flinch. Look at me. Look into my eyes. Do you think you can hurt me? Am I as stupid as my master? I will protect his work. I lay down and covered the roll with my body.

'The devotion of a saint,' said the mounted soldier. 'Brings tears to your eyes, doesn't it?' He laughed. 'Get him up.'

The soldiers lifted me up. I struggled.

'Pass me the roll.'

The roll was picked up and handed over.

I cringed.

Turold was coming round.

The mounted soldier kissed the roll. We were the best luck of his life. 'Bring them,' he said.

There was nothing I could do.

7

We were taken back to Winchester and locked in a cell. Turold's chains were removed. He sat and rubbed his wrists.

My feet ached.

There was a window, high in the wall. The stones wept with damp, the floor was covered with rank straw. Rats gathered at a corner hole, the sound of wailing carried from another cell to where we were.

Turold said, 'Forgive me.'

For what?

'I should never have led you here.'

I am part of you, as much of you as your head or your hands. I will never leave you.

'You should never have left home.'

You are my only father.

'You know what?'

What?

'I think about your pigeons.' He took a deep, painful breath. 'Will they live without you?'

I nodded.

He looked at me, then moved towards me. He hesitated, put his arms around me, and hugged. I felt the power of this man, and I was thinking, what is going to happen to us? A rat scuttled from the corner and sniffed at my foot. I kicked it away. It squeaked and ran, the others disappeared into the wall and scratched along their burrow.

'Do you forgive me?'

I nodded.

'I was a fool.' He shook his head. 'How could I have been such a fool?' He tapped his head. 'You know what I've been called?'

I shook my head.

'The greatest. My work could seduce women, calm insanity, but sometimes,' he said, and he lowered his voice, 'I think I am two men.'

Two men.

'In here.' He tapped his head again.

Another rat came from the hole. Fresh air blew in the window and I heard a dog bark. The wailing in another cell stopped, then started again.

'Hello?' said Turold.

I squeezed his arm.

He was looking at me, smiling. I closed my eyes.

'Go to sleep,' he said, and his voice was soft as straw.

I dreamt. There were horsemen galloping across a plain, and in their wake, foot-soldiers carried lances. The lances were tipped with fire and the horses rode on fire; battle was joined at a fork in a river, steam rose all around, flames burst from holes in the ground.

And a hand came down from heaven and blessed the armies. The hand did not bless just one army or another, it blessed both, and the light of God shone on all the men. They looked up to see, but as each stared at the hand, they were blinded, they were struck dumb and unable to fight.

Weapons fell into the river. The horses threw their riders and bolted for woods on hills that bounded the plain. A village stood to one side, and when I looked, I saw women standing on the roofs, wailing.

A window opened in the sky. I was awake and the window was in the cell. I closed my eyes again, and the armies were folding into themselves. Each man was part of the man he stood next to, the weapons on the ground melted, I opened my eyes again, light was shining through the window and Turold was looking down at me. He had held me through the night, he had not slept at all. He had cursed himself and worried about his sketches. He wanted to continue with the work, he would work with a scribe, he had no choice, but he would not have his design dominated by text. He was wasting time in a cell. I heard the sound of approaching feet, rattling keys and a key in the lock. The jailer brought bread and water and said, 'Someone is coming to see you.'

The jailer was an idiot.

Turold smiled, picked up some bread, took a bite, folded his arms, sat with his back against the wall and chewed.

'Someone is coming to see you,' said the jailer, again.

'Can I eat in peace?' said Turold.

The jailer glared at him. The jailer only had one eye, but he carried keys, and keys were big magic. He did not know how locks worked, he did not know how iron was forged, he put his hands on his keys, as if they were his balls.

'He will be here soon.'

'My visitor is a man?' said Turold, pretending to be disappointed.

The jailer bent down and said, 'If I had my way, I would draw that tongue from your mouth and slice your fingers to ribbon.' He stood up straight and held his back. 'But I have orders.'

'You have orders?' Turold laughed now.

The jailer clenched his fists. 'You must be someone special.'

'I am.'

I nodded.

Wailing began from another cell. The jailer turned to the sound, smiled and left. Turold passed me some bread. I took some, and sipped some of the water.

At midday, as the sun cut barred lines across the floor, the air was filled with the sound of commotion, doors were opened and slammed, keys rattled and heavy footsteps stamped along the corridor that led to our cell. Turold wore a calm face, there was nothing anyone could do to him. He had sketched his greatest work, his Tree of Life hung in St Pierre sur Dives, his chasubles and copes were worn by great men of the Church, his girdles were admired by the Queen, her Ladies longed to lay them out. He was not frightened, so I was not. A key turned in the lock, the door swung open and Bishop Odo stood on the threshold. He sniffed the air.

'How can you stand it?' he said, and strode in. Three men followed him, one carried a chair. This was placed in the middle of the cell, we stood up, he sat down and with a faint wave of his hand, dismissed the others. 'I'll call,' he said. 'Wait outside.'

One of the men looked at Turold and grinned an evil, yellow smile. He bowed to the Bishop and joined the others.

We were alone.

'Turold,' said Odo. 'Turold.' He sighed. 'What am I going to do with you?'

Turold shook his head.

'You disappoint me.' The Bishop spoke as if addressing a boy. He was indulgent and quiet, and looked at my master with sorrow and a kind of longing. 'There was no need for it...'

'My Lord...'

'Quiet!' Suddenly Odo's face flushed and his voice grew a hard edge. 'Only speak when I tell you to!'

Turold opened his mouth, began to form a word, then closed it again.

'Take a lesson from your boy!'

Turold looked at me and nodded.

I nodded.

We are nodding. We are like a pair of chickens. Here is the corn, here is the straw, but do not lay any eggs. The rats were in the wall. Bishop Odo looked strange, sitting on a beautiful chair, wearing his fine clothes in the middle of the cell. He took a deep breath, looked away, then looked back.

'What am I going to do with you?' he said again, quietly.

I wanted to scratch my leg, but did not.

'You are a dilemma. If I do not make an example of you, my enemies will think me weak; but if I do, I deny myself your talent.'

It is talent.

'I could have the hanging worked without your further help; the sketches are enough, but do not think I do not know that it needs your supervision. Your touch from beginning to end.'

Turold bowed his head.

'That does not mean that I will dispense with the scribe.'

'But...'

'Silence! We have already discussed the subject, and I do not need any more from you!'

I know Turold knows he has no choice. He has explained to me, he simply wants to explain to Odo.

'You have no choice,' said Odo. 'My respect for you can easily be betrayed by my desire for your neck. I swear to you...' and the Bishop leant forward so his face was almost touching Turold's, '...last night I would have had your balls sooner than blink. You may thank God He persuaded me otherwise.'

God talks to Odo.

Balls.

Neck.

Text.

'As it is, I think I'll just scar you; something to match the one you already have?'

Turold put his hand to his face.

'And then you can meet Brother Lull.'

'The scribe.'

The scribe.

'My Lord,' said Turold.

Odo's hand flashed and he caught Turold on the chin. Turold did not flinch, his eyes were lowered, Odo hit him again, this time on the nose. A dribble of blood came from one nostril. The Bishop smiled at this, his eyes were red, his lips were wet. He swung between such piety and this violence, Turold swung between stupidity and brilliance, I swung whichever way I had to. I was the boy; if I had not been in the cell, the interview would not have been conducted any other way.

'What did I tell you?'

'Only speak when you ask me to.'

'And did I ask you?'

'No, my Lord.'

The Bishop hit Turold again, this time with enough force to make him sway on his feet, but he made no move to defend himself.

'You are a lucky man. I think you know how lucky. Not all patrons have my appreciation. A true appreciation.'

This was true.

Turold nodded.

'Never forget my indulgence.'

Turold looked at the floor.

I scratched my leg. Bishop Odo looked at me. I thought about Martha.

Our packs had been taken at the gate. Her strip of linen was folded at the bottom of mine, wrapped in a clean rip of sacking. I never thought that I would not see her again. The story of our flight would be known by everyone in town; as Normans we had been shunned, as Normans who refused to obey our masters we were noticed. Craftsmen were bonded by their secrets and cunning; bakers, masons, carvers or designers. All had boys, all the boys loved girls they had not approached. All the girls had fathers. Odo said, 'William has heard of your escapade; as I say, your actions reflect on me. He had the grace to laugh, but I was not sure whether he was laughing at me or you. I think you know; he is a master at disguising his true feelings, and I think he was indulging me. So, as he indulges me, I indulge you.' The Bishop looked at me. I looked at him. 'I think your boy indulges you,' he said, and then he spoke to me. 'Do you indulge your master?'

I nodded.

He smiled.

'Robert?'

I nodded, opened my mouth and formed the word 'Yes.' I felt tears behind my eyes. I formed the word again, forced air through my mouth and almost heard the word. The Bishop spoke to God, God spoke through the Bishop, I was closer to God than I had ever been. God took my voice, God could return it to me. I saw God holding my voice in His hand, all the words I had wished to say and all the words I will say. My voice can be seen, it is a ball of blue air. God has to toss it in my mouth, I tried to say, 'Yes' again, but when I tried, when I thought about it, nothing came. Nothing but the wish and an echo in my head. Odo said to me, 'Robert?'

I nodded again.

'Your master is lucky to have you.'

I looked at Turold. He wiped his nose and said, 'He is a good boy.'

I had tears in my eyes.

'Men dream of boys like you.'

I heard shuffling feet outside. Odo turned to the noise, tapped the side of his head and said, 'I have other matters to attend to.'

'My Lord.'

'You will be allowed to return to your lodgings, but please, Turold, do not be so foolish again. You will return to work in the morning.'

'My Lord?'

'Yes?'

'My sketches...'

'They are in the workshop, and will not leave the precincts again. They will be under lock and key when you are not working.'

'May I...'

'You,' said Odo, and now he stood up, 'are in no position to request anything.'

'I...'

'No!' Odo walked to the cell door and banged it. 'I have given you my thoughts.' The door opened, a man came in and picked up the chair. 'Remember,' said the Bishop. 'I indulge you, but I only indulge once. Pray, Turold, then go back to work.'

8

Rainald was waiting when we returned to the lodging. He wore a disappointed face, disappointed that his advice had been ignored. Rainald was not like other men. His mind was fixed. He knew the outcome of things, he had faith, he did not drink or swear. He said, 'Were you hurt?'

'Hurt?' said Turold. 'It would take more than Odo to hurt me.'

'So you have learnt your lesson?' Rainald crossed himself. 'May the Lord protect you.'

'I've learnt one lesson. I'll be more careful next time. I'll play along with his wishes, but he'll regret not listening to me in the first place. It's easier to make a scribe look foolish than it is a man like me.'

'What is a man like you?'

Oh God.

I opened my pack and rummaged to the bottom. I pulled out the sack, laid it on my cot, opened it and took out Martha's linen. I held it to my face. It smelt fresh and clean.

'A man like me?' Turold smiled at his friend. 'I am the sort of man who makes the world.'

'The pride of fools.'

'Rather the pride of fools than the humility of the pious.'

' "By humility and the fear of the Lord are riches, and honour, and life." '

'Another dead prophet?'

'The Book of Proverbs was not the work of a prophet.'

'Priest, semanticist, philosopher. Do your talents ever cease?'

Rainald looked away. 'I am a humble man,' he said. 'It is enough for me to honour God. It is left to men like you to express His will, His thought.'

'I express God's thought?' Turold laughed at his friend. 'Me?'

'Of course. We all express God's thought, but you have been especially blessed. Few are.'

'Maybe...'

'Not maybe...'

'Flattery...'

'Truth...'

Martha.

Night was falling. Turold and Rainald loved as brothers. They argued and fought, they rarely found good words for each other; when they did, the words were not believed. One envied the other's talent, and believed that the other did not understand that this talent was a gift. Gifts should be accepted with grace and used to honour the giver and the thought behind the original deed. The other scorned the one's absolute belief, the certainty of faith and the calmness of his nature. Rather than be angry, Rainald was 'disappointed' with Turold. Turold wanted anger, but he knew enough to know that he would not get it. He got a long, steady stare instead, and said, 'I know.'

'You know,' said Rainald, 'but you don't care.'

'How can you say that? I cared enough about the work to resist a text's intrusion. I risked my life for my convictions; have you ever done that?'

'You know I have...'

'Forgive me...'

'You are.'

Ten years previously, a fire had consumed the greater part of the monastery of St Denis. Against advice and order, Rainald had returned to the burning library to rescue a Bible, a History of Saints, a History of St Denis and twelve rolls of sketched parchment. His courage showed in scars that covered his back, his hands and his right ear. They required the daily application of butter.

'You were brave.'

'I was God's instrument.'

'God's instrument...' mumbled Turold.

'Believe and you will understand and fear nothing, no one.'

'I'm not afraid of anyone now. Belief has nothing to do with fear.'

'You are wrong.'

Turold laughed.

'You fear the scribe.'

Turold stopped laughing.

'Don't you?'

Turold did not answer.

'Do you fear words?'

'Pictures have more power.'

'Pictures never changed the world.'

'Have words?'

'The Bible,' said Rainald, 'has changed the world.'

'So words can suit any man for any purpose. Pictures can never be so two-faced.'

I looked down at the yard below the lodging. Martha came from her door. She was carrying a bucket of swill. She tipped it on to a heap, poked it with her foot, a dog came and sniffed the fresh pile. She said, 'Shoo!' then she turned and looked up at me.

Her face reflected the stars, her eyes were blue and her hair was long. I held the linen in my hand, I turned it over and sniffed it. As the material touched my face, she held up her hand, smiled and waved.

I looked over my shoulder. Rainald was saying, 'Faith is...', Turold was shaking his head. I looked back at Martha. She opened her mouth, licked her lips and waved again.

I waved back.

She put her hand down. She held her empty bucket as someone else would hold a tray of eggs. Her fingers were white and tiny, I wanted to shout to her.

'Sheep...' said Rainald.

I held up the linen, but she would not know why or what it was for. I saw the shadows her breasts made, I saw her tongue in the dying light. A voice called from the bakery, she put her hand up again, closed her fingers and walked away.

'The Lord watches over His wayward sheep,' said Rainald.

'Do not compare me to a sheep and I will not compare you to a goat.'

Eight wooden frames were set in the workshop. Each measured nine paces in length and four spans in width. The linen was stretched on these frames. There was room between each pair of frames for benches. The embroiderers sat on these to work. Small boxes were provided for needles and wool. At the far end of the workshop, Turold arranged a trestle. Here he laid the sketches, his brushes and quills, his inks and cloths.

Oblong boxes were arranged on small trestles beneath the windows. These contained the stock of wool. Five main colours had been dyed. These were:

Terracotta red.

Blue-green.

Dark green.

Sea blue.

Gold.

Two other colours were prepared in smaller quantities. These were:

Sage green.

Night blue.

Empty of people, the workshop resembled a scene from a dream. The frames were solid and well built, the linen was white and trembled slightly when a breeze blew in the windows, the benches were neatly rowed and the baskets of wool breathed an air of promise. I was with Turold when he transferred the first sketches to the linen.

He used charcoal sticks for the outlines, and marked letters to indicate colours. The folds of tunics, the harnesses, roof tiles and windows were carefully drawn, the first boat was launched on to lines of waves, while in the borders, the first fables were put in place.

Ermenburga came as we were working. A week had passed since our last meeting. When she entered the workshop, Turold put down his charcoal, rubbed his hands in a cloth, approached the Abbess and said, 'You have been hiding from us.'

Ermenburga's face was thinner than I had ever seen it, her eyes were red, she took Turold's hand and said, 'You were forgiven?'

'Does the Bishop forgive? Can he?'

'That is for you to tell me.'

'Maybe,' Turold said, 'maybe not. He forgives if it is in his interests. If he believed he could complete the work without me, he would have had my hands, at the least.'

'I am glad you kept them.' Ermenburga had not let go of Turold's hand. She rubbed its back with the tips of her fingers, he bowed his head towards her and for a moment, I thought he would kiss her. 'Is Mildred safe?' he said.

'Yes.'

'And our escort?'

'Your escort?'

'Three Englishmen. They acted as guards.'

Ermenburga released Turold's hand. 'She said nothing about them, but I am sure they are safe. She would have said if they were not.' She looked around.

'And you?'

'I?'

'Mildred told me.'

'She should not have done that.'

'No,' said Turold. 'She should. And I will…'

'Please.' Ermenburga put her finger to her lips.

'Please what?'

'Forget what you know. I do not want to…'

'This,' said Turold, 'is just another job for me.'

Ermenburga laughed now. I had not heard her laugh before. She covered her mouth with her hand, her eyes cleared, she reminded me of a girl. 'I know you do not mean that. You cannot.'

'I don't,' he said. 'But your laugh was worth the lie.'

'Please,' said Ermenburga.

Turold took her hand and drew it towards him. She turned away, bowed her head and said, 'No.'

No.

Turold.

He picked up a stick of charcoal and went back to work. She did not move. I passed him a cloth, the sun shone through the windows, through the linen and on to the floor. The Abbess took a step towards Turold, then she walked to the door. He turned as she opened it and said, 'Forgive me. I was proving that I can be as stupid as you think.'

'You are not as stupid as you think.'

'A part of me is more intelligent than anyone.'

'Stupidity is intelligence's shadow.'

Look at me. I am standing to one side. I pray for a voice, and I pray for the chance to leave my mark. I am not stupid, I am not intelligent, I had the luck to be there. I was there from start to finish, and when I think about it now, I do not think I paid enough attention.

My pigeons flew. They took a path from their loft to the woods. I watched them go. The English summer was hot. They flew lazily. There were six of them. Each knew its place in the kit, none jostled another.

Here was the sun and here was the sky, there are the trees and my birds flew towards them. They are my birds, I have power over nothing else. They respond to the only sound my mouth can make. I whistle three times and they come, I click my fingers and they rustle in their basket. They will never be free, I will never be free, Turold will never be free, Ermenburga will never be free, Odo will never be free, William will never be free. Rainald thinks he is free in God, Martha's breasts are free, free as the birds.

This story is not complete. The rambles interrupt the story. Is the story more important than the rest? Are my pigeons more important than anything? In their minds, do they think the same as us? They are dumb, they coo and squeak, but that is all.

Now they are flying back from the woods. If they wished to fly over my head and not come back, I could not stop them. They are flying fast. They are their own arrows, I am holding Martha's linen in my hand.

I have cut two holes in the strip, and with two larger circles of linen I cut from the ends, I am going to stitch a bowl over each hole. Her breasts will be able to sit in these bowls, like puddings. I would not think of her breasts as puddings, but this is one way to explain.

Turold's job is to explain.

Here I am.

My pigeons are back from the woods. One is perched upon my head. It has shat in my hair. This is the kiss of pigeons, and this, as the day spins and I allow it to, is the gate of cunning.

If you have seen Odo's hanging, all the lengths stitched together, the story complete and balanced from beginning to end, the colours of the wool, the life in the horse, the strength of the ships, the expressions on the faces of important characters, it is easy to imagine the look of the linen as it filled with the outlines. It was the ghost of art, the end of Odo's dream. The lines of charcoal were applied thinly, the linen was stretched tight and easy to work. It was my job, as Turold reached the end of the first strip, to complete the borders. He had sketched the outlines of a pair of birds here, a pair of bears there, a fable here, a hunting scene where a hunting scene should be. Diagonal lines of colour would separate these scenes. He had put a line of dots where each solid bar would be, and in a generous moment, allowed me to choose the colours of the bars. I am about to leave my mark, and here, about to leave his mark, is Brother Lull. Odo has offered to accompany him on his first visit to the workshop, but the scribe says he can look after himself.

It was a warm day in the middle of August. Rainald was sitting at a window, listening to bird-song. Turold and I were fiddling with this scene: Westminster Abbey is completed, the weathercock is erected, the Hand of God blesses it. Edward's shrouded corpse is carried by eight men. Two acolytes carry bells. Turold was trying to find room for four pairs of legs at the front of the bier, and four pairs at the rear; he struggled, he gave up, Lull knocked on the door, Turold shouted, 'Who is it?' and the scribe opened the door.

Lull's robes were stained, he had a paunch, ink on his fingers, bad teeth and a beard. His beard was thin and scraggy, and there was a bald patch over one cheek. His eyes were dull, I do not think there was a muscle in his body.

'Master Turold?' he said.

Turold thought the man was a messenger. 'Yes?' he said. 'What do you want?'

'I am Brother Lull. Bishop Odo's scribe.'

'Lull?' said Turold.

Rainald left his place and came to where we were, but he did not say anything.

'At your service,' said Lull, nervously.

'If you were at my service,' said Turold, 'you would not be here.' He began to draw a row of cobbles for the bearers to walk upon. Lull narrowed his eyes and watched.

'I heard,' he said, 'you were unhappy a text was to be added.'

'Unhappy,' said Turold, 'is not the word I would have used.' The cobbles stretched from the eastern end of the abbey to the foot of the walls of King Edward's palace. 'I was insulted.'

'Bishop Odo and I have…'

'Bishop Odo and I!' Turold mimicked Lull's high, weedy voice. 'You enjoy a special friendship?'

'I think so.'

'Do you?' Turold finished the cobbles, dropped his charcoal into a box, turned and faced the man. 'You like to think?'

'Yes.'

'I thought scribes hated to think.'

Rainald tapped Turold's ankle with his foot.

Lull did not rise to the bait.

Turold looked at the scribe. Turold does not dislike often, but he made an exception for Lull. Lull shuffled from one foot to another and looked away. I felt sorry for him now; he was following orders, he did not want to irritate the designer. He said, 'Will you choose the style of script?'

'I have not been asked to.'

'You are the designer.'

'Thank you for reminding me.'

Rainald took Turold's arm, led him to a corner of the work-shop and said, 'Listen.'

'What?'

'You and Brother Lull will be working together for many months. It would be wise to remember this.'

'Wise?'

'Yes.'

'How could I forget?'

'You misunderstand me. If you mean to antagonise him from the start, you will allow your work to suffer. You remember Abbot Nicholas's cope?'

'How could I forget?'

Lull was leaning forward, straining to hear.

The Abbot Nicholas's cope was designed by Turold in the eighth year of the conquest. In an effort to impress his loyalty to Odo, the Abbot demanded the orphreys embroidered with arms of Norman knights; for this reason, a secretary, expert in the study of arms, travelled to Bayeux.

This pale and slimy man insisted on interfering in the general design of the cope, a servant who believed himself above other servants. Turold wished to depict twelve scenes from The Life in frames of cloud. The secretary suggested that twelve was an inappropriate number. Turold hit the secretary, broke his nose and lost the commission. Later, he was thanked by Bishop Odo for blooding the man, but the thanks were tempered by a warning. Upset his servants and you upset the Bishop; at that time he was indulged because Odo disliked the Abbot Nicholas. Rainald said, 'You remember what Bishop Odo said at the time?'

'Not what he said.'

'Upset my servants and you upset me.'

'I am his servant now, and I am upset. Did that count for anything?'

'He forgave you.'

'I have already discussed his idea of forgiveness with Ermenburga.'

'I know.'

Turold fixed Rainald's eyes; he held them for a minute, then turned and said to Lull, 'If you do not try to interfere with my design, we will be able to work together. But...'

'I was never...'

'But we will fight if you begin to voice any opinion on this.' He pointed at the outline of William's council with Odo, and the order given to build the invasion fleet. 'You know where the text is to be placed?'

'I have an idea; if I use your sketches, I could ink on them.'

'You could what?' Turold raised his voice, Rainald bowed his head and whispered something I did not hear.

'I should say, this was Bishop Odo's suggestion.'

'Odo can…'

'Turold,' said Rainald.

I heard a dog, barking beyond the precinct walls.

'Odo,' said Turold again.

Lull lowered his eyes, I saw him smile.

Lull.

He was liked by no one, had only been loved by his mother, he would take payment for anything from anyone, he did not owe people anything, he wanted his revenge on the world. He pitied himself, for no one else would, his faith had dried up years before; greed and a desire to hinder others' progress had filled the place where faith had been. He imagined his Bishop's favour when news of Turold's attitude was delivered. Rainald said, 'I think then, you should see the sketches.' He put his hand on Turold's shoulder.

'It would be a good idea.'

'One man's idea is…' Turold began.

'Turold!' said Rainald, and the monk's eyes flashed with a look faith could not control. When we flew for the coast, he had never sprung like this. Now he turned Turold towards him and said, 'It is a good idea. The hanging will have a text, that is final. Brother Lull will be unable to place it without reference to your sketches, and then you will be able to make whatever changes you wish.' He turned to the scribe. 'I am sure that would be Bishop Odo's wish?'

'Yes,' said Lull, softly. 'I am sure he would not like to think that his designer was unhappy in any way. An unhappy man is unlikely to produce the best work, is he?' He raised his eyebrows and looked straight at Turold. He had no talent, no talent at all, but for the ability to disturb Turold's mind. The one man's head was full of pictures and colour, the other's was a jumble of words. Words come in black and white, they can only be read by those who understand the language. Pictures can be understood by people of all ages, faiths and races; words are more dangerous. They hold secrets better than pictures, they can fly like pigeons. Pictures hang like hawks, and there it is.

9

Here is Martha's linen, stitched and ready to give. I am waiting by the bakery door with it tucked in my waist, I am holding the most beautiful pigeon I own.

Her feathers are flecked with red, her eyes are bright as jewels, she sits in my hand as Martha's breasts will sit in their bowls. I am stroking the pigeon's head when she comes out, she saw me standing there, I did not move.

'Hello,' she said.

I nodded.

'Robert?'

Yes.

'I see you every day.'

I opened my mouth, and for a moment it was filled with the shadows of words, as it had been when Bishop Odo spoke to me. William's half-brother has spoken to me, and has asked for my opinion.

'You cannot talk, can you?'

I shook my head.

'I am sorry.'

She said this as if it was her fault, and she would do anything in the world to give me a voice.

I put my hand to my waist and felt the linen. The more I thought about it, the more impossible it was to give.

'How long have we lived next door to each other?'

I do not count.

'Oh!' she said suddenly, and looked at my pigeon. 'Can I hold him?'

I shook my head. He is a she.

'Why not?'

I nodded my head now and passed the bird to her.

Our fingers touched as I gave the bird to her. She held her as the nest and said, 'She is so warm.'

Her cupped hands were bigger than the cups I had stitched to the linen. I put my hand to my waist and looked at her eyes. They were filled with wonder, big and blue as sky. 'I have seen you fly them. Do they always return?'

I nodded.

'They must love you.'

They know me, if that means love. I put out my hand to take the bird back; when she was in my hands again, I pointed to the city wall and opened my mouth.

'Are you going to fly her?'

I pointed to the wall again, and walked away. Martha followed me, I could hear her footsteps next to mine, and the rustle of her clothes. Her hair was fine and shiny. She was the same height as me. I stood back to let her climb the steps and followed her up.

Her ankles were tiny, and I was thinking how could such fragile things hold up her body? Then I was thinking they make such a nice sound as the bones click together, and her calves are so white and smooth, and I was squeezing my bird. She squeaked, I relaxed my grip and stroked the top of her head. A pigeon's head feels so light to touch, and then we were on the wall together. It was early in the evening, and children were playing on the rubbish below us.

The sun was sinking, the forest was covered in light that turned the leaves gold, the sky was as high as it ever was, and bluer than the sea.

'Are you going to let her go?' said Martha.

I nodded and held the bird to my lips, pecked her lightly on the top of her head, then held her above my head and opened my hands. She sat in my palms for a second, lifted her tail, then opened her wings and flew, tipped slightly in the air then righted herself and went like an arrow, over the rubbish to the trees. I whistled once and she adjusted her flight; Martha said, 'She can hear you?'

I nodded.

'I can hear you,' she said.

I looked at Martha. There was nothing I could do. I moved towards her, and as I had done with my hen, I pecked her lightly on the top of her head. As I did, she lifted her face and kissed my lips. We held each other's gaze, I forgot about the bird. Her hair blew towards me and brushed against my cheeks, children yelled below us, but I did not hear them. I put my hand to my waist and pulled out the linen, and gave it to her. I said, 'I made this for you,' in my head, I opened my mouth, forced the words into it, but they stuck there. I prayed for them, I prayed for a sign, she took the linen and said, 'What is this?'

I smiled.

She opened the linen and held it up. 'For me?' she said.

I nodded.

She turned it upside down, she held it the right way up, she put her hands in the bowls. 'What is it for?'

I could not say.

'Did you make it?'

I nodded.

'Is it for straining? For cheese?'

Oh God.

'My father uses bags like this, but they are not so small.'

Size has got nothing to do with it.

She held it to her face. 'This is fine stuff,' she said.

I am smiling.

'Where did you get it?'

I shrugged.

'I have never seen finer.'

I held my hands as cups and placed them over my chest, but as I did this, she turned towards a noise below us. Suddenly I was red, I scratched under my arms and she said, 'Did you steal it?'

I shook my head.

She shook her head.

We are shaking heads together.

This was my prayer. Dear God, Take my sight and give me voice in its place. I will never forget what Martha looks like, her face will always be behind my eyes, whether she is with me or not.

I have my eyes closed, and I am thinking about God in heaven, and his thoughts. All men have gifts as all men have been denied. Some men never know what they were denied, others can never forget; as Turold was His instrument, so I was Turold's instrument, and useless blind. God did not reply, I opened my mouth, said the words, 'It is for you, to hold you,' but not a sound came.

Martha said, 'Is this your way of pleasing my father?'

It could be.

'He'll be pleased with it, I'm sure.' She folded it and tucked it into her waist, then kissed me on the lips again. This time, we did not move away from each other, the tip of her tongue flicked into my mouth, I touched it with mine, her arm pulled me tight, then we broke apart and she said, 'A boy who does not talk.'

What could I say?

'Does everyone love you?'

I do not think so.

'I think they do,' she said.

This is stupid.

'Who do you love?'

I turned away from her and whistled. The forest was vast and stretched from coast to coast. My pigeon appeared as a speck, then grew as she approached, the red feathers on her wings were tinted by the sun, and she held her neck out. She folded her wings before dropping down to me. I scooped a handful of corn from a bag, and held it up. She landed on my fist; I brought her down, let her feed, then stroked her head.

'Do you have a girl?' said Martha.

I shook my head.

'Would you like one?'

I nodded my head.

'Would you like me?'

I looked at her face. Her chin was small, her ears were like flowers. Her nose was straight and covered with freckles. Her shirt was open to the top of her breasts. I nodded again.

She smiled.

I bent down and drew a sign in the dirt.

She said, 'That is pretty. What is it?'

I can draw.

She talks, I do not.

'You are so clever,' she said, and she took my arm. She stroked the hen's head. 'I never thought I would meet someone like you.'

No.

I put my hand on hers and squeezed her fingers. A voice called 'Martha!' from below. She shouted 'Coming!' and said to me, 'My father. Would you like to see him?'

I shook my head.

'He would like to see you.'

I pointed towards the nunnery, and made a scribbling sign with my hand.

'You have to work?'

I nodded.

'And such beautiful work, I know.'

It is beautiful work. I am with Turold and he is with me. I lifted Martha's hand to my mouth and kissed it, then I let her go and I walked to the loft, bedded the hen and then followed the alley to the gates of Nunnaminster.

The transfer of sketch to linen continued for weeks. Occasionally, the twin fowl came to the workshop to inspect the work, but most days Turold and I worked alone, while Brother Lull sat at the far end of the workshop, writing sentences, cursing quietly, scratching out words, inserting different, battling with the sense. I know the form and style of the embroidery had appeared to Turold by magic. The story was well known. Harold was not a bad man. He was brave, he was dignified; his mistake was to swear on the Relics of Bayeux and then break his oath. He paid his price, as anyone will pay the price of betrayal. Harold was a hero, now he is dead, and the man who helped him become a hero — William — is King of his lands. Turold's vision of the story slipped quietly on to the linen. Lull's vision was clouded, the clouds would not clear.

Turold came to him as he snapped a quill, wiped his hands and pushed the sketches away.

'Are you struggling?'

'Yes.'

'Why?'

'Why?' Lull stood up, tossed the broken quill to the floor and said, 'Have you any idea of the size of my problems?'

'Are they big?' said Turold.

'And you mock me.'

'You have so many problems...'

'The only thing you and I have in common is orders. If I had the choice, I would be away.'

'No!' said Turold. 'Don't leave us!'

Lull turned away and looked at the sketches.

Here, above the ships being dragged to the sea, Lull has written, 'Here the ships are dragged to the sea.' Turold followed the words with his finger and laughed. 'I'd never have known that this is what is happening.' He traced his fingers along the ropes that run from the ships to the men. The men are barelegged, wading into the water.

'That is my biggest problem.'

'Ah...'

'Why do I have to state the obvious?'

'That is what I asked Odo.'

'And his reply?'

Turold shrugged. 'He did not convince me, but his mind was made up. It defied reason, he was most insistent. The more I tried to persuade him otherwise, the more fixed he became in his ideas.'

'Did he?'

'Yes,' said Turold, 'he did. It is a habit of his.'

I am wondering; does Lull mean what he says, or are his problems created for our benefit? Does he want us to believe that he considers Odo stupid so we express our true thoughts about the man? Turold does not trust Lull. He wears a knowing smile as he talks to the scribe. He said, 'Leave the story to me and do as Odo requests. I am resigned to your contribution; if I was not, then you would have problems.'

Lull thinks Turold is playing with him. He does not know what else to think. Bishop Odo has told him to keep one eye on the master's work and an ear to his talk; now he thinks that he and the master have more in common than not. All Odo's servants live under a black cloud; it is how to see the cloud that counts. It covered Lull, it was hardly noticed by Turold, I saw it once or twice, but the Bishop had winked at me, he had asked my opinion, he saw no threat from me.

'My contribution,' said Lull, and he turned back to the sketches, sat down and let out a sigh. He picked up a fresh quill and mumbled to himself. He looked grey and sad. He had rejected the divine master for an earthly, while all the time he wanted no living master at all. Turold's only master was his work; Lull envied this. Lull was a slave to his work. Once he had loved words and seen truth in the way they could lie, now he hated them. His head was boiling with uncertainty and guilt. Once he had loved, now he was lost. He wanted to obey Bishop Odo but he wanted to give some trust to Turold.

He was in a crisis. He buried his head in his hands and said, 'These men are carrying arms to the ships.'

'Do you like the way they strain?' said Turold.

Lull did not answer.

Look at the expressions on the faces of the men who carry the arms and haul the cart. They are walking slowly, it is a hot day. Turold sketched his scene in no time at all, he saw it in a dream, he heard the sound of the cart wheels on the ground, and the curses of the men.

10

In the night, Turold was joined on the wall by Ermenburga. They stood next to each other. They did not touch, their cloaks did not brush, the moon was down, wind blew through the forest. She said, 'I have two weeks left.'

Turold did not say anything.

'I do not know what to do. My life is here, I have only left Winchester...' she stopped for a moment, '...four times. I would not know what to do if I was forced to leave.'

Turold ran his fingers through his hair.

'I have been raped,' she said, 'but never by the Bishop I kneel before. If he had me and I was permitted to stay, I would have to leave. Either way I am trapped.'

He put his hand on her shoulder, she did not move away. 'I have some influence,' he said.

'How?'

'When the sketches are complete, William will inspect them.'

'So?'

'I may speak to him.'

'About me?'

'Yes.'

'No one speaks before being spoken to. You would...'

'I speak when I like.'

'Please…'

'Why not?'

'No!' Ermenburga became agitated. She took a step back, put her hand to her mouth and shook her head. 'They have no secrets. They would…'

'William does not trust Odo. You know that. The Bishop is too ambitious. If he is trying to find favour through my work, he will be disappointed.'

'I do not believe you.'

'Abbess,' said Turold, and he turned her towards him. 'I never talk unless I know that what I am saying is the truth.'

'Ha!' Her profile cut the night, we had knives like that in the workshops. Knives for linen, knives for life. 'However much William mistrusts Bishop Odo, they are half-brothers. You would be meddling in family business.'

'William holds strong views. He sees the immorality of his court reflecting upon him. He would be convinced.'

'Of what?'

'His brother's lust threatens his own position. William knows that control is best achieved through example. Convince conquered people that you lead an exemplary life and they will respect you. His own marriage is proof of this.'

Ermenburga pulled her cloak around her and said, 'What you suggest is…'

'The only way,' said Turold. He was firm. 'There is no other.'

'I wonder. If I am to survive…'

'You will.'

Ermenburga moved towards Turold, hesitated and then laid her hand on his arm. They looked at each other, and in the black gap between them, a star appeared. I thought they would kiss, I thought he would take her head in his hands, but he was the first to move away. She gathered her cloak, turned and walked away. Turold watched her go, then, as he passed my hiding-place, he said, 'Come on, Robert. Martha will be going to bed.'

I stood up.

He put his hand on my head and ruffled my hair. I looked into my master's eyes and they were as kind as Martha's, as kind as a pigeon's, they were deep and I thought they knew everything.

The last sketch was transferred to the linen on the first day of autumn.

The frames stood in their places in the workshop, each covered with the charcoaled outline of the story. Men, ships and horses floated on the linen, as if they could fill themselves with colour. There was life in them, a quiet, hardly breathing life, drifting between heaven and earth.

The linen snapped in the breeze that blew through the workshop, falling leaves gathered in small heaps at the door.

Turold and I stood on a table, so we could look down and see the entire work, one strip behind another. He held my hand and said, 'Be proud of yourself.'

Pride.

Those horses; did they move? Did they whinny?

The dogs are barking.

Men enjoy a meal.

Men wade into the sea carrying dogs.

The ships sail across a faint sea.

Men ride.

Men are questioned.

Below us, on the first strip, Turold had sketched himself, as is the custom, as a dwarf. He is holding the reins of two horses, floating above the ground, as if supported by cunning. His beard is tidy, his feet are small, he holds his head up.

Below him, in the border, a boy is slinging stones at a pair of birds. This is me. See how I am aiming wide of the birds, see my big hands? I stitched my own hands, I stitched the sling, I left my mark on the world, as the world touched me and I touched Martha.

I was thinking about Martha as we tidied the workshop. We met each day on the wall, and she talked about baking, asked questions about home, wanted to know who my mother and father were, and she kissed me. I kissed her, I put my arm around her waist, but I would become fixed there. The more I wanted to slip a hand beneath her dress so the more difficult it was to do. I imagined the feel of her stomach, I wanted to touch her breasts. I did not want to hurt her, I wanted her to want me. She was not the girl I had imagined her to be; she was shy, and not at all confident. She told me I gave her confidence, but only when I was with her. She said I reflected my master's greatness, and that I had some of it myself. I sat quietly with her, her hair smelt of flour. As Turold and I were in the workshop, I took a deep breath, as if I could draw the thought of her smell to me. Turold was saying, 'Put those rags for the wash,' when I heard a commotion outside, horses and the shouts of men, the clank of arms and the heavy rustling of armour.

'Dismount!'

'Whoa!'

'Steady!'

There was more shouting.

I began to walk towards the door but Turold took my arm and pulled me back. 'Quiet,' he said.

Why?

Give it to me! It is no use to You. You have a thousand voices, and each of them speaks a thousand languages, and each mouth holds a thousand tongues. And as I pleaded — I am almost on my knees, blood is rushing into my legs and out again, my eyes are screaming with tears and my mouth is full of salt — King William entered the workshop.

What will I say? The stories and legends I have heard, the love and fear and hatred. The cruelty and the forgiveness, his understanding and courage. His presence filled the workshop, his clothes were magnificent, his face was large and grave.

His hair was the colour of rust. I could not look at his eyes. I stared at his hands. They were huge, and covered in hairs. He said, 'This is it?' His voice was low and quiet, like thunder rolling over hills. Bishop Odo appeared behind him and squeaked, 'It is.'

Odo was rubbing his hands together, nervously. He was sweating.

Turold took a step.

I stayed where I was.

'And this,' said Odo, 'is Master Turold.'

'Master Turold,' said William.

Turold moved forward, bent and kissed the ring.

'Yes,' said William.

Turold stood.

William studied his face. They were equal in height, their eyes met, the King said,'Show me your work.'

William walked along the strips, Turold followed two paces behind, I was at Turold's elbow, Odo was three paces behind me, clerks followed him. William's men stood at the door and scowled; leaves blew against the backs of their legs.

As I followed the King, I felt power in the air. It followed him like foam in the wake of a ship, it smelt of fire and blood. His shoulders were huge, he stopped and stared at himself in conversation with Harold in the palace at Rouen. The palace arches were carefully outlined, William appears calm as he listens to two men's opinion. He is pointing in the sketch, he is pointing at himself and he said, 'This is fine work.'

Bishop Odo said, 'The best.'

'We will wait and see.'

Turold swallowed hard.

I touched his coat.

William turned around and said to Turold, 'Your reputation is justified.'

Turold was speechless. He tugged his beard. I did not let go of his coat. William coughed, and then he looked down at me.

His eyes were big and brown, and pierced me as if they were reading my thoughts. I was thinking, 'If I touch his coat, I will be given my voice.' This is a truth. His hands were folded in front of him, I looked away from his face, then he went down on his haunches, took my face in his hands and said, 'And who are you?'

I gagged, breath shot to my mouth in spurts, I put my hands out to steady myself, his hand was cold, it froze my skin, I wanted to run. His beard had crumbs in it, my legs could not move, my mouth was open. I had to say who I was. Turold said, 'This is Robert, my boy. He is dumb.'

'Dumb?' said William.

I nodded at the King.

The King's eyes softened. He loves children and dogs, he believes they are unlikely to scheme. 'Why?'

'He has never spoken,' said Turold. 'He was found by the monks of Bayeux. As a baby he never cried; the physicians could not explain it.'

'Physicians cannot explain anything,' said William, and he stood up straight. He laid his hand on my head, I gasped for breath, no words came, he turned away and said, 'And here,' pointing to the linen, 'I give arms to Harold.'

'Yes,' said Turold, smiling. The text had not been sketched in.

William walked slowly along the linen, nodding here, scratching his head there, stopping to look closely at the image of Harold crowned at Westminster. By the time he had reached the eve of the battle, Odo was ten paces behind, discussing a detail with two clerks, strangers to the nunnery. So Turold dared say, 'Your Majesty?'

'Master Turold?'

'Your Majesty...'

William looked from the work and said, 'You have something to say?'

'If I may be allowed.'

The King looked into Turold's eyes. There was no trace of deceit in them, or worry. 'You are.'

'I have promised a helpless woman, and only you can help me keep my promise.'

'How is that?'

Turold looked towards Odo. The Bishop was squeaking at his own image. He was advising William, his face was thinner than real life, and appeared to radiate love and understanding. The clerks were indulging him, congratulating him on his taste, envying his appreciation. William said, 'Does what you have to say concern Bishop Odo?'

Turold nodded.

'He is too keen to impress me; he must be shown that I am chosen, he was merely picked.'

'He,' said Turold, 'has demanded the Abbess of Nunnaminster screw him, and if she does not, she will lose her position.'

'He has what?' William's voice was raised. Odo and the clerks looked towards him, he held a hand up.

'The Abbess Ermenburga…'

'He wishes to screw the Abbess?'

Turold said, 'Yes.'

William's clenched his fists. 'Odo,' he hissed.

'Your Majesty…' said Turold.

William's eyes were white with anger, spit was at the corners of his mouth. 'What do you want?'

'I told the Abbess I would speak with you, but she was afraid.'

'And you were not? To approach me in this way?'

'I am your servant.'

'You are.'

'Forgive me.'

William looked hard at Turold, his face relaxed and he said, 'She has nothing to fear.' He licked his lips. 'Nor you.'

'The embroidery will not suffer?'

'No. I will make sure of that.'

'Thank you,' said Turold. 'We thank you.' He put his hand on my head.

'No,' said William, 'I thank you.'

Turold bowed, William clapped him on the shoulder, then turned and hurried from the workshop. Bishop Odo watched him leave, he looked at us, Turold smiled, the Bishop's face was crossed by question, then panic, then he hurried after the King, but the King was gone, spurring his horse across the precinct yard to the gates.

11

I lay on a hill with Martha and my pigeons. I rested my head on their basket, she sat with her legs crossed and played with leaves.

'Do you love me?' she said.

I nodded.

'How much?'

I stretched my arms as far as they would go. She moved towards me, I wrapped my arms around her and nestled my face in her face. I opened my mouth and breathed her in. There were cows on the hill.

'I love you,' she said.

I tried to get my hand on her stomach. She took the hand and held it.

I looked hurt.

She raised her eyebrows. I held my hands over her breasts. She slapped them. I smiled. I loved her, and I loved her because she could give me voice. I had touched a bishop, I had been touched by a king, neither had given me the power. The messengers of divine and temporal power were powerless, only virgin love would do. I thought this, I imagined that I had belief and some sort of belief lay upon me. Martha lay upon me, and as her hair covered my eyes, I kissed her.

Bishop Odo's anger was greater than any I had seen. He came to the workshop as Turold was removing a man and adding a cow to the scene inscribed, 'And here the soldiers hurried to Hastings to seize food.'

Look at this cow. This is not the work of a worried man. Turold was at peace with himself. He had spoken to the King, and the King had responded. He had saved Ermenburga from Odo, the cow is jumping with joy.

'Your foolishness,' screamed the Bishop, 'exceeds all others!'

'My Lord?' said Turold, as if the fat man was whispering.

'And do not use that tone!' Odo's mouth quivered, his chins bounced up and down. He held himself upright, his stomach was like a barrel. 'You forget who I am!'

'You are a bishop,' said Turold.

'And your King's brother! Whatever you dared say to him, do not think you can come between us.'

'I would not dare…'

'But you dared speak before being spoken to.'

'I listened to my conscience.'

'Did you?' said Odo. 'And it spoke?'

'Yes.'

'And it told you to betray your patron?'

'Betrayal,' said Turold, 'was not mentioned. Hypocrisy and…'

'Hypocrisy?' Odo's face was red, and covered with sweat. 'You accuse me of hypocrisy?'

'I did not accuse you. I informed the King that his servant's morals reflected on him. He was grateful for the reminder.'

'You have the impertinence to claim that?' Odo slammed his fist on a trestle, the trestle buckled, its legs snapped, sketches slipped to the floor.

'I am only reporting what I believe to be true.'

'True?' Odo kicked at the trestle. 'The truth is this! You and I were patron and designer. We were as close as men of different stations could be. Maybe, and I remember the time, we touched the edge of friendship, but now…' he drew himself up to his full height and licked his lips, '…now we are enemies.'

'My Lord.'

'William humiliated me before the court.'

'I am sorry.'

'You will be.' Bishop Odo's voice was hard and sharp, it cut the workshop air and burnt the pieces. 'When the hanging is finished, when William sees that I honour him, and when he has forgotten that you ever spoke to him, then I will take pleasure in watching you plead for mercy. You will regret that you ever spoke...'

'And Ermenburga?'

Odo laughed. 'Ermenburga is nothing. I could have her whatever the circumstance.'

Turold did not move. He said, 'Could you?'

Odo narrowed his eyes and lowered his voice. 'Why don't you learn, Turold?'

'We are all learning, all the time.'

'That is true, but some of us learn the wrong things and forget what they should remember.'

'I agree.'

'So you have some sense?'

'I have more sense...,' began Turold, then he stopped.

'You have more sense what?'

'I have work to do.'

'No!' Now Odo took Turold's shirt and pulled him towards him. 'You have more sense than who? Me?'

'My Lord...'

'You walk a fine line, Turold. Finer than any you could draw, and more dangerous.'

Turold did not flinch. He believed he was protected by truth. Though he lacked faith he saw God looking down at the world and considering all men equal. Why should he be afraid of someone because they had one kind of power? He had another, and it would last longer than any. He said, 'The only lines I care about are these.' He turned towards the linen, and as he did, Odo struck him on the chin. As soon as the blow landed, Turold pulled himself away, his eyes flashed and he hit back.

His fist caught Odo on the cheek, the fat man's face appeared to throw itself away from his head, he staggered, he was out of condition. He could barely mount a horse unaided, his chins bounced up and met his mouth. A sound came from him, like a dog's bark; he put his hand to his cheek, he was bleeding. The blood trickled through his fingers, he looked at it, he looked at Turold and yelled, 'You dare hit me?' He took a deep breath. 'You hit your Bishop?'

Turold shook his head. 'I do not consider a man's position before I hit him.'

'You should,' said Odo, and he lunged towards Turold, who side-stepped and pushed him in the back as he went by. The Bishop could not stop himself tumbling into another trestle; it collapsed beneath his weight and he lay on it, on his stomach, his cloak thrown up to cover his head. Turold smiled at me, he did not care. I thought he had gone too far now, too close to the heat, you could not humiliate Bishop Odo and live. You cannot expect William's constant support. The protection of the realm was more important than the resolving of petty quarrels. Odo was a greater part of the system than Turold could be. William would tolerate Odo's immorality rather than see the ripples it caused threaten stability. William could, Odo would, Odo struggled to pick himself up, but caught his feet on the cloak and went down again.

Turold took a step towards him and said, 'My Lord, I...'

'Never!' yelled Odo and he ripped his cloak from his neck, threw it to one side and pulled himself to his feet. 'I will never forget this!' I thought his face would explode.

Turold did not say anything.

'You may worry now, but when this work is finished, then you will sweat.'

'I...'

'Do you understand?' Odo picked up his cloak and flung it over his shoulder.

'I think...'

'And that is your problem! You think but you do not allow your head to consider your thoughts before your mouth opens.' He brushed past me. I smelt bad eggs in the air, he had blood on his lips. He stopped in front of Turold and hissed, 'Work well; this will be the last mark you make.'

The last mark you make. The expression on Turold's face did not change. He looked at Bishop Odo, but I do not think he saw him. The patron provided the means, the designer provided a glimpse of heaven and a glimpse of heaven was stronger than a draught of poison or the strength of arms. Turold wore a calm and satisfied face, his eyes were clear, his lips were moist, his beard was thick and black.

Ermenburga said, 'I never intended to lead you into such trouble.'

Turold still did not care. 'The only trouble that bothers me is this; do we have enough night blue?'

'Night blue?'

'Wool.'

'I think,' said Ermenburga, then, 'Turold...'

'Yes.'

'Do not mock me.'

'I am mocking no one.' He stood over the Abbess, he put his hand on her shoulder. 'I know Odo's threats are real. I know he will have his revenge, but I cannot regret what I did. I cannot deny my convictions. Maybe I should worry, but I cannot. I can express my cunning in more ways than you think.'

'I am sure you can.'

'I was blessed.'

'You are blessed.'

'As you are,' said Turold, and then he left the Abbess and came to where I was hiding. He stood in front of me, reached down and pulled me up. He held me so my face was in front of his and said, 'Leave us, Robert.'

I am looking into his eyes.

Ermenburga looked at me. She raised her hand slightly, then turned away.

'Go and watch your girl.'

I nodded.

'Or listen to Rainald.'

I shook my head.

'Choose one or the other, but do not stay out here.'

Bishop Odo, touched by a light fear of Turold, took his anger out on Brother Lull. The scribe, who never meant to do anyone any harm, who was simply weak. He would go wherever his master wanted, do whatever his master required, he had opinions and true feelings but kept them hidden behind a mask of insecurity and terror. Now, as the final touches were made to the transferred sketches, as the colours of the horses that won the battle were chosen, Lull struggled to find the words to describe William's speech to his men. Harold's army had been sighted along the ridge; 'Do I mention the ridge?' he said.

'No,' said Turold, 'keep it simple.' He pointed to the sketch. 'Put "Here Duke William exhorts his soldiers to prepare manfully for the battle.' "

'...against the English army.'

'That is obvious,' said Turold.

'And that, as we know, is the problem.'

Lull looked at Turold and Turold looked back. 'I am sorry,' he said. 'If I could...'

'That they prepare manfully and wisely for the battle,' said Lull. 'I think it would be wise to say this.'

'Wise to say what?' This was Odo's voice. He had crept into the workshop in the hope of overhearing slander. His patience was exhausted by talk of simplicity and wisdom.

'My Lord,' said Lull.

'What?' said Odo. He ignored Turold, who stood to one side while the Bishop stood over the scribe and cast his eyes over the inscribed sketches.

'I was explaining, my Lord, that here, as William prepares for battle, he exhorts his men to prepare not only manfully, but also wisely. I believe the King places great store in correct thought. Moral thought...'

'Does he?' said Odo, quietly.

'As I said...'

'I heard you.' Odo gathered his cloak around him and took a deep breath. He was caught between real life and wishes. At one moment he wished that he had never commissioned the hanging, at another he thought that it would bring him favour he had lost. To tolerate Turold proved that he was above petty feud; he could take his frustrations out on Lull. Turold could be dealt with later, all the Bishop needed was patience. He would train himself; he moved along the trestle, pointed to the scene when he encourages the knights in their panic, and said, 'I will be named here?'

'I have the text prepared,' said Lull, 'it is simply a matter of placing it in the design.'

'Simply?' said Odo. 'It is that simple?'

'My Lord.' Everything Lull said took him to the edge of the Bishop's anger; all this worried him, it turned his mind upside down, he wanted to return to the quiet life he had known before. He would rediscover his faith if it meant that he could be free of the Bishop; he would escape but he did not have the courage, he would have to accept his role, he could not change it. He said, 'It is simple when you know how.'

'Is it?' said Odo, meanly.

Lull only wanted to please the Bishop. He said, 'I think so.'

Turold shook his head. He did not approve or agree. Designers and scribes studied hard to learn their skills. Nothing was simple about it.

'Are you saying,' said Odo, 'that this is, for you, easy work? Trivial, even?'

'My Lord, I did not say that. I did not mean...'

'I know what you did not mean!' Odo rose to his full height and pushed out his belly. Lull shook with fear, he did not know what to say now, he forgot what he had said, his ambition did not match his instinct. His ambition was to cling to Odo and ride with him to the centre of power, his instinct was to lock himself in a cell and scribe the Lives of Saints, and Histories of the Church. His only courage had withered with his faith, he was the shell of a man, waiting for whatever would pour into him.

'You meant that you are above this work?'

'I never said I...'

'I will tell you what you never said!' Odo banged the trestle with his fist, colour drained from Lull's cheeks. 'You never said that you were honoured to inscribe this work!' He turned to Turold and said, 'At least he did.'

Turold did not take pride in this. Odo was work for him, monied means behind the cunning. He had never considered the Bishop a step to greater power. He looked at Lull and pitied him; the scribe's eyes were damp with fear, he was picking at his sleeves.

'But you!' Odo turned back and jabbed his finger in Lull's face. 'All you wanted to do was use me.'

'My...'

'Quiet! For you, I was the gates of heaven on earth!'

'I have sworn holy orders. I never...'

I swore the same orders!' screamed Odo. 'But that did not stop me...' The fat man took a breath, fisted his hands and licked sweat from his top lip.

'I am...'

'You are nothing!'

'My Lord...'

'Silence!'

Lull wished he was dead.

'Have you seen,' said Turold suddenly, 'the cunning way in which Brother Lull has inscribed this scene?' He pointed to the outline of the council William called before battle. William, Bishop Odo and Robert sit together, their names do not intrude upon the design, they could be there, they might not be. Odo looked at his image, touched the inscription with his finger and said, 'What is cunning about it?'

'Brother Lull gave great thought to the…'

'And why do you suddenly support him? He was the reason you flew for the coast!'

'He wasn't the reason. The inscription was.'

'You dare,' said Odo, and he clenched his fists again, 'interrupt and contradict me?'

'My Lord,' said Turold, mockingly.

'Do I have to remind you?'

'Of what?'

Lull was still white, he was looking at Turold. His eyes were dog's eyes, he would follow whoever was the kindest master.

'William's favour can be removed as easily as it is given. His mind is occupied by many thoughts, great thoughts. Ambition. Power. Enemies. He will have forgotten you long before I do.'

'I'm shaking,' said Turold.

Odo kept his temper, but loaded his voice with poison. 'You will do more than shake,' he hissed, and then he turned to Lull and said, 'and you will do more than piss yourself.' He looked down at the pool that was growing around the scribe's feet, pulled his cloak around him and left the workshop. He left a smell by the sketches, but the wind blew it away.

Rainald, who was in England to intercede, calm and heal, spent less time applying himself to these tasks. First the flight for the coast, then Turold's fight with Bishop Odo convinced him that he was wasting time. He had tried to be of use when Lull first appeared; the experience had frustrated him. Now he spent more time in the forest, 'It is God's own cathedral,' he told himself. Then he rebuked himself. Cathedrals were built by men to glorify the Father, nature's work was of the Father, He could not glorify Himself. He was all glory. Doubt touched

Rainald, confusion came to him in the night and said, 'What are you doing here?'

The night was warm and close.

'Turold has angered Bishop Odo, Odo has sworn revenge, because of Turold William has taken against Odo, Ermenburga has appeared to melt for Turold, Lull is going mad with fear, Robert chases the first girl he sees, the hanging will not be finished in time. These things are beneath you. Retreat and you will advance. Do not become infected by the hatred, greed and lust that surrounds you. The hanging touches everyone with trouble. You are marked for greater things.'

And Rainald went down on his knees in the forest, and he prayed. What was his prayer?

Did he pray for the birds to come from the trees and rest on his head, did he pray for the animals of the forest to accept him as one of their own? He was tired, he wanted to disappear and contemplate the goodness in things, none of the bad. Too many nights were disturbed by Turold's complaints, his ramblings about finer points of the design, his musings on my worth.

Too few nights were spent in peaceful sleep, nights that came dreaming in calm clothes. Once in his life, long before he had met Turold, he had enjoyed many nights like that, now he remembered that time and wondered why he had lost it. Had he earned a divine retribution, and if he had, why? 'The Lord shall give thee there a trembling heart, and failing of eyes, and sorrow of mind; and thy life shall hang in doubt before thee; and thou shalt fear day and night, and shalt have none assurance of thy life.'

Rainald could live with a trembling heart, failing eyes and a sorrowful mind, he could cope with fear, but he was lost when doubt began to cloud his mind. Doubt was his worst nightmare; without it, he could live with any trouble or pain. With it, all trouble and pain took his spirit and swamped it. Doubt suggested the worst, it suggested that God's eye was not upon all men, that His interest could wane, that He could forget. But how could God forget, how could He allow His flock to scatter? Were men doomed to see the light but never hold it, were they, as the prophet warned, the architects of their own destruction, given the gift of free will but not the sense to understand the gift? Rainald sat on the city wall and looked towards the forest. The trees were shedding their leaves, a cold wind was blowing from the east.

'What doth the Lord require of thee, but to do justly, and to love mercy, and to walk humbly with thy God?' Micah's words troubled Rainald, they struck his heart and rattled in there. They were the words that had convinced him of the right of a monastic life; now they returned to remind him that a humble walk with God was simply that, it was a walk with God and no one else. I heard him sniff. I think he was crying. Then he called me. 'Robert?'

I did not move.

'Robert?'

I stood up.

'Don't be afraid.' He beckoned me. 'Come here.'

We stood together on the wall.

He said, 'Have you considered that God's gift to you was silence? I sometimes think a dumb man has greater opportunity for the deepest thoughts. Is this true?'

I shook my head.

He carried on as if I was not there. 'I sometimes wish I was not required to answer questions, soothe arguments and calm troubles.'

You are required to but you never do. You have ignored your responsibilities. Maybe if you took more interest in the world around you, God's world, you would not be so confused. We all follow His plan, but only He knows what that plan is. Madness is the price you would pay for that knowledge. There are more mad men than mad women. This means that men are more inclined to impossible thoughts, more likely to wish for a truth they believe hangs in heaven but actually lies at their feet.

Rainald said, 'I believe the life of a hermit would fulfil me.'

Yes, Rainald.

'I am drawn to the forest. I could draw closer to the Lord if I lived in the shadow of His works. Works untouched by man, places where men have never been.' He looked at me now. 'Do you ever have such feelings, Robert?' His eyes were milky and his eyelids drooped.

I shook my head.

'You are satisfied?' He looked away. 'Satisfied to do His work, to move amongst the heathen…' He put his head in his hands. 'Did you know the heathen see signs of fate in the flight of birds, the fall of a leaf?'

I shook my head.

'They do.'

I was sorry for Rainald. Everything he said was true for him; he should have stayed in Bayeux. His talent was at home, moving quietly about the monastery, smoothing the ripples that disturbed the order of the place. But he had to obey an order; the temporal betrayed the divine. The divine must floor the temporal, he had to banish fear and embrace the greater will. 'As each leaf dies,' he said, 'it falls and covers its own shadow. A fallen leaf has no shadow.'

Rainald. Go and live in the forest.

Turold said, 'I am worried about Rainald.'

I buried my head in my hands and followed him out. We sat on benches, he shooed a dog, drank and said, 'And I am worried about Lull.'

Lull. The inscriptions changed every day, they did not need to change at all, but he made them. The longer he stared at the words, the more he hated them. He had changed 'Here Duke Harold returned to English soil' to 'Duke Harold sails for England' to 'A ship carries Harold to England' to 'Here Duke Harold returned to English soil' again; he was not satisfied, he was frustrated and cursed himself. It was dan-

gerous to curse anyone else; such a simple task, so difficult
to execute.

'I think,' said Turold, 'he'll go mad.'

I sipped.

'And when I look at Rainald, I think he'll disappear into thin
air. Have you noticed?' Turold swayed towards me. 'The life
seems to have left his eyes.'

No.

'Has he spoken to you?'

I nodded.

'What did he say?'

Turold is using his stupidity to avoid madness and doubt. He
engages a sensitive and imaginative mind when he is required
to work, he leaves this mind in his work and takes an empty
head away.

'What did he say?'

I shrugged.

'He didn't care?'

I nodded.

'He did care?'

I nodded.

'Robert...' said Turold. I know he says the same prayer as me.

I pointed out of the door, towards an orchard, apple trees
and birds.

'What?' Turold finished his second drink and clapped for
another.

I made the shape of a tree with my hands. Rainald wants
to be a tree.

'What are you doing?'

I pointed again.

He looked towards the orchard, then back at me.

I nodded, opened my mouth and showed him my tongue.

'What about it?' His left eye was half-closed.

Best to do nothing now. I put my hands on my lap and bowed
my head.

The drink came.

'What?' said Turold again, and he took my face in his right hand.

I am shaking my head. His hand hurts. He is pinching my cheek. I try to wriggle away, but cannot.

'Robert,' he said, quietly, 'speak to me.' He picked up his drink with his free hand, and drank half.

I wanted to cry.

Suddenly he let go and slapped my cheek. 'Speak to me! Speak!' His right eye was wide open, his left was tightly closed, his mouth did not believe what his voice had said, but it did not hold him back. 'Don't just sit there!'

I cried.

'And don't cry!'

People were looking at us; when Turold looked at them, they looked away. He finished his drink and shouted for another.

I put my sleeve to my eyes and blew my nose on it.

'What are you? Boy or man?'

I looked at Turold. I stared into his eyes and did not blink; I drew in my lips.

'Nod if it's a boy,' he said.

I did not move.

'Man?'

I did not move. I stared until I had had enough, then I looked away. I saw his hand flash in front of my eyes, then he had me by the throat and we were on the floor.

He hit me once in the back of the head, I tried to squirm away, it was useless, he turned me over and sat astride me, my arms pinned back by his knees. My head was between his thighs, he lifted his fist again and then I began to bleed.

The sight of my blood froze Turold, the colour of it transfixed him, he lowered his fist, shook his head and said, 'Robert?'

I pulled my arms out.

He put his fingers to the cut, dabbed at the blood, looked at the end of his fingers and said, 'It's so red.'

I began to squirm my legs out from beneath him. He was a heavy man. I think he had forgotten I was there. He was staring at my blood as if he had never seen blood before. Colour is the son of his gift. People went back to their drinking. We were known in town; the Norman designer was unpredictable, liable to fits of anger, waves of remorse, acts of foolishness, words of stupidity, works of brilliance, cunning art in a cunning head. His boy was dumb, his boy had power over birds, his boy was after Martha the baker's daughter. I pulled my legs out and waited for Turold to see me again. My blood began to dry; as its colour faded, so his face began to change, his left eye opened, his mind came back from the place it had been and he said, 'Robert?'

I nodded.

He pulled himself up. 'Did I hit you?'

I nodded.

He put his hand on my head and then pulled me into his waist. It was like this, it was like this in Winchester. He forgot and he remembered, and when the time was right, and he had taken my hand, we went back to the lodging.

12

The first stitch was sewn on a Tuesday in October, in 1075, in red wool; the first flip of the scroll that borders King Edward, throned and instructing Earl Harold.

It was Turold who threaded the needle, Turold who chose the colour, Turold standing at the frame. He leant over the embroiderers at their benches; they sat in pairs, each pair two paces apart. Twenty-six worked the main field of the hanging, and eighteen apprentices stitched the borders. They were all sisters of Nunnaminster, each chosen for speed, nature and care.

The translation of the sketch, the folds of a man's cloak, the branches of trees, the fall of a horse's mane, the wind in the sails of ships across the sea; all had to be stitched with delicacy and confidence. The movement behind the pictures must be felt, and the passion behind the story leap from the stitches.

A calm nature, a mind of pious thought, eyes cast to heaven when they were not upon the work. Steady hands, slim fingers, perfect sight, no need to gossip. So the only sound in the workshop was a hissing, as the needles pulled the threads through the linen, day after day, week after week, each outline filling with colour and life.

The stitches were simple. The sketches were defined by stem stitches, then filled with laid and couched work. None of the embroiderers could not sew these stitches in her sleep, and none of them, though they all marvelled at the way Turold's brilliance lifted their own work, allowed admiration for the designer to cloud her mind. The embroiderers lived in the Lord. I was watching them but they did not watch me. They would allow me to stand behind them, I could have been born a dog.

The work was to be finished by Christmas of 1076, to be hung around Bishop Odo's hall in celebration of ten years of William's reign. 'What does my hall lack?'

'Whores, my Lord?'

'The greatest work you can produce, Turold. A hanging.'

'When do you want it finished?'

'By Christmas.'

I am standing behind Turold when he hears that he, I and forty-four nuns have fourteen months to finish the work.

'Impossible.'

'What is impossible?' said the Bishop. He held Turold with his eyes, the two men circled each other, like primed cocks. 'Do you think William listened when he was told a crossing to England was impossible?'

'That was a different situation.' Turold waved his hands. 'You cannot compare the two. The embroiderers cannot work faster than they already do. Fingers can only go so fast…'

'Waves can only be so tall,' said Odo.

'I'm sorry?'

'You will be.'

'I cannot...'

'You can, and you will! Forget any other threats I have made to you,' said Odo, and he moved on Turold, so their faces were a fist apart. 'You have failed me in many ways, but if you fail to complete within the time, you will wish you had only failed as you did before...'

Turold was tired of threats. He shrugged, he could do no more, sunlight was in the workshop. 'I could find more embroiderers.'

'Do it.'

'Their work might not be as fine...'

'The work will be the finest!' Odo's eyes popped and the veins on his neck rippled. The embroiderers did not stop working. The shouting washed over them, their minds were on the Lord, their fingers followed the sketches as if they had eyes at their tips.

'It will never be less,' said Turold.

Here is Martha and here I am, and we are standing in the yard beneath our lodging. We can see Rainald. He is kneeling at his cot. He has been kneeling all day. He will not leave the lodging during the day, I have to bring him food. Martha says, 'Is he sick?'

I shrugged.

If I had her now, I would be given my voice, but the more I know her the more difficult it becomes. We are in the dark, her father and mother were asleep, her father snored like a bull.

Rainald's head cast a shadow on to the wall. This shadow was sad, I could tell: he was screaming. Peace, the removal of doubt, a vision of the Lord enthroned, flights of angels in triumph; Martha said, 'Do you ever think about me while you work?'

I think about your paps.

I nodded.

'What do you think?'

Why do people ask me questions like this?

I looked into her eyes and I tried to tell her that way. I pulled her towards me and kissed her lips, and then, thinking that there was no reason to wait, I slipped my hand beneath her shirt and ran it up to her breasts. She blew air into my mouth, she twisted away, then came back again, she pushed at me but did not try to move my hand. My hand is on her now and her breast feels as I imagined it would. It feels exactly this way, I knew it would, as if I was spoken to by a bird. It feels like holding a pigeon. Her skin is feather, her pap fits between my fingers like a bird's neck. I push it up and wait for it to squeak.

'Robert,' she whispered.

I smiled.

'What are you doing?'

I am not waiting for you to lay an egg.

'Is this all you want me for?'

Do not be stupid, Martha. I want you for many reasons. I shook my head.

'What is going on in there?' she said.

I had my eyebrows up, and then I put my other hand to her other tit, and I was holding them like a pair in their basket, and I was the perfect birdman.

'Robert,' she whispered.

I whistled, softly, and I felt her paps stiffen.

'Are you whistling at me?'

Her breasts were fluttering in my hands.

My pigeons are locked in their loft. I am not whistling at anyone but you.

'I know what you want to do,' she said.

She knows.

I know.

I could feel her knee against mine, and when I slipped my thigh between hers, Rainald let out a scream, as if he had been attacked by demons. We jumped apart, looked up, and he was standing at the lodging window, naked, his mouth wide open. A moment later, Turold appeared behind him and pulled him back.

'He is in pain,' said Martha.

I put my hands to my nose and smelt her on them. Then I pointed up, kissed her once and climbed to our room.

Rainald was on the floor now, his head resting in Turold's lap. 'He thinks God has deserted him.'

I knelt down. The monk's head was covered with sweat, he glowed in the dark. He was breathing heavily, his eyeballs were swinging beneath their lids. Turold said, 'He should never have left Bayeux.' He stroked his friend's hair. 'Why did Odo think he would be of any use here? He was only ever meant to patrol the edges of his own pond. This place, my work; he doesn't need the trouble.'

I looked out of the window, I could see Martha in the yard. I waved to her, she waved back and went into the bakery. Leaves blew around her feet, Turold whispered, 'He never deserved this. He never did anyone any harm.'

Turold wonders if the embroidery curses, then dismisses the idea. Some people make their own fate, he thinks. Other people cannot stop other people's fate affecting them. 'Men with a faith built on a sheltered life do not need the suggestion that God's eye can shut.'

I do not know what he is talking about. I can still feel Martha's breasts in my hands, as men who lose their hands say that they can still feel them attached. Here are their sides and here are their paps, they are warm and smell of flour and feathers. Rainald opened his eyes, then his mouth, Turold put a finger to his lips and said, 'Don't say anything.' He bent towards him and whispered, 'Go to sleep. You are safe here.'

Rainald turned his head towards me, his eyes were full of tears. He looked at Turold, then closed them.

'You go to sleep too.' Turold put his hand on my head. 'I think you need it.'

I could not sleep. I lay on my back with my hands on my chest; Turold sat up all night with Rainald's head in his lap. They were both still, the air was filled with the smell of ripening apples and burning leaves. There were ghosts in the lodging, there were voices in the night that came from no mouths. No mouths had no heads; the voices came from thought. Martha would be sleeping in the next house, if I listened hard enough, I could hear her breathing. She is as kind as Turold, Turold is as kind as a nursing mother. He cares and he loves, he is only riled by injustice, and only forgets when he has drunk too much. He could go one way or the other; when he has people to care for, work to complete, pictures in his head of horses picking up speed for battle, then he shows his best. Here he has a cloth, and is wiping Rainald's brow. He smiles as the sun breaks over the forest and shines through the branches of the tallest trees and he says, 'Sleep on, Rainald. No one is expecting you.'

Here is Lull.

Oh Lord.

He has finished the text, he has placed it on Turold's sketches, and it has finished him. He is agitated, hopping from one foot to the other. He is waiting for a horse that will take him miles from Winchester. He will return to Canterbury, where there is one person who will listen and understand.

Turold worked his way along the sketches. In places, the text had been placed carefully and with a degree of cunning, but in others it ranged clumsily through the action with the grace of drunk sailors dancing on benches. I saw the expression change in his eyes, but he did not allow Lull to see this. He wanted to see the scribe go, but he did not want him to think that his text had failed. Any partnership, whatever its foundations, can create a miracle; with Lull gone, he could place the text exactly as he wanted. Bishop Odo would never know the difference; he said, 'This is good.'

'You think so?' said Lull.

'Of course. I might place some words differently, but...'

'Please,' said Lull. 'Do whatever you want. I am happy to have finished.' He looked over his shoulder. His pack was at the door, rain was blowing across the precinct yard. His face was white, Turold put his hand on his shoulder and said, 'Strength, Brother Lull.'

Lull jumped at the touch. 'There is none for me here,' he said. 'Only when I'm home; when I'm home, when I'm at my own desk again.' He looked to his place at the end of the workshop. 'I was never even given a desk here.'

'Fix your mind on home,' said Turold. 'Forget Winchester.'

Lull laughed. His laugh sounded like metal on metal. 'I will never forget Winchester,' he said. 'It will haunt me for ever.'

'Rather it haunt you than you have to stay here.'

Lull looked at Turold. 'I'm sorry for you,' he said.

'Why?'

'If I had half your trouble I would rather die than face another day.'

'If I die, the world will lose my vision.' Turold looked at me, smiled, looked at the work and narrowed his eyes. 'My vision freezes my fears; I don't have to worry.'

'Modesty never worries you?'

'What do you mean?'

'Nothing...'

'Modesty has nothing to do with it.'

'I know...'

'Then why mention it?'

'Forgive me,' said Brother Lull.

Turold looked down at the thin monk. The sound of hoofs echoed across the yard, and voices called out. The workshop door opened, a stableboy called for Lull. We shook hands with him and watched his back as he left. I am sorry to see anyone go, the sisters worked without stopping. The first completed figures appeared on the linen; they came slowly, they seemed to move, they would live for ever.

Rainald ate some bread and drank some water, but he would not take anything else. His body was weak but his mind was strong. He had made a decision, and no one was going to persuade him that he was making a mistake. He sat up in his cot and stared from the lodging, over the bakery roof, past the city walls to the forest. He said to me, 'I meant what I said.'

What did you say?

'The forest will be my home. I will put my life behind me and another before me.'

What are you talking about?

'I have learnt an important lesson.'

Tell me what that lesson is.

'God may be defiled by man, only nature allows Him to be pure.'

I heard the bakery door open. I looked down. She was in the yard with a bucket. I listened to her footsteps.

She stopped to look up at our window, but I did not show my face. I had promised to watch over Rainald, Turold had made me swear that I would not leave the lodging. He held my hand over my heart as I followed his lips with mine. 'He is weak, you will not allow him to become weaker.'

I looked at our friend. His eyes were on my face, but I do not think they saw me, not as Turold's boy. I could have been a stranger or I could have been a spirit. 'The Word,' he said.

I moved my head towards him, so I could feel his breath in my ear.

'The Word of the Lord came to me, and said, "Set thy face toward the south, and drop thy word toward the south, and prophesy against the forest of the south field..."'

What are you saying?

'These are God's words, and they are directed at me.' Now his eyes widened and he could see me. 'I trust you,' he said. 'You would not betray me.'

No.

'Would you be my help as you are Turold's?'

I nodded.

'Would you be my raven?'

What do you mean?

'The Lord ordered Elijah to hide himself by a brook. You remember the story: the prophet drank from the brook, and ravens brought him food.'

And you are a prophet?

'Do not misunderstand me. I do not believe I am Elijah, but I know the Lord has called me. I recognised His voice. I heard it once before, when I was your age.'

I have never heard the Lord. I know He is guilty, He knows I would turn against Him if He spoke to me, for I know He speaks with the voice I have been denied. Yes, I will be Rainald's raven, I owe him more than anything I could do for him. In Bayeux, he taught me to count and he told me how Turold could be helped. He showed me the stairs to the top of the abbey tower, from where we could look down and see pigeons nesting below.

Rainald loved to be so high, to look out across the country and watch the weather change.

'Do not do this because you think you owe me something, but because you love me. I think at the heart of my doubt lies the idea that God's love can never be complete, for He cannot love as one person loves another.'

Rainald, go to sleep.

'I have chosen a place. It is a hollow beside a stream, an hour's walk from here. It is sheltered, obscured from view on all but one side, and that side cannot be reached without difficulty. A narrow path leads down to it. I will be able to build a roof over the narrowest part of the hollow. A hole in the bank will serve as a larder.'

Have you told Turold?

'I will leave in the morning. Will you come with me, so I can show you the way?'

I nodded.

He put his hand on my head. It was warm and sticky, like air before a storm. 'You will bring me food?'

Yes.

'And butter for my burns?'

Yes.

He smiled at me, then looked away and faced the wall. I heard a noise behind me, and turned around. The shadow on the door moved, Turold took a step towards me and put his finger to his mouth. He took my arm and sat me on the far side of the room. 'You are,' he said, 'willing to help him?'

I nodded.

'Good boy.'

We looked at Rainald.

'I will come when I can.'

I heard a dog barking on the wall, and the sound of wind as it rushed through the room. There were smells in the air and a light in the night, but my senses froze, and the light shone in a different place in the world.

13

In November, Bishop Odo came to the workshop, ignored the hanging, took Turold away from the face of Guy as he captures Harold, and said, 'I am leaving,' he coughed, 'for Kent.'

Only idiots and men on urgent business travel in November. I twirled some night blue around my finger. We were going to run out of it.

'We'll miss you, my Lord.'

'Don't!' said Odo.

'Believe me...'

'How can I? I don't trust you, so how can I believe you?'

Turold turned away, looked at the row of embroiderers, the hiss of needles filled the air. He looked back at the Bishop and said, 'All I want to do is produce the finest work...'

'And all I want you to do is finish. Finish, Turold, come back to Bayeux with me and enjoy the reception I have planned.'

Turold is holding Odo's stare. He is not afraid. 'Kent?' he said.

'Yes.'

'You are leaving today?'

'Yes; I will be back for the new year.'

'Two months?' said Turold. He spoke quietly.

'You can count?' said Odo.

Turold nodded.

'Good. Then you will notice that from today, there will be an extra face in the workshop. Someone to watch over you.'

'Another Lull?'

'Lull was a scribe.'

'He was more than that, but it did not help him...'

'If you say so.'

'It is the truth.'

'Truth again, Turold?'

'I think...'

'And thought!'

Turold turned away but Odo pulled him back and said, 'His name is Stephen, and he doesn't like you already.'

'I will try to like him.'

'And he doesn't understand jokes. I've never seen him laugh.'

'I never saw Lull laugh.'

'Scribes never do,' said Odo.

The sisters bent towards their work, they pursed their lips and steadied the linen with their little fingers. Their sewing fingers moved like maggots wriggle on flesh, never still, moving for only one reason. Their eyes were wide, they breathed slowly and quietly.

Here, on the first strip, is the completed scene of two messengers, sent by William to demand Harold's release from Guy's custody.

The horses are flying, but they are tired. You can see this in the eye of the one in front, and in the way it is overreaching its stride. The ground is poor, the messengers are wearing spurs.

The sisters stitched the colour, Turold stitched the messengers' heads. All important heads and faces were stitched by Turold. I was behind him, I passed him the wool and he turned it into the men's hair, and sent wind rushing through it. He made the speed of the galloping horses appear in stitches, the messengers' heads are thrust forward, their faces are written with William's order. The picture did not lie. Bishop Odo said, 'Turold?'

'My Lord?'

'Kent is closer than you think.'

Stephen was a weasel, thinner than Lull, and taller. He could hide behind a pole, he could listen to talk at a hundred paces. He was always in the workshop but it was as if he was not there at all, just the echo of a man. He never spoke, I never heard him cough, he could stand and watch for hours without blinking. I ignored him, Turold ignored him and the sisters ignored him; this was not what he wanted. He wanted to scare people, he wanted to keep us on edge, he wanted to be the weasel at the mouth of the vole hole, and the moon was bright.

I am with Martha. She has given me bread for Rainald, and I have some cheese from the nuns. Turold has given me apples, it is morning, I have not been to the workshop.

Martha thinks I am wonderful and brave, and that I understand people. I do not understand anything at all. It is my job to take this food to Rainald, it is my job to stand behind Turold and know when he is going to need the length of wool.

'I could come with you,' she said.

I shook my head.

'Why not?'

Rainald only expects me; he is close to the edge of madness, I think the sight of a girl would throw him over. All he wants is the bread, the cheese, and the chance to talk to someone who

will not answer back. I am his perfect friend, the holy man's
bird. I come and I go, I do not threaten at all.

'Please.'

I shook my head again. Now I do not want to shake it again,
I want to leave the yard and get on the path.

'I could follow you.'

I took her head in my hands and shook it backwards and
forwards. I opened my mouth and let out a blast of air. Her
eyes opened wide, and her tongue flipped out of her mouth.

'Stop it!' she cried. 'You're hurting!'

I stopped. I never wanted to hurt her. What have I done?

I was alone in the forest, walking the path to Rainald's hollow. The trees were bare, their branches rattled in the wind.
Sleet blew in my face and stung my skin.

We have had our first fight, and I am ashamed. I had been
taught never to use strength as a substitute for words, but
I had forgotten the lesson. She forgave me but I could not
forgive myself. I looked over my shoulder though I knew she
would not be following. She could have come some way with
me, Rainald would never have known, I had not given her the
chance to suggest that.

Here are the trees. The trees in the embroidery were grown
in the mind. They have a life beyond plant life; see how the
ones logmen are about to chop for William's ships are standing
tense and fearful, as if they want to run. Before the battle, three
trees on a hill appear to be talking to each other, but they are
not afraid, only resigned. Trees whisper, they stand in gangs
and watch the solitary traveller as he passes. They have all the
time in the world but you have none, that is what scares me. I
know they are saying things about me, but I do not know what.

When I sit with Rainald, an hour seems like a day, and I grow
tired though I am doing nothing. I am listening to him, I am
watching the brook bubble at our feet, I am listening to birds
in the trees. I am listening to Rainald, but he is not saying

anything I understand. His hair has grown, his beard is longer than Turold's, he does not ask about Turold. I do not think he knows who I am, or who I was when he knew me in Bayeux. I am a miracle who appears every day with food; maybe he believes I am a messenger from God, muted by knowledge, followed by no one.

He breaks bread, takes some cheese and places it on a rock. He kneels before his meal, places his hands in prayer, closes his eyes and whispers a long grace. The sound he makes reminds me of the needles in the workshop, the wool through linen, the creak of the benches and the rustle of the sisters' cloaks. It is cold in the workshop, but our work keeps us warm, as if it was bred in the sun.

Turold sat alone in the workshop at night, and Ermenburga watched him from outside. She did not want him to know she was there, she wanted to look at him as if he was a statue. She could stare like this at the Cross; a feeling of peace and security filled her body and lightened her eyes. We had thought she was sour and cold, but she gave thanks to Turold for saving her from Bishop Odo. I was watching her from inside a barrel, and heard her whisper under her breath.

'...and shield him from the forces of darkness, and give him the wisdom to understand Your mercy.'

The barrel had a fleece in it. There were maggots in the fleece, and they began to crawl up my legs. I could feel them wriggling on my skin, and sucking at the creases behind my knees. I bent down to brush them off, the barrel rocked. The noise it made echoed across the yard, then two hands appeared over the rim and steadied it. Ermenburga stuck her head in and said, 'Quiet, Robert! Why do you have to make so much noise? He is thinking!'

She reached in and lifted me out.

I stood up and brushed the maggots off. Some were squashed, others wriggled away.

'Did no one ever tell you about bad barrels?'

I shook my head.

'Come,' she said, and she took my hand and we stared in.

Turold was stitching the first word. A burning candle, set in a metal clamp, illuminated the work. From where we were, we could see his hand, a circle of linen, one completed figure, two horses' heads and half his face, floating in a sea of darkness. The light shone on the scene, as if it was a painting.

Turold's hand stitched his name over his image, six letters bordered by two lines. He blew on his work, he touched it lightly with his fingers, as if he was waiting for it to dry.

'How can he stitch so finely?'

People ask me questions. I know the answers, but I am not saying. Turold is not two men, he is a man and a woman. He knows this, women he has known have known this. I knew the moment he took me as his boy, that he was my father and my mother. He could move in any direction, the needle drew the wool, and a bat flew through the workshop.

We love the bats. People say they blow from hell and return to hell at dawn, but I know they roost in the workshop roof. They are blind but see by singing. I am dumb but speak by looks. They hang while they sleep, Turold needs less and less sleep, I am in bed before him, and he is up before I am awake. Dogs bark, and their message carries over the city walls to the forest; it is lost in the trees, and its pieces fall to the ground.

14

Ermenburga, the once stick-faced queen of Nunnaminster, grew plump cheeks in Bishop Odo's absence. She spent an hour of each afternoon in the workshop, and as each day passed, we watched her fatten.

Turold was afraid the weasel Stephen's presence would upset her, but she ignored him as we did. He was born to be ignored;

his efforts to wear a threatening face were clever but did not convince. We began to pity him as we had pitied Lull, but at least Lull had done something. Lull could do something, all Stephen did was lurk.

Ermenburga's hour in the workshop was a daily gift to herself, she believed that she had earned it. No one argued with her, she sat in a chair Turold placed for her, he placed it with care, and never in the same place twice.

I could see the feelings he had for her in his eyes. He was thinking the things he thought about a woman he wanted, but was held back. He had never wanted an abbess, he had never had a thin woman. He was confused when he looked up and saw her face at rest, her eyes half-closed, her hands folded in her lap. The urgency of the work was forgotten, I saw him stare with longing in his eyes. Maybe I was wrong, and maybe he saw her as his mother, or his sister; maybe he did not want her in any other way.

I was not around them all the time, so how can I tell? One morning I was in the workshop, the next I was carrying to Rainald, the next I was in the yard for an hour with Martha. How long have I been with Martha, and how many loaves has she taken for me? How long has Stephen watched us, and can he be distracted? If Bishop Odo meets with an accident in Kent, will the work ever be finished?

Martha has taken dozens of loaves. Rainald thinks his food comes straight from God, and he could be close to the truth. He never asks me questions, he does not want to know anything. The weather is cold, but I have never seen him shivering, he never complains. God has wrapped Himself around the monk, His protection is greater than the armour of kings, the angels are in heaven, but they come to earth. They do not touch the ground for they know it would burn them. The angels are pure, and Rainald gives them messages. He is losing his face as his mind runs out of his head, and I am afraid that all that will be left will be a mad man. I think it is easy to go mad; doubt is the seed, solitude is the earth, unwashed clothing is the water and stolen bread is the sunshine. Sometimes, I want to cry for him, and pull him back to town, but I know he would not come. Everyone thinks they are found and others are lost; I look into Rainald's eyes but they are not there. They could be in the trees, looking down at me, they could be in a beast's head, and the beast is waiting for me on a hidden corner.

The sisters had left, only Turold and I were in the workshop. Stephen might have been there, he might not have been. We did not care, we were busy men, working on great art, we were above the ordinary. Even our lies could express the truth, and our mistakes would never need correction. But we were never satisfied. Turold believed he could do better; there is not a scene in the hanging that he did not find fault with. Even the most carefully planned and wrought were missing something. Sometimes, he did not even know what that something was, but he knew it was missing.

It was one of these evenings; dark before it should be, and here, Harold saves two of William's men from the quicksands of the river Couesnon. He was strong and brave. Turold was stitching his face, giving him wide eyes and a long moustache. He had been William's companion in arms, he had proved himself worthy of the honour bestowed upon him. Greed had betrayed him, bad advice had sealed his fate.

Turold was not happy with the man on Harold's back; was this a man or boy? I was not asked. The workshop was quiet, candles burnt around our work, I held a box of wool on my knee.

'What would I do without you?' he said.

I did not know. When I thought about my work, it was nothing. I was another pair of hands for him, but they were not connected to his mind, they could have been anyone's. Maybe me just being next to him was enough, maybe he was so used to my presence that I was a solid, living shadow. Shadows serve no useful purpose, they are cast, they shorten and they lengthen. There were no shadows in the hanging, no shadows at all, for it is a shadow itself. A shadow of the story it tells, not even the story itself, for it is full of lies.

'Master Turold?'

The voice was low, the workshop door was open, and a cold wind blew in.

'Are you there?'

Turold left his place, took a taper from the wall, and left me where I was. I put the box of wool on the floor and stood up.

'You work hard.'

'I have to.'

'Because you need to, or because Bishop Odo makes impossible demands?'

'When I am in the middle of any work, I become obsessed. I cannot leave it alone. Bishop Odo's orders are the wheels of the cart, but they cannot make the cart move by themselves. A horse is required...'

'I think you could have been a bishop. Your mind is full of the most imaginative ideas...'

Turold laughed, the workshop door slammed shut and the King came to where we were working. He was visiting alone, his men were standing at the gate. He had been hunting. His clothes were covered in mud, his hair dripped, his boots squidged as he walked.

'Robert,' he said to me, and he crouched down. The candle-light flickered across his face. 'How are you?'

How do you think I am? He is so big, I could fit inside him twice. The darkness made him bigger, it thickened the power that surrounded him, I felt his breath upon my face. It smelt of meat, I opened my mouth, but I could not say anything.

'Would you like to talk?' he said to me.

I nodded.

'One day,' he said, 'I think you will.'

When?

'What will he say? What would you like to ask?'

I would like to ask the King why he married a midget. Queen Matilda is the smallest woman I have seen. She is the size of a large child. I have seen her and heard her voice; she makes up for her lack of height with it. It has the power of three, it can range from the highest a woman can manage to the depths of a large man; she has changed William's mind more times than anyone alive. I want to know why he married her.

The two men looked at me. I felt small and cold. I held my hands tight, but I never wanted to be sent out. I was standing in the presence of two great men, and between them, they were baffled by me. They wanted to understand something about me, and this made me important. I had to take a step back, then William put his arm on Turold's shoulder and said, 'Tell me. Do you work better without Bishop Odo looking over your shoulder?'

'Better is not the word I would use.'

William stared at Turold. No one told him that he was using a word another would not. What the designer said sounded strange to him.

'Bishop Odo,' said Turold, 'does not know what he wants.'

'He wants too much...' said William, as if to himself.

'And his problem becomes mine. It is easier to work with him away, but I do not believe the work is improved by his absence. The work is above argument.'

'You believe that?'

'Yes.'

William nodded, and for the first time, I saw him smile.

William's smile exposed his face, for it was thin and showed his teeth. These were better teeth than I had ever seen on a man, few were missing and they were a yellowy white, as if he polished them. He ran the tip of his tongue over them, then rubbed a knuckle on them. 'So,' he said, and the word hung in the air.

'Yes,' said Turold.

William leant forward to examine the march past Mont St Michel, the quicksands of the Couesnon and the attack on Dol. He touched the mounted figure that represented him, he traced the outline of his horse's neck and said, 'Your horses are magnificent.'

'A horse,' said Turold, 'represents the best of nature; the most expressive of animals, quite predictable, but only when they want to be.'

'Is that you, Turold?'

'Me, Majesty?'

'You.'

'I was talking about horses...'

The King looked away from the work.

'I am,' said Turold, 'like a horse.'

'Bishop Odo called you a reptile.'

'Bishop Odo...'

'Bishop Odo what? You cannot tell me anything I do not already know.'

'He is a good patron, to me and many others, but for the wrong reasons.'

'Are there right reasons? You are paid?'

'Yes,' said Turold.

'So?'

'So I wish we could discuss the work without argument, but when I...'

'Would you,' William interrupted, 'make room for a scene of my own design?'

'Your Majesty.' Turold tugged at his beard and mumbled, 'I would have to...'

'Answer me. Yes or no.'

'Yes. Yes, but I think Bishop Odo would...'

'My scene will be my present to him.' He pointed to the scene of his palace at Rouen, where he meets Harold in audience. It was half completed; he and Harold had been stitched, the palace arches and the columns that supported the roof were only sketched in. 'There would be room for it here.' He made a circle around the outline of Harold's entourage. 'Remove some of these men and leave a space between them and this horse.' He pointed to the rearguard of the column that passed Mont St Michel.

'A space?' said Turold.

'Yes.'

'What will it be filled with?'

Now William turned to the designer and laughed. The laugh was huge and stank, his eyes twinkled, he had planned something that gave him great pleasure. Bishop Odo was not worth the severest punishment or the most obvious; he would be hurt more by being reminded of the only occasion in his life when he exposed himself as a loving man.

'It will be filled, as I said, with a scene of my own design.' William smiled as he spoke. 'Now I know you are willing to accept my idea, I may think more exactly about what I wish to show.'

'Surely my willing has nothing to do with it.'

'You are right, but I was anxious not to upset you. Odo said that you do not care for interference...'

'As I have said...'

'As you have said,' said the King.

I hoped Stephen was remembering this. He was in the workshop. I hoped he was awake. To miss the only conversation his master would be interested in. I think, if I had a voice, I would have called out to him. Wake up, Stephen! Do not make a mistake!

'I wish you to leave room for two figures and an inscription.' William raised his eyebrows. 'You will be happy to do an inscription for me?'

'I am happy to stitch Bishop Odo's. I have allowed him that.'

'For which he was grateful.'

'Was he?'

'I know he was.'

Turold stood by the palace of Rouen, narrowed his eyes, raised his hand to the linen and said, 'From here…' he moved his hand to the right '…to here.'

'Exactly,' said the King.

There was a snuffle in the workshop, by the wool stock. I took steps towards the noise, and when I reached the window, I felt my way along the far wall. The bats were flying, William and Turold's heads were thrown into massive shadow, up the walls and into the roof. Their faces were illuminated by candles, a jewel at the King's neck flashed colour on to the linen, through it and out again. I walked backwards towards Stephen, who was asleep on the floor. He was snoring lightly, and his face was free of the meanness it usually displayed. He had a slight smile on his lips, he was dreaming of a dog. He was the sort of man who would always have a dog and never a girl; I poked him in the ribs, he opened his eyes, blinked once and jumped up.

I held my finger to my mouth.

He looked fierce, as if he might bite my neck. He grabbed my arm and pulled it around; I ducked underneath him and pointed into the middle of the workshop.

He let go of me and took a step towards Turold. Then he stopped, his arms went down by his side and his chin jutted out. He stared for a minute, then turned and whispered, 'The King?'

I nodded.

These were the first words I heard him speak. His voice was as I had expected it to be, thin and flat as ice. There was panic in his face. 'How long has he been there?'

I shrugged.

'What has been said?'

Stupid Stephen. He is another. Please.

'Idiot,' he hissed.

Me or you, pig breath?

He began to creep along the first frame towards the men, crouched low, testing the floor with his hands before taking a step. He looked like a huge spider on the floor, his coat dragged behind him and his fingers were very thin.

I walked back to the King as he was leading Turold to the workshop door. He said, 'When this work is finished, the Queen wishes to see you. She has plans for her chamber.'

'I would be honoured.'

'You will be,' said William, and when he turned to me he bent down and said, 'And you will not be forgotten, Robert.'

I was smiling, half at the King, half at Stephen. He was making too much noise in his approach. The King looked up and said, 'You have mice.'

'They do no harm,' said Turold.

The King banged on the workshop door. It opened from the outside. A blast of sleet blew in, we drew our cloaks around us and followed him into the yard. 'No,' he said, pushing us back. 'Your fingers will freeze.' He blew on his. 'Keep them warm for my scene.'

I turned around. Stephen was by the door, he mouthed the words, 'Keep them warm for my scene,' and looked at me. I shrugged, William stalked across the yard, his men followed him, they slammed the precinct gates. Turold said, 'The Queen is a very small woman,' to me, and went back to work.

December was cold, snow lay on the path to Rainald, the brook was frozen at its banks, icicles hung from the trees. The silence in the forest was deep enough to slow my time to the hollow.

I was afraid, but I did not have to be. Rainald had made his shelter as warm as any lodging. A carpet of ferns and mosses had been added to the wooden frame that covered the place where he slept, and he had woven hurdles of sticks to keep out draughts. The bank retained warmth, and the prevailing wind blew snow away from the place, so he was dry, and as we sat around a fire, and I dried my feet, I felt content and I think he felt so too. We ate bread, and I offered him some cider I had carried. He smelt it, thought about it, smelt it again and then said, 'No.'

I put the bottle to my lips.

'But you have some.'

It was sour.

'I never see anyone indulging in their own pleasures, their own faiths. Faith; is that pleasure? Faith, is it within or without?'

I took the bottle from my lips.

'Pleasure needs no proof, faith needs no proof, you need no proof.' He looked at me.

Do you want butter on your burns?

He looked away. 'Forgive me,' he said.

I put the bottle on the ground.

'How is Turold?'

I smiled at him.

'Good. Please, never think that because I am here I have forgotten you or him, or the work you are doing. I pray for you every hour. I hope you understand that I do not have your courage. I could not live another moment in the hanging's shadow, or its spell.'

It casts no spell. You were homesick, you were struck by the first doubt of your life, you needed to go away and think. This happens to everyone. You are not so special, Rainald.

'Would you do my burns?' he said.

I nodded.

A clot of snow dropped off a tree and landed in the hollow. 'I wash in snow,' he said.

I picked up the bottle and had another drink.

15

December was cold; cold for my birds and cold for Martha, who felt cold badly. She grew blue circles around her eyes, and when she had to run from the bakery door to the rubbish, she ran like a rabbit, hunching her shoulders and skipping between the pools of ice. I met her in the lodging, we lay in Rainald's cot, I held her breasts but I was not allowed to touch any other part of her body.

It is a good way to keep warm.

Oh God.

Please.

Give me strength.

I will go mad. I will follow Rainald to the forest. His doubt has stolen the certainty of his voice, You have stolen my voice, I cannot be certain of anyone because I cannot speak to them. I cannot ask, reassure, lie or joke. So why do I need people, when all they give me is frustration?

'Do you love me?' she said.

Yes.

'As much as your pigeons?'

Yes.

'More than your pigeons?'

Yes.

'How are your pigeons?'

Well.

'And you do love me?'

I opened my mouth, lowered it to her ear and took a breath. As I did, I concentrated on the word. I forced it from my head to the back of my throat, gave it solid form and waited for my breath to catch it on the way out. I blew, Martha wriggled beneath me and I heard the very start of the word, the sharpness of the top of the first letter, but then my breath was out, it was in her ear, and I was on my back again.

'What are you doing?'

I am talking to you.

'When will you take me to Rainald's?'

I do not know.

'Please?'

Martha.

'Please?'

I looked into her eyes and they were kind. I was going to take him honeyed cake for Christmas, her father had baked it for me. She could carry it for me, I would warn him that she was coming, we could celebrate the feast together. He would enjoy it; I gave her my best smile, I took her in my arms and kissed her. She was warm and I was so warm. Rainald's cot was comfortable, I do not know why he did not take it with him.

Poor Stephen. Like Lull but not like Lull at all. He changed our memories of Lull, so we began to remember the scribe as a good man. Stephen had to know what Willam had said, he would kill to know, but could not stand the sight of blood.

First, he asked Turold, 'How was the King?' and Turold said, 'Well.'

'He looked well.'

'Did he? When was that?'

'When I saw him.'

Turold let his needle hang and said, 'You have just said more words in a minute than I have heard in six weeks.'

"Words,' said Stephen, 'are expensive.'

'Lull said that.'

'Lull?'

'A scribe. The scribe who wrote this text.' Turold pointed to the work. 'This is a nice word,' he said. '*Parabolant*.'

'What do you mean?'

'It rolls off the tongue.' Turold stitched into it. 'Right off the tongue,' he said, and Stephen walked away.

Next time, Stephen said, 'What did the King say?'

'When?'

'When you spoke. I was there, do not think I…'

'If you were there, why didn't you show yourself?'

'Your boy saw me…'

'And if you were there, why don't you already know what the King said?'

'There were some words I did not…'

'Besides,' said Turold, he threaded some wool, 'what the King and I have said is between ourselves.'

'The Bishop would not agree with that.'

'What Odo agrees with and what he disagrees with mean nothing to me.'

Stephen smiled.

'You find me funny?'

'No,' said Stephen.

'Odo said you do not understand jokes.'

'He was telling the truth.'

'And our Bishop always tells the truth?'

'He likes to hear it too.'

'Please,' said Turold, 'tell me something I don't know.'

Next, Stephen buried his pride and asked, 'What is the King's scene?'

'Now you are asking the right question,' said Turold, 'and I can answer truthfully.'

'What?'

'I do not know.'

'He has not told you?'

'He is King.'

'I know that.'

'He does not have to tell me anything.'

'But as the designer…'

'As the designer, I do as I am told.'

Stephen laughed.

'That was not a joke.'

Stephen said, 'I know.'

'I mean what I say.'

'Deceive yourself, but you will not deceive me. I know more than you think.'

'I am sure you do,' said Turold, as if he were talking to a child. He reached out to pat the spy's head, but the spy backed off.

'Don't touch me!'

'Are you afraid?'

'No.'

'Afraid of another's touch?'

'I prefer to keep to myself,' said Stephen.

'Why?'

'You do not need to know why.'

'I would like to.'

'You would like to? That is a good reason?'

'Reasons lead to mistakes.'

'Not just reasons.'

Turold shook his head, Stephen waited, Turold said, 'The King's scene is the King's business. His reasons are his alone. When I have to know them, maybe I will call you.'

'You will not.'

'Maybe…'

'You cannot play with me…'

'But I do.'

Stephen looked hurt now, he turned away and shook his head. He was tired of talking, he was tired of trying to understand the workshop, he was afraid of what Bishop Odo would do to him. The spy's job was to stay awake, he had fallen asleep at the wrong time. He looked at me, and I thought he was going to spit in my face, but he looked through me instead, and walked to his usual place by the window.

In celebration of Christmas, Turold and I attended Matins in the abbey church. We were allowed seats behind the choir; I was given cushions, so my head was level with his. When I looked to my right, I could trace the tiny lines on his cheeks, when I looked to my left, I could count the heads of the nuns in the nave, and all their faces. When they stood, they rose like waves coming on to a beach; when they knelt, their habits rustled and the sound carried into the abbey roof and disturbed the pigeons that roosted there.

It was warm inside, and the candles cast a thousand different shadows on to the walls, so another abbey and another service appeared inside the real, following in its path like a bad brother. When Ermenburga stood to read from the Gospels, Turold watched her without blinking, his eyes were on her, she turned towards us so her voice was clear as water, and as pure.

We know the story — Mary is visited by the angel Gabriel, Cæsar taxes the world, Mary and Joseph travel to Bethlehem. There is no room at the inn, Ermenburga read slowly, she did not allow the occasion to worry her. I never saw her look so well, she was queen of her land, and every word she said was heard by that congregation.

King William and Queen Matilda sat enthroned beside the altar. He sat still, his eyes fixed on the floor, then on the roof, then they stared at the floor again. He was a satisfied man; fresh from London, where he had used his power in ecclesiastical council. As Christ built his Church on Saint Peter, so William would build his kingdom on the solid ground of a disciplined Church. The spiritual nourished his people, it gave them a purpose and hope he could not provide. He provided what the Church could not, his Queen fidgeted and picked at the sleeves of her gown.

Her throne was the same size as William's, though the seat was higher, raising her body so her head was level with his shoulders. A tall footstool provided her with a step up, she sat on two cushions. Her arms were smaller than the rests, her crown was too big, and almost covered her eyes. Her face was small, like a nut. Her hair was black and tied in a ball. She swung her legs beneath her gown; William glanced at her, she stopped. She held up the fingers of one hand and inspected them; jewels on her collar sparkled, the story of the Nativity ran like a stream through the abbey, over our heads, around the columns and on to the floor.

We know the story, it was warm inside, I began to feel sleepy. When I tipped towards Turold, he jabbed a finger in my side, and I sat up. Incense was burning, the smell went to my head.

I stared at the ears of an old nun who sat in front of me. They were shaped like cabbage leaves, and tiny hairs grew out of them. At first, I thought these hairs were mould, then I saw them move in a draught. The more I looked at them, the closer they seemed, but I did not move forward, I allowed the praise to cover me, and all I felt was warm.

In celebration of Christmas, Turold, Martha and I carried fresh milk, cream and honeyed bread to Rainald, through the snowy woods to his hollow. I walked in front, Martha came behind me and Turold last.

'Do trees talk?' he said.

Martha was worried by him. The stories she had heard, lies, truth and nonsense; she laughed nervously.

'Are you laughing at me, or the idea?'

There had been fresh snow in the night. My old tracks had been covered, the noise our feet made comforted me.

'How could trees talk?' she said. 'They do not have mouths.'

'What does having a mouth have to do with it?'

I felt her eyes in my back. She was pleading with me to talk, she felt trapped, and wished she had not come with us.

'You need a mouth to talk.'

'Do you?' said Turold. 'Robert has a mouth, but he cannot talk with it, he talks in different ways. Have you ever felt that you are listening to his voice in your head?'

Tell him.

'Maybe,' she said. 'Yes.'

'What has he said to you?'

I turned around and looked at her. She blushed and said, 'I would not like to say.'

Turold laughed and said, 'You would not like to say?'

'No.'

'Naughty boy!'

'No,' said Martha, 'he's not.'

'Why not?'

'He's a good boy.'

'You're a good boy!'

I quickened my step. They kept up.

'He is!'

'You are!' Turold had a bottle with him. He drank from it and passed it forward. Martha would not touch it, but I took it and drank more than I should.

'Ssh,' said Martha.

'What's the matter?'

I knew what she wanted to say, but she did not want to embarrass me. She understands what it is like for me. She knows my head is screaming but my tongue will not answer. I am trying to tell her that I would have her in the evening. I am shouting this to her, but something is blocking her mind. The words are there, but she is deaf. The snow was crisp, and where sunlight lay upon it, holes formed over coins of mud and grass.

Rainald welcomed us with open arms, he never appeared more holy. His hair was long and white, his beard grew from his face like fog, his eyes were pale and his voice was soft, as if it came from beyond him. He took the bread from Martha and held it as if it were a child. He cradled it in his arms, bent his head towards it and touched it with the tip of his finger. 'Bless you,' he said, and he touched Martha's head. She stared at the ground. I thought she was going to kneel. 'We will share it.'

Turold stepped forward. 'It is for you,' he said. 'Save it.'

'As it is mine, so shall it be yours,' said Rainald, and we sat down.

I poked the fire.

Turold said, 'If you say so.'

'The Lord has taught me so.'

'That was good of Him.'

'Turold.' Rainald shook his head. 'You never change, do you?'

'I change all the time. My mind never stops changing its mind...'

'About what?'

'My work.'

'Your work,' said Rainald, so softly I could hardly hear.

Martha broke the bread, and passed pieces around.

'And as my work is mine, so one day it shall be yours.'

'How is it?'

'Good.'

'And our Bishop?'

Turold snorted. 'No word. I do not think he will change...'

'I think,' said Rainald, 'that he is most likely to change. There is more good in him than bad, but the bad is stronger. This is, I believe, a problem in men, one which power feeds.'

'Remove his power and the good overcomes the bad?'

'I did not say that.'

'But you think it?'

'No.'

'Then we agree,' said Turold, and he ate some honeyed bread, and it was good.

Here, after Harold's rescue of the men from the quicksands of the Couesnon, William rides against Duke Conan of Brittany. A group of horsemen attack Dol, flames spout from the keep while Conan escapes the town by climbing down a rope. Turold has allowed him to keep his hat, but he is wearing a worried look as he shins to the ground. He has no baggage, and escapes unarmed.

With great discipline, four armoured knights attack Rennes and charge on to Dinan. Their horses are flying, their faces are grim, they are wearing spurs. Sheep are grazing on the fields below Rennes, but at Dinan, foot-soldiers are sweeping the fort with fire brands, lances pierce the border, a group of three defenders, trapped in the keep, are panicking. They have fought in vain, William is determined, his support for the rebels of Brittany had not been foreseen by Conan, who, in this delicate scene, surrenders the keys of the city to William.

The space around the tips of the lances, the pennants and the keys was carefully considered. The keys must be on Conan's lance but closer to William. Conan holds his lance with both hands, and leans over the moat. He is afraid he will fall. William halts his horse, and with the most humble expression, it bows its head and closes one eye.

William looks grim. When he leaves Brittany, he will leave Conan and his jealous nobility to themselves; it is enough for them to know that their northern neighbour is capable of conquest. Turn south, Conan, and I will take these keys.

So William gave arms to Harold. William was anxious to trust Harold, he never wanted an ally more, and he believed he had one. Harold was brave, he was honourable, he was armed, I stitched cobbles beneath their feet, from the ruins of Dinan to the relics of Bayeux.

16

In the new year, we asked Stephen to join us for a drink. We would wait for the sisters to leave, take benches to a corner of the workshop, light candles, drink and eat the remains of a chicken.

Stephen did not want to drink, but he wanted to eat chicken. He could eat all day and not put on any fat. He burnt it in his head. His face shone, he sweated in the cold, he was a freak. He was shy too, his fearful look was a mask. He wanted to be friends.

'Our Bishop is a day away,' said Turold. 'Celebrate his return!'

'Do not mock.'

'Would I?'

'You are indulged, but not for long.'

'Sit down.'

Stephen stared at the bench. I moved it for him and pointed to the spot.

'Robert has even warmed a place for you.'

I smiled.

'He is a good boy.'

Stephen looked at me, nodded and sat down. Turold passed him the chicken. 'Have a leg,' he said.

'Thank you.'

'And I will tell you about the King's scene.'

Stephen held the chicken in his hands and took a couple of short, squeaky breaths. Then he took a deep breath and more of the squeaky ones; I thought he was having an attack, then I realised he was laughing.

'I mean it.'

'You said,' said Stephen, 'he had told you nothing about it.'

'We have spoken again.'

'When?'

'Last night.'

'I watched you all night...'

'Not all night,' said Turold. 'There was a time after Compline.'

'You never left your lodging.'

'I did not have to.'

'The King visited you?'

'Yes.'

Stephen let out another squeaky breath, then a deep one. 'I do not believe you.'

'Ask Robert.'

Stephen turned to me and said, 'Did the King visit your lodging last night?'

I picked up a bottle, shrugged and had a drink.

'He is worse than you...'

'I know.'

Stephen took a bite from his chicken and chewed slowly. He pulled some of the skin away and sucked it into his mouth, pointed at Turold with the bone and said, 'So...'

'Do you want to know what the King said?'

'So why are you asking me?'

Turold put his arm up as if to put it around the spy's shoulder, but stopped himself. 'I want to help you.'

'Help me?'

'We are always anxious to help Bishop Odo's servants.'

I nodded.

'For we are his servants too, and know how cruel he can be.'

'You are mocking me.'

'I am not!' Turold raised his voice. 'It was the same with Brother Lull. Brought in to provide a text I never wanted; at first we hated him, but then we grew to understand him.'

'I know nothing about Brother Lull or his art,' said Stephen. 'My job is to be the Bishop's eyes and ears; I am not required to have opinions.'

'But that is an art in itself.'

'What is?'

'To be another's eyes and ears.'

'Maybe,' said Stephen.

Turold picked up a bottle, and drank. Beer dribbled into his beard, he wiped his mouth with the back of his hand and said, 'So the King sat on my cot and passed me a sheet of parchment.'

'Did he?'

'He did.' Turold took another drink. When he put the bottle down, he almost missed the table. '"There," he said, "that is my design."'

'The design for what?'

'His scene, Stephen. The King's scene. You see? He is King, he gave me his design.'

'I am not an idiot.'

'An idiot?'

'Go on...'

'So I was holding this parchment in my hands, and I opened it, and studied the design.'

'And what was the design?'

'Ah!' Turold tapped the side of his nose. 'That is between him

and me. I swore not to reveal it to anyone else. Even Robert.'
He turned and touched my head with his thumb.

'But you said you would tell me. You said you...'

'And I have.'

'You've told me nothing!' Stephen threw his chicken bone away. 'And what you have told me are lies.'

'How can a man tell another man nothing but still tell him lies? Are lies nothing?'

'Bishop Odo will hear about this.'

'As he will hear about your dozing in the King's presence.'

Stephen looked at the ceiling. I know he wished the world would close in, he wished to return to the certainties of life at Odo's hall. There, he was required to listen for murmurs of discontent and wayward ambition; here, he was afraid that all he heard was spoken at his expense, mocking to his face. The designer was mad. Mad Turold, dumb Robert, this hanging. He looked at the chicken, he looked at a bottle of beer, he reached out, picked it up and took a long drink.

'And then,' said Turold, 'the eagle returned to the lodging, and after the King had given me his crown, he climbed on to its back and flew away.'

Stephen looked up, the candles guttered. 'Liar,' he said.

'Me?' said Turold.

'You know no more about the King's scene than I do.'

'That is the truth.'

Stephen stood up and walked to the door. 'I will not play,' he said, and he left. He returned in the morning to collect his pack, and had to step over us as he crossed the workshop. We never saw him again. We had slept on the floor; the sisters were the next to find us, but they did not say anything.

While the sisters stitched the campaign against Conan, Turold moved to the twenty-five faces that appear between the city of Bayeux and Edward's admonishment of Harold. I was behind him, he stitched the heads and no more, so for sixteen spans of the work, the faces stared from nothing at nothing, floating on the linen like clouds in the sky.

William's face is calm and serious, but heavy with respect for Harold's face, which is indistinct, hiding a lie. Behind William, two lesser faces warn; behind Harold, two faces are suggesting that the Earl hurry. There is a ship to meet, and here is the row of eight faces in the ship.

The tillerman is shouting an order, the man in front of him offers advice, the next is watching the wind, the next tells a joke, the next is watching for land, the next watches the wind, the next is listening to the tillerman's order, the last face in the row is Harold's, still indistinct, and he is gazing at the face of his wife, who gazes back at him with a look of foreboding.

Behind her, Turold stitched the craned faces of four wakeful children, and Harold's face again, and the face of the nervous servant who accompanied him to Edward. In four final faces, he created four expressions in a way that caught my breath and held it inside. I was away from the workshop for a time; when I returned I saw for the first time what you may see, in wool.

Edward's first servant is wearing an expression of pure contempt, condemning Harold with his eyes and his black, crooked mouth. Harold uses his eyes to plead; he was forced to swear on the relics, he could not refuse. He is begging Edward's forgiveness and understanding, swearing that he is his servant, not William's.

Edward is pained to hear Harold's news, but has been expecting it, and his face is heavy with resignation. It inclines down and to the side. The old man is unwell, his eyes are weak, the crown is heavy. Behind him, a second servant has a furious face; the King is hurt, so he is. If this servant were King, Harold would be dead, but Edward is forgiving, he understands.

The twenty-five faces floated above the outlines of their bodies, the ship, the horses and the palace. I touched Edward's, Turold slapped my hand, the workshop door opened and Bishop Odo stepped in, fresh from Kent, a meal and two women.

'Turold!' he yelled.

I had not forgotten his voice.

'I have returned!'

He was bigger than I remembered, fatter, redder and louder. He stamped mud on to the floor, smiled at the embroidery and slapped Turold on his back.

'How is my work?'

Oh God.

'That is for you to judge, my Lord.'

Odo laughed. He was in a generous mood, big and powerful. He had been welcomed by William with open arms. 'And you, surely,' he said.

'Good,' said Turold.

'Good?' Odo unbuckled his belt, handed it to a man and said, 'What does that mean?'

'I cannot say the work is the best, but...'

'Why not?'

'Modesty...'

'Modesty?' Odo roared. 'Modesty never prevented you before.'

'This,' said Turold, turning and leading the way to the completed scenes, 'is the finest work.' He winked at me, patted my head as he passed and pointed to Harold's oath on the relics.

'That is more like it...'

'I am sure you agree.'

'I do,' said Bishop Odo, 'I do.'

Harold swearing on the relics is the hinge of the work, the scene the rest spins around. If Harold had not agreed to swear, he would never have left Normandy, he would not have died in battle. The relics are as holy as relics anywhere — the small shrine contains a knuckle of Christ, the other contains the bones of Saints Rayphus and Ravennus, Englishmen martyred in France — the magic fumes from them, Harold is weighed down by his deed. The scene is a warning to everyone who sees it. Harold's fate is a lesson. He knows what he is doing.

Though his indistinct face hides the lie, his men's warning faces are our warning faces. Beware, people. The Church is charged with the stewardship of ultimate power; that power may seek its revenge at any time, in any place. You are warned, do not forget. The most difficult lessons are the shortest ones, they hide truth in ceremony. Ceremony is the Church's clothes; only God can stand naked before you. He is your Father, he is your Judge and your Saviour. Deceive yourself and you deceive Him. You cannot lie to Him, for he is Truth.

'And the text?'

'Does it suit your purpose?' said Turold. 'Brother Lull was anxious that it did.'

'He is an anxious man...'

'I have stitched it as clearly as I can; I did not want to...'

'Allow it to intrude?'

'I was resigned to its intrusion long ago. That no longer bothers me.'

Bishop Odo snorted.

'Now I wish to blend it with the main field. I have to blend it, so it appears to complement the original designs. I must not allow it to interfere, that is all.'

'You do not mind interference, but you resent intrusion. Another of your fine lines, Turold.'

'The finest lines are the best.'

'Are they?'

'My Lord...'

'Sometimes,' said the Bishop, and he turned away from the relics of Bayeux and walked to another scene, 'you talk non-sense. Most of the time, when I think about it.'

'Talking is not my strength.'

'You need not remind us of that. I think your boy speaks more sense than you ever could.'

Very funny, you bastard.

Bishop Odo is in a good mood. Kent has been satisfactory, the travel was unhindered, his wealth is increased, he sees his future opening as it never has before. William's power in the north, Odo's power in Rome. The axis unbreakable, they will be unstoppable, he would lose some weight first. The hanging will seal the bonds of allegiance. It will point the way and teach lessons that must be learnt by powerful men.

'And how are you, Robert?' said Odo. He crouched down as William did, but I was not thrilled. His face was too big for his head, the edges of it spilled over like water in a basin. His nose was smaller than I remembered it, his lips shinier.

I nodded at him.

'Still not talking?'

I hate him in this mood. I am not a child. I have feelings. I am growing.

'You have grown.'

I nodded.

'Are you going to catch your master?'

I do not know.

'You have a long way to go.'

I know that.

I once looked at Bishop Odo with awe, and called him a great man. Now I have met a truly great man, I recognise the imitation. Some men are born to power, others wear it as a cloak, and any cloak can be stolen. A man's birth can never be stolen from him.

Odo stood up, touched my head and said, 'And you have a long way to go,' to Turold. 'You will be finished in time?'

'Is that a question or an order?'

'Both, as you know.'

'I will not let you down.'

'Good,' said Odo, and with a glance at the growing scene of Edward's death he turned towards the door. As he came to it, Stephen appeared from behind a frame, the two men nodded and left together. It was a freezing day, the wind was loud and blew darts of sleet across the precinct yard.

'Good,' said Turold, 'and not even midday.'

I visited Rainald but he was not waiting for me at the foot of the cliff above the hollow. He usually waited there, though he never looked towards the direction I would come from. He looked ahead, his hands folded, his lips moving. Now, in the coldest time, he was lying at the back of the hollow, shivering. His shelter had collapsed under the weight of snow, his food had frozen in its larder, the brook was iced over. He had been sucking stones, he had stared at the snow for too long. He was half blind, and when I tried to sit him up, he yelled with pain.

'Let me down!'

No.

'Don't touch me!'

I gripped him around the waist. This time he hit me. He was not strong, but the surprise of his blows was enough.

He looked towards me, but not at me. I think he saw me as a cloud, nothing else. 'Leave,' he said. 'I am going to die here.'

You do not mean that.

'I do.'

We must get you back to the lodging. You will be warm there.

'I am warm in the body of Christ,' he said.

We could look after you.

'And He looks after me as no one else can.'

He does not feed you.

'The food He provides is all I require.'

Don't be so foolish.

'There is nothing foolish about it.'

It? Is that all it is?

'Though I would like to see Turold again.'

I will bring him. He will talk to you.

'You talk to me, Robert.'

Do I?

'Yes.' Rainald's eyes floated in their sockets, like feathers on water. 'You have for a long time, and what I like about your talk is that it is spoken by your heart, not your mouth. You never lie, you never say what you do not mean.'

You can hear me?

'Have you gone deaf now?'

No.

'I can hear you, Robert.'

No one can hear me.

'I can.'

Rainald could hear me, but not my chosen words. He can hear my thoughts, whatever comes into my mind. I could be thinking about Martha's skin, and he will know, stealing an apple from a tree, he will know, any sin I commit, any blasphemy. God is not fair.

'Someone has the gift to understand you, and you say God is not fair.'

I thought it.

'Your thoughts are mine.'

Are they?

'Believe me.'

I do.

'And leave me...'

I cannot.

'Go!'

All right, but I will return, and if we have to, Turold and I will drag you back to the lodging.

'Do not try,' said Rainald, and I was scared by his voice. 'I will stay here.'

Now I wish I could not speak to him. I am confused, and I want to see Martha. She does not complicate my life, she hovers above me and wants me happy.

'Go!' he said, again.

I am going! Christ!

'Robert!'

What?

' "For the Lord will not hold him guiltless that taketh his name in vain." '

Rainald.

'Away!'

Martha, I want you.

'It was warmer today.' She snuggled up to me.

I will warm you.

'But now I am as warm as I could be. Are you as warm as you could be?'

No.

'I know you are.'

I held her breasts. When we meet, I always hold her breasts. I hold them and she smiles up at me, and when I put my lips to them, she closes her eyes and pushes towards me. They appear from a gap in her clothes like mushrooms shining in a muddy field. I cannot see anything wrong with them, I cannot see anything wrong with that. We love each other, but do not know why. She is there and I am here, but we will always be together.

'Do you love me?'

I opened my mouth and nodded. She made a buzzing sound, poked her finger in my mouth and touched my tongue.

'How much?'

Why do you want to know how much? This much. I opened my arms as wide as I could. She grabbed my neck and pulled me back to her; I lay on her like a bird. She smacked me and I pinched her side. She squirmed, I put my teeth on her neck, we turned over and fell out of Rainald's cot. A mouse scuttled by my ear, sniffed it and ran away. 'You watch it!' said Martha, and she pushed me off, put her breasts back and brushed her skirts.

Threaten me, Martha.

17

'What is the King's scene?' Bishop Odo clenched his fists. He had snot on his top lip. 'What does it mean?'

Turold shrugged. 'I don't know.'

'Liar!' Odo spat, the snot flew across the workshop and landed on the embroidery. 'What are you and William planning?'

'There is…'

'As soon as my back was turned…'

'I swear to you. I know as much as you.'

'You don't deny that it is something? The King wishes to
add his mark?'

'I have been ordered to leave a space.'

'A space?'

'Yes.'

'What space?'

Turold led Odo to the palace at Rouen.

'And you have no idea?' Odo held his chins in his right hand
and stared at the gap between palace and horse.

'There must be room for two figures.'

'Two figures?'

'And an inscription.'

'What does it mean?'

I do not know what it means, and I do not care. I am worried about Rainald. He is worse, he does not talk any more,
and I am afraid to be with him. He knows my thoughts. He
sits in the snow and stares with his blind eyes. I cannot be
there longer than it takes to leave the food. He eats some,
but not enough.

Bishop Odo was thinking. He forgot where he was, he forgot
we were there, he leant towards William's image, enthroned at
Rouen, and whispered, 'What are you planning?'

'My Lord?' said Turold.

'A little surprise for me? I will be sent away while you arrange
it, I will return to enjoy it?'

'Bishop?'

'Am I close?'

Turold put his hand out, I thought he was going to touch
Odo's shoulder. He held it over the man, then took it away. He
turned me around and marched me back to the other side of the

workshop, the death of Edward, Harold's coronation and the star over England, shooting across the sky with fire in its tail.

I showed Rainald's cot to Turold, and stuck my fingers down my throat. Immediately, he found a sledge, he found a pony, he packed fresh bread, fresh milk and butter, and we left for the hollow. We were away so quickly that I forgot to worry about what the monk would say. He had scared me when he told me not to try and take him from the hollow; now I was leading the pony and Turold was behind with a stick.

'How long has he been bad?'

I held up three fingers.

'Weeks?'

I nodded.

'You should have told me before.'

I shook my head.

'Has he been difficult?'

Yes.

This is Turold; he does not think about the consequences of his actions. He does what he believes is right, and considers his mistakes afterwards. I think Rainald should be allowed to die where he wants. He is sick, but he has found peace in the forest. He is a holy man. I am regretting that I told Turold, I should have kept quiet. I could have found Rainald dead, he could have died in peace. We could have buried him in the forest, that would have saved a lot of trouble, and pleased him.

The trees were his friends, but did not move to help him. They did what they could, but did not interfere or judge. He lay beneath them and his bones began to lock, his blood ran thick, his muscles withered and his eyes closed. Turold put his hand on his shoulder, shook him and said, 'Rainald?'

He did not move.

'Can you hear me?'

I think he is dead.

'No I am not,' he said, and he opened his eyes. They were all white, stared straight at me. They were pigeon's eggs, they were round and dry. He said, 'Not today.'

'Not today what?' said Turold, and he threaded his arms beneath the monk's shoulders and lifted him up before he could complain. 'You are coming home.'

'Home?'

'Yes.'

'This is my home.'

'Are you going to argue?'

'Yes.'

'Why?' Turold had picked him up like a child, and carried him to the sledge. There were skins and rugs to cushion him and keep him warm. I arranged them before Turold laid him down. 'There is no point.'

'I want to die here.'

'No one is dying anywhere,' said Turold. 'Talk about something else or be quiet.'

'I hurt.'

'Where?'

'Everywhere this sledge takes me.'

'Thank God for it.'

'You still know some jokes, Turold.'

'You are the biggest joke.'

'I,' said Rainald, 'am no joke.' Turold cracked the stick on the pony, I pulled the rein, we headed away from the hollow, on to the track and through the forest to Winchester.

We laid Rainald in his cot, and while Turold arranged the monk's rugs, I fetched Martha. She was going to sit with him while we worked, and if he showed signs of unusual kinds, she would call us. I kissed her at the bottom of the stairs to the lodging and she said, 'Is he in his cot?'

I nodded.

'No more tit for you...'

142

I shook my head.

'It's not for you to shake your head. That's my job.'

I put my hand over her bush, she slapped it away.

'Stop!' She pushed past me and began to climb the stairs. I followed close behind, teasing her as she went. She waved her hands behind her, but I would not stop until we were at the top, and then we went quiet and serious, and waited before opening the door.

Turold was sitting over his friend, telling him a story that was not listened to. 'Martha,' he said, 'is Robert bothering you?'

'Yes.'

'Stop bothering her, Robert.'

Mind your own business and get your hair cut.

Rainald's eyes were open, but they saw nothing. He was not shivering, but his skin was blue.

Turold stood up and Martha sat down where he had been, and smoothed the covers. 'Has he eaten today?' she said.

'No. He had some water, but nothing else.'

'Is he dying?'

'Yes.'

'How much longer?'

'Who knows?'

Martha took a cloth and wiped his brow. When she touched him, his lips moved, and a ribbon of whispers came from his mouth. 'What is he saying?' she said.

'The Words of God.'

Martha looked at Rainald with wonder. She folded her hands on her lap and bowed her head. I believe we were in God's presence. The monk lay with his head lit by a shaft of sunlight, the girl sat in reverence, Turold stood by the door with his arms crossed, one hand stroking his beard. I stood at the foot of the cot, put my hand out and touched Martha's shoulder. The room was cold but I felt the warmth of compassion in the air, and a swirl of protection breeze never offers. The sunlight was pale and slight, it gave Rainald's face some colour.

On Bishop Odo's return, Ermenburga retreated to her cell, she refused herself a daily hour in the workshop, she suffered from lack of daylight. She did what was required, she concentrated on a deeper understanding of the Scriptures.

Turold went to her cell, argued to be let in. I was in the corridor, and when they were together, at the door, he said, 'Forget him.'

'How can I?'

'He has forgotten you. His mind does not work as other men's; his ambitions change daily. Now he has decided to chase the greatest…'

'What is that?'

'You know.'

'I know nothing about him.'

'Everyone knows.' I heard Turold's feet shuffling.

'Rome?' Ermenburga laughed now, I heard the sound as it popped out of her mouth and bounced against the walls of her cell.

'You,' said Turold, '— and forgive me when I say this — were never more than an idle thought to him. It was not that I deprived him of you, it was that I deprived him of something, and approached the King…'

'I will never forget what you did, but I pray you will not live to regret it.'

'I will live and you will never live to regret it. Bishop Odo is a simple man. He is driven by simple instincts; he rarely allows thought to bother him, least of all regret.'

'Now you are underestimating him.'

'I know him,' said Turold. 'He has done nothing in England I haven't experienced before.'

'At his hands?'

'At his hands.'

'Then you do not learn your lessons. I am trying to learn mine.'

'I learn my lessons,' said Turold, and he raised his voice, 'when they are worth learning. Odo can teach me nothing; I only regret that I react to his stupidity. I should ignore it.'

'As you are asking me to ignore him?'

There was silence now, only the sound of nuns passing across the yard below, and the chattering of my teeth.

'Ermenburga.'

'Fool.'

'But you understand me?'

'I do.'

'And you will come back to the workshop?'

'You want me there?'

'Yes.'

'Why?'

'I don't know.'

'Turold doesn't know?'

'No one knows.'

'No one knows what?'

'What makes one person want another.'

'I know why Bishop Odo wanted me.'

'Lust is no reason for anything.'

'I will take your word, but I have heard different.'

'Lust is only an end in itself. It is the mayfly of emotions.'

'And you want me for...'

'Your presence strengthens me. It gives me confidence.'

'I give you confidence?' Ermenburga laughed again.

'Yes.'

'Your mockery gets worse.'

'Believe me. I mean what I say.'

There was silence again.

It was cold.

'I mean what I say,' said Turold, again.

'I heard you.'

'Come back to the workshop. You have my protection, so you have William's.'

'Protection is not what I need.'

'What is?'

'Respect.'

'Odo has little respect for anyone; don't imagine he will make you an exception.'

'I don't want to be an exception.'

'You are,' said Turold.

Ermenburga sat in the workshop again. Here is the death of Edward, and his burial.

The sun, warmer that it had been for months, bathed the hanging with fresh light, it picked out the arches of Westminster Abbey, the Hand of God and the bier.

Dying Edward's face is pleading. His faithful friends must be strong. They must support Harold, whom he touches. Queen Edith holds a kerchief to her face, her eyes are heavy with sadness. Stigand has not shaved, he knows the King has less than an hour to live, he listens patiently. Robert the Staller offers support, and here is the King dead.

Stigand has shaved, servants wrap the shroud. Immediately, the crown is offered to Harold, who is crowned King.

Harold's face, as he sits upon the throne, is blank but firm. He knows his crime, but cannot resist Edward's wish and the power of his position. He believes William will not invade. The Duke is threatened at home, he cannot risk leaving Normandy, the sea is too wide, he can only fight with horses, horses cannot travel by ship, the south coast is fortified, dogs eat their own tails. Here are two dogs eating their own tails, in the border beneath Harold's throne.

Here is Bishop Odo, and he thinks people are plotting against him. He is standing with Turold, he has glanced at the death of Edward, but it does not interest him. He has seen Ermenburga sitting in her chair, but does not recognise her. The more he thinks people are planning behind his back, the more he thinks people are planning behind his back. When he first heard about the King's scene, he was flattered, then he was worried, then he was scared, then he was terrified, then he decided Turold was to blame, he said Turold could have refused the King's request.

'Refuse the King?'

'You are on intimate terms.'

'I am not!'

'You are arguing?'

'Please,' said Turold. 'I cannot tell you more about the King's scene than I have...'

'He has not approached you again?'

'No.'

'Has he?' Odo swung around and asked me; then he shouted, 'Has he?' to the others in the workshop. I shook my head, the sisters shook their heads, they would not stop work. They would not listen. 'Who can I believe?' he said. 'Who can I trust?'

'Trust me,' said Turold. 'He has not approached me; when he does, I will tell you. Until then, I can do nothing but continue with the work I know something about. Your work...'

'Do not try to placate me, Turold. You do not have the time.'

'My time is yours.'

'And why don't you kiss my arse?'

Turold gave Odo a hard look. He was trying to keep the Bishop happy, he did not want to waste time. 'I would rather not,' he said.

Odo laughed now. 'Whose would you, rather?'

'No one's.'

Odo threw back the look with one that came from his eyes in fire. I took a step back, every sister dropped a stitch. He yelled, 'You will kiss mine!'

'I would...'

'You would rather not but you will! I will have you on your knees, Turold. William's enemies are plotting; he will leave for home, then you will taste the fruit of my suspicion.'

'Will that be an apple?' said Turold. He was tired of the Bishop, he knew him too well, a dog barked in the yard.

'An apple?'

'As Eve offered Adam.'

'You compare me to Eve?'

'I compare you to no one, my Lord. You are quite unique. There is no one like you.'

'No one likes me?' Odo's face twitched, and his right eye blinked five times.

'I did not say that.'

'You did!'

'I did not. I...'

'And you contradict me again.'

'I said that there is no one like you, not that...'

'And you repeat it!' The Bishop was pale now, he was blinking again, and rubbing his forehead.

'My Lord...'

'Guard!'

'May I return to my work?'

'Here!'

'We have a great deal to do.' Turold was close to Odo, Odo was boiling red, I felt cold, the guard clattered his sword.

'Take this man and lock him up!'

Turold put his arm up, the guard grabbed it, he said, 'What are you doing?'

'Following my instincts.'

'I have done nothing! You cannot...'

'Cannot is not a word I use, and you should not use it either.'

'Why? Why am I...'

'Why is another of those words!' Bishop Odo was looking mad now. His chins were up and down, his eyes looked like fried nuts. 'This is my hanging! No one, whoever he is, should interfere. I would not interfere in his plans, he has no right to interfere in mine.'

'You have done nothing but interfere in mine,' said Turold.

Odo hit him in the face, then slapped him across the back of his head. 'Take him away!'

I took a step forward.

'You!' he shouted at Ermenburga, 'are in charge! Do not make his mistakes, or you will join him!'

Ermenburga looked straight at the Bishop, she was not afraid of him. Turold gave her courage, Turold's face was tired but his eyes were wide. 'My Lord,' she said.

'Bring him!' yelled Odo, and he swung around, and led the way.

18

Martha nursed Rainald, I sat beside her and worried. There was nothing I could do. I was trapped, all my thoughts could do was circle themselves, like buzzards on warm air. Bishop Odo's threats were warm air, Turold was locked up, the sisters continued to work but the workshop lost its eyes.

Rainald had lost himself, only the body remained. His mind was taken by God, he lay and waited for his flesh to give up. His flesh was stubborn, hardened by the forest. Martha was patient, she kept a bowl of bread soaked in milk for him, but he never ate.

We are sitting together, Turold had been locked up for a week, there was a knock on the lodging door.

I answered it.

It was King William.

I was very afraid.

Martha fainted.

I was afraid he would break the floor.

William went to her.

There was nowhere for him to sit.

His tunic creaked.

His eyes were wide and red.

'Help me,' he said. He picked her up and laid her on Turold's cot. He propped her head, undid his cloak and spread it over her. I stood behind him, I am standing behind the King, now I am straightening the hem of his cloak. Martha's hair is covering her face, he stroked it away from her eyes. His hands were big, he said, 'Does she do this often?'

I shook my head.

'I startled her.'

I stared at him but did not move.

'I could have sent a messenger, but I did not have a message.'

I did not believe this.

The King sat on Turold's cot and looked at Martha. His eyes were full of regret, he shook his head and said, 'I have not forgotten Turold, but I must allow Bishop Odo to punish him.' He talked slowly. 'I must allow him to think that he has the power. If I deny him now, he will only store up the resentment, and I cannot allow that to happen.'

I looked straight at the King, he looked straight at me. His power was chipped in his eyes, his brow was covered with lines.

'He will not be hurt.'

You will hurt his mind.

'And when he is released, he will be free to work to the finish.'

Martha opened her eyes. She looked at me, then at the King. She closed her eyes, opened them again, felt the cloak that covered her and licked her lips. The tip of her tongue shone like a jewel. I wanted to touch it. She said, 'Where am I?'

'Safe,' said the King.

I am standing behind the King. I do not believe that I am here, I do not believe anything. Kings do not knock on doors and wait for a reply. This is the real world and we are all in it, whatever our names. We live our lives and cannot escape; even Turold and Odo know that. The King leads a blameless life, though he is cruel and dangerous. He is also kind, thoughtful and full of grace. He is a huge man, I stand back from him, so I can see his face and Martha's.

'Who are you?' she whispered. Her voice was so quiet it came after her mouth had closed, he narrowed his eyes at her, opened his mouth to speak, she put a finger to her lips, he closed his mouth. 'What do you want?'

'Turold,' he said, 'is in no danger. He will be released, but I want Odo to think he can still do as he wishes; within reason…'

I am looking at the King. He does not have to explain to anyone. There is a bell in the tower, and it rings at midnight.

It has rung. He is looking at me. I believe him, but what he says does not comfort me. I want to see Turold now, I want him in the workshop in the morning. If Odo knew anything, he would want him in the workshop too. The sisters are unhappy without him to watch their work; they know what they have to do, but they need his approval, even if all they have to do is complete a border. Nothing about this work is easy.

'What did he do?' said Martha.

'What he did is not the point,' said the King. 'It is who he is.'

'I do not understand.'

'Nor do I.'

'Who is he?'

'A man with a way that offends; Bishop Odo believes he is laughing at him…'

He is laughing at him.

'I am sure…'

'What you are sure of,' said the King, 'is of no consequence.'

I am thinking of the angel Gabriel's visit to Mary. I blinked. I was there and they were too, one on the bed, the other beside her.

Turold sat in jail, quietly. The jailer smiled at me, then at him, then left us alone.

I sat on a stool beside him, he lay on a blanket and stared at the ceiling. Drops of water fell on us, the cell was cold, rats stayed in the walls. The first thing he said was, 'How is Ermenburga?'

I shrugged.

'Is she looking after the work?'

I shook my head.

'Do you see her?'

I shook my head.

He folded his arms across his chest. 'And the hanging?'

I smiled at him, but could not hide my thoughts.

'Do the sisters miss me?'

I nodded.

He sighed now. 'And Odo?'

I shrugged.

'Do you know how long I am to stay here?'

I shook my head.

He shook his head. 'You…' he said, then he stopped.

What?

'You are the first friendly face I have seen since I saw you last.'

He hated to be alone, he hated having no one to talk to, he hated silence he could not control. Odo knew this. Turold could make his own torture. Force him to face himself and he will learn respect, he will become a better man.

'How is Rainald?'

I shrugged.

'I think about him every day. Tell him I want to see him on his feet.'

I looked at Turold.

'I will be released soon.' He put his hand on my shoulder. 'Spring is coming, the work will never be less than I planned.'

He wanted me to believe him, but he did not believe himself. He was not drowning, but he was losing strength. His arms were flailing in the solitude, he was screaming for another voice. I tried to tell him something, I was cursing inside, I put my hand on his. His eyes were half closed, his breathing was slow, he tapped his fingers. 'And for nothing,' he said.

Odo will take nothing and turn it into something. This is the alchemy of power. Nothing can be anything if the result pays. The pay can be gold, respect, fear, love or land; Odo needs no reason to throw anyone in jail. There is a line between you and him, there are flights of angels in the clouds of hell. This is one day, there is another and here, resting in the palm of my hand, is Turold's cheek. I think he is listening to me. He is warm. I laid my head on his shoulder and heard the blood in his neck.

The workshop was cold and damp, the sisters worked slowly, the air was heavy. Turold's voice haunted the walls but was trapped in them.

I pretended to be in charge, that I could be the one who, at the last minute, changed the colour of a horse's legs. I could stand at the linen and stitch the worried faces of the men as they marvel at the star, I could imagine the terror in their hearts. I could look across the sea and imagine the ships as the wind filled their sails, I could be a man on the beach, and seagulls wheel over me. I wish I was a man on a beach; I cannot be anyone but who I am, I cannot be anywhere else. I am lucky. I can touch the heart of power, I am trusted, my dead voice is my best friend, but I am not happy. I am Turold's, I cannot work without him. I try, but I fail. I leave the workshop, cross the precinct yard, go through the gate to the alley and the lodging.

Martha was in the bakery, Rainald was asleep. I sat beside him, his breath came like a pigeon's. His hands lay on his chest, his fingernails were yellow.

Behind his beard, his face had collapsed into hollows. I reached out and touched his shoulder. His body was still.

I looked away. Outside, birds were singing, white clouds drifted in a deep blue sky. The sun was bright, the smell of fresh bread filled the air.

Turold had been jailed two weeks and five days. I hated to think of him alone for so long. William protected him, I believed William, I prayed for him, Rainald's hands moved, he opened his eyes and said, 'Two more days.'

I pissed myself. Rainald had not spoken for weeks, he had not opened his eyes, his hands were always folded. I was holding myself and thought, 'What?'

'Turold will be released in two more days.'

How do you know?

'God has told me.'

God?

'God. His protection is the only one. William will die, Bishop Odo will die, Turold will die, you will die. When you die, who will protect you?'

God?

'Yes.'

And Turold will be released in two days?

'Yes.'

And will complete the hanging?

Rainald closed his eyes and did not answer. The birds did not stop singing, they were on the roof. A dog barked in the alley, I heard Martha singing in the yard. Her voice was high and breathy, her skin was white, from her feet to her head.

I sat alone on a hill outside town. I held my favourite cock. He was big and proud, and carried all my wishes. He pecked at my fingers, I nuzzled his head, he bubbled at me.

Could a pigeon give me voice? I held him to my face, opened my mouth and put his head in. I closed my lips around his neck, I felt his bones with my teeth, he began to panic, he opened his beak and blew into me.

I tasted his breath, and it tasted of corn. His beak cut the inside of my cheek, I closed my teeth so there was the smallest gap between them. He shat into my hand, I put my tongue to his eyes and licked them.

I was thinking: the bird feels as I do, it is trapped, it is dying in the dark. It can give me no voice for it has no voice to give, all it does is breathe. Its feathers are soft, its bones are thin, it can fly fast as an arrow. Its feet scratch my hands, its head is going mad, my mouth is bleeding. I opened my mouth, let him out, opened my hands and he looked at me. His head was wet and spotted with blood. He lifted his tail and spread one wing; he opened his beak and his tongue poked out. It was sharp and red. I held him up, he looked at me but did not hate me. He knew I was troubled, he understood and did not want to leave me. I tossed him up. He flipped on to his back, opened his wings, turned over and then flew away, over the side of the hill towards town and the forest beyond.

Soon, he was a spot in the sky, and then I lost sight of him. I whistled but he did not hear.

Smoke rose from town, the abbey shone in the sun. I could see men on its roof, hauling blocks of stone along scaffolded walkways. To the north, pennants fluttered over William's hall, and the sound of shouting carried to where I was. Turold was in the dark, I was in daylight, there was no star in the sky to warn, no omens, only the incomplete figures of the men of Odo's hanging, staring from the linen.

19

Turold was released as Rainald said he would be. The sun blinded him, he steadied himself on my shoulder, the jailer said, 'Be back soon.' Turold did not reply. He was not afraid, he was resolved, he was a strong man. He wanted a drink. I sat him in the lodging and fetched two jugs.

He drank half a jug quickly, asked for some cheese, ate that, drank some more, pointed at the monk and said, 'How is he?'

I do not know.

'I am in the Lord.'

'He still talks, does he?'

'I do.'

Turold looked at Rainald. As his friend died, so he became scared. They had been young together. 'Do you remember,' he said, 'when we used to argue?'

You never did anything else.

'We never meant it, we were doing it because we loved each other. We never fought, we never hurt each other. We were never like real men, we did not have to prove anything to each other. He had his faith, I had mine.'

'Has,' said Rainald.

'See what I mean?' Turold took another drink, wiped his beard and passed me the jug. 'He can hardly move, but he has the strength to correct me.'

'I have the Lord's strength.'

Turold laid his hand on his friend's head and said, 'You have the Lord's strength.'

A smile came to the monk's lips, he opened his eyes and said, 'Turold.'

'I am free.'

'Free?' said Rainald.

'Yes.'

'What is that?'

'I can work.'

'Work well.'

'I do,' said Turold, and he took the jug from me before I had a chance to drink.

A murmur went through the sisters as Turold returned to the workshop; they stopped work to look at him, he went to where they were stitching, and inspected the progress.

'Happy?' he said.

None replied.

'Missed me?'

They missed you; you do not need to be told.

He looked at Harold's coronation, traced his finger along the border to the empty ships of Harold's omen, rubbed the dead King's blank face and said, 'Do you need me?'

We need you.

'Do you need me?' Now he raised his voice, he wanted an answer, he needed it, but the sisters did not say anything. 'Why don't you answer my questions?'

They are busy.

'Why don't you talk? Have you taken vows of silence?'

You know they have not.

Turold picked up a needle, I fetched a box of wool, he whistled through his teeth. 'Why won't anyone talk to me?' he said.

He had never asked this before, he had not cared. His eyes had a look I did not recognise; his mind was burning, then it was frozen, then it charged around his head. 'Why?' he said.

'Because they have work to do,' said Bishop Odo.

Turold pricked his finger and stared at the blood as it oozed out and dripped on the floor.

Oh God.

Odo came from the door to where we were working. 'As you have,' he said. 'Three weeks to catch up.'

I passed Turold a cloth, he dabbed his finger on it.

'Were you comfortable as my guest?'

Turold bit his lip.

Odo said, 'I would not like to think you did not enjoy my hospitality. And now you are free to come and go as you please.'

Turold put his finger in his mouth.

'And you complain that no one will talk to you! Are you following your boy's example?' Odo reached out a hand to touch me, but I moved away. 'Boy?' he said to me. 'Are you afraid?'

'No one is afraid of you,' said Turold.

'Ah...'

'For the harder you try, the more you fail. I see that now.'

'And what am I trying to do?' said Odo.

Turold took some wool from the box, licked it and concentrated on the eye of the needle.

'What am I trying to do?' Odo held his temper, he held his hands behind his back.

The wool would not go through the hole. Turold narrowed his eyes at it, shook his head, took a deep breath and tried again.

'Do you think I cannot throw you back in jail?'

'I already have three weeks to catch up...'

'The example I must make of you is worth any number of weeks.'

'Forgive me,' said Turold, softly, 'but...'

'Forgive you?' Bishop Odo was boiling now, I was tired, I wanted to live in the forest.

'Forgive me,' said Turold, and now he put the needle and wool down and turned to face Odo. He fixed the fat man with a powerful stare and folded his arms across his chest; six nuns dropped stitches, he said, 'William does not want me locked up any longer. He is as irritated by you as I am; you should tread more carefully than I.'

For the first time, I saw Odo turn his eyes away from Turold; he looked at the floor, then at the hanging, then at the floor again. He shuffled his feet, rubbed his hands together and said, 'How I tread is my own business, whatever rumours you have heard.'

'These rumours come from the King.'

Now Odo looked at Turold with fear in his eyes, and belief. Turold did not care, he had seen the shadow of the worst Odo could do to him; now he would live for nothing but his work. William gave him this confidence, I showered in it, I stared at Odo, and for a moment, held his gaze.

His eyes were glassy, the right one blinked madly, a trickle of sweat ran from his forehead, down the side of his face and across his cheek. He opened his mouth, his tongue lay inside it. It was small and pink, he ran it over his teeth and said, 'The King has many concerns.'

'You are one,' said Turold.

'I think,' said Odo, 'that his favour will go as soon as it came.'

'His favour is no longer the question.' Turold farted. 'Your behaviour has persuaded him that you are the question.'

'The way I treat my servants has never concerned him before.'

'I will be the Queen's; she dislikes you more than anyone...'

Odo's face darkened now, and he wrung his hands. 'The Queen,' he hissed, 'has no power, no influence at all.'

'Fool yourself,' said Turold, 'but no one else. She has more power in one hand than you will ever hold in both.'

'She is...' said Odo, but then he stopped. The sisters stopped work, Ermenburga's face was at the window. She turned when she saw us, and walked across the precinct yard.

'She is?' said Turold.

'Queen,' said Odo, and then he walked away.

The sisters went back to work.

Here are Harold's dreamt ships, here is the star in the sky. I tasted salt in my mouth, but I swallowed and it went; I swallowed and I felt a pain in my belly, a pain that caught me suddenly, as if I had been stabbed. I put my hand to the place, took a deep breath, when I let it out, I squealed. I sounded like a kicked dog. All the sisters looked at me, then their faces turned back to their work. Their fingers did not stop moving. Turold said, 'Robert?'

I shook my head, picked up the wool box, sat on the bench beside him and followed his fingers as they stitched Harold's worried face, as he leans towards his adviser.

20

The days grew longer, the forest trees burst their leaves, and as birds collected for their nests, Rainald died in his cot.

An hour before it came, he opened his eyes and said, 'Fetch them,' to Martha. 'Bring them, and I will tell you what I have seen.'

She ran to the workshop, we left the nuns building and launching the fleet, the fleet sails, look at the horses in the ships. People said it could never be done, but they were secure, not one was lost in the crossing.

We sat around Rainald and he said, 'I have seen heaven and I have seen hell, and I have seen between the two. You...' he pointed at Turold '...will triumph, die and triumph again.'

Turold looked at Rainald but could not say anything. There were tears in his eyes.

'Triumph will be yours. I have seen this written in stone. Stones line the walls of the House of God, and all things are written on them. The Lord sits before them, and knows. Past, present and future life. Nothing escapes Him.'

Martha was on her knees, shaking. I put my arm around her and she fell towards me. She felt small against me, her eyes were closed, she did not want to look at Rainald. She believed everything he said was true, there was no doubt that he had seen heaven. There were angels in the air above him, and clouds to carry him away. I took her hand and held it. It was cold. She whimpered and pressed herself closer to me.

'She understands,' said Rainald.

I know.

'You know but you do not understand.'

What is the difference?

'If you do not know then you know nothing. But you are young, you will learn. You have the Hand of God upon you, and His angels protect you.'

'I am young?' said Turold.

'I am not talking to you,' said Rainald.

Turold looked at me.

I looked at Rainald.

I like the name Rainald. It sanctifies itself. Martha sanctified me. Her tears soaked through to my skin, the closer I held her the tighter she held.

'Who are you talking to?' said Turold.

'Robert.'

'He replies?'

'Yes.'

'How?'

'I hear what he thinks.'

Turold laughed.

I looked away.

'I can.'

'Since when?'

Rainald shook his head. 'What has when to do with it?'

'I would like to know.'

'Why?'

'Because...' said Turold, and then he patted his friend's shoulder. 'We're arguing. We have not done this for a long time.'

'Yes we have.'

'When?'

'When you tried to take me from the forest.'

'I remember no argument.'

'You wouldn't,' said Rainald, 'But there was one.' He stared at Turold, then turned to look at me.

'Maybe in your head. I said nothing...'

'Look after him,' Rainald said to me. He put out his hand and touched my knee. His fingers were like roots.

'I can look after myself...'

'He needs a guiding hand.' Rainald's voice was breaking, cracks showed in his words, and the edges of them dropped off and fell to the floor. 'I am sorry I failed him.'

'You never failed me!' said Turold. His voice was up, he wiped his nose.

Rainald bowed his head and closed his eyes. Martha looked up at him. Her face shone with tears, her hands shook in mine. She took deep gulps of air and sniffed. She wanted me to protect and comfort her, she felt safe in my arms.

'Not once,' said Turold, quietly.

I watched Rainald's mouth as he took his last breaths. They came slowly, his lips hardly moved. He lay back, and as he did, he cackled. A smile crept on to his face, and as it did, I wondered where his voice would go when he died. Where do dead voices go, do they wander, looking for a home, would I be luck for Rainald's voice? I opened my mouth, I moved closer to him and laid one of my hands on his. I held Martha with the other, Turold smiled at me, my father and my mother.

He did not know what I was thinking, Martha could only guess, Rainald was too tired now, and wished to go. I remembered him in Bayeux, I remembered him pointing from the abbey tower, and scuttling through the cloisters. I remember him telling Turold that the rent was fair, the house had expenses to meet, its income was limited. I remember him holding his hands together, praying across the table, willing us to see sense. There was no point arguing.

'Please,' he said, and I took my hand from his and put it on Martha's head. She trembled, I put my nose in her hair and took a breath.

'Rainald?' said Turold.

'Turold?'

'I'm here.'

'You must,' said the monk, 'not be so quick to…' His voice trailed away, he coughed, raised his right hand, it fell back.

'To do…'

Rainald gulped, opened his eyes wide and stared at the ceiling. He saw something there; I looked up, but there was nothing. 'You are too quick too judge.'

'I know…'

'Do not forget. God is watching you…'

'God is watching me…'

'Nothing you do escapes his notice…'

'Nothing…'

'Nothing at all,' said Rainald, and with a longing sigh, he died. His face sank into an expression of peace, his hands relaxed. I leant forward, I tried to catch the breath, but I failed. It slipped past me, it buckled in the morning air, and then flew away, out of the window and into the sky.

There is no reply to death, no peace at a funeral. Turold spun with regret. He wished Rainald had stayed in Bayeux, he wished the monk had never become involved, the hanging was to blame, the hanging was poison. It ruined, it twisted and it spat in its creator's face. It had a life of its own, it raced across the linen, it did not need an excuse.

Turold drank in the workshop, something I had never seen him do. He believed art and drink mixed, but not in the same room. Now he said, 'I do not care.'

Ermenburga was in her chair, but she did not chide him. She never drank, but she knew. She saw the grief in his eyes, she watched his face grow thin, she watched him stand over the sisters and shake his head but say nothing. Before Rainald's death, even during the worst times, he had never stopped coaxing them, changing colours at the last moment, adding a man where no man had been before. Now he slouched around the frames, a bottle in one hand. His eyes were dying, he walked to where Ermenburga sat, and leant against her chair.

'Are you pleased?' she said. She pointed at the finished strips and the growing scene of the building, launching, loading and sailing of the fleet.

He stared blankly.

'Turold?'

Turold is a strong, male name. It comes from the back of the throat and drops out of the mouth slowly. I should concentrate on saying one word; his name would be a good choice. I should build his name in my head, and when I have finished, I would carry it to my mouth without dropping it. There is no secret to talking, there are no secrets a dumb man knows.

'Pleased,' he said, 'is not the word. How can it be?'

Ermenburga touched his arm and said, 'What do you mean? It is beautiful, everything you said it would be.'

Turold shook his head. 'Consider,' he said, 'the trouble it has caused, and now the death of my oldest friend. He did not deserve to die here. He should have gone home.'

'His home is in the Lord...' Ermenburga put her hand up to stop his interruption '...and the hanging had nothing to do with his death. Believe me. Doubt and the folly of his hermitage hastened it, not your work. He was proud of you.'

Turold snorted.

'Do you think he would have wanted you to give this up?'

'What he would have wanted means nothing.'

'Doesn't it?'

'How can it?'

'Memorialise him in the work. Would that mean something?'

Turold continued to stare at something else, but slowly came back from that place, his eyes widened, he shuffled his feet, focused on the scene in front of him and said, 'A picture of Rainald?'

'Yes.'

'Where?'

'That is for you to say.'

'And do.'

'And do.'

Turold turned to Ermenburga and said, 'You have the best ideas.'

She bowed her head.

I looked away.

'No...' she said.

'You do...'

'Will you do it?'

'Maybe...'

'Do it.'

Here is Rainald, stitched by Turold, carrying a sack of corn. He is at the head of a column of men who are carrying arms and provisions to the invasion fleet.

He is tall and upright, with a pear-shaped, open face. His eyes hover between innocence and knowing, his arms are strong, the sack is heavy. He is in his prime, he believes God is true, there is no doubt in his mind. The men behind him, though their faces are straining, look up to Rainald. He is a good man, worthy of imitation.

He has a slim waist, the creases of his clothes are picked out in gold, stitched as though they were drawn. There is purpose in his stride. Before him, a group of horsemen lead the way to the fleet, and here, as the fleet sails across the sea, I am reminded of when I sailed across the sea, and Turold and Rainald argued about the fear of God. Affliction is a signpost on the road to truth? Affliction is affliction.

Bishop Odo in the workshop. Here he comes, walking between the frames, dragging his feet, winking for no reason and tugging at the hair at the back of his neck. He has food stains on his tunic, his chins are covered with stubble. He looks mad, he looks tired. When he speaks, his voice comes in squeaks.

'William leaves this morning,' he said, 'as I said he would.' He smiled, he thought he was safe. His smile was thin, his breath stank.

'His enemies have shown their hands?' Turold stitched into the face of William's tillerman.

'Yes.'

'All of them?'

'Those who think the time is right.'

'Do you think the time is right?'

'No...'

'You count yourself one of his enemies?'

Odo looked at Turold, rubbed his chest, then looked away, picked at his fingernails and said, 'Me?'

'You.'

'I,' he said, quietly, 'am his Bishop. It is my work to advise, never antagonise. And as his brother, I am privy to his more personal feelings; we could never be enemies...'

'Two heads on one body?'

'If you like,' said Odo. 'If you like.'

I took a breath. As I did, I felt a quick pain in my belly, as I had before. It banged into my lungs, it fingered towards my heart, then it dropped and faded away. I bent over, let out a soft rush of air, put out my hand to steady myself and Turold said, 'Robert?'

I stood straight.

'Are you sick?'

I shook my head and took a step back.

'Two heads on one body...' Odo liked this. He smiled and said, 'Yes, I know.'

'And one head is leaving for the coast,' said Turold.

'Which means,' said Odo, 'it is you and I again, and no one to come between us.'

'The King never came between us...'

'Didn't he?'

'His request was for the smallest space. Maybe he will use it to honour you...'

'Honour me, through you?' Odo laughed. 'I have all the honours I want.'

'Do you?'

'Yes...'

'Honours or honour?'

'Is there a difference?'

'Of course.'

'And you would know what that is? You could tell me? You could throw some light on the nature of the scene?'

'No...'

'You could not?' Now Odo was closer to his old self than he had been for months. The chins were going, the lips were trembling, his tongue flicked out. 'Turold cannot throw light on something?'

'My Lord...'

'Patron!'

'I...'

'And designer!' Odo jabbed his finger in Turold's chest, the sisters concentrated as the ships sailed across the sea, the wind filled their sails, the horses stood in rows.

'I am...'

'Yes!'

'And I wish to get on with my work,' said Turold. 'There have been too many interruptions.'

'And whose fault were they?'

'Please!' Turold held up his hands. 'Let us call a truce. I am tired, all I want to do is work...'

A truce?' Odo twitched his head and narrowed his eyes.

'My Lord.'

'And my designer...'

'For my benefit, and yours.'

'Meaning?'

'Meaning nothing but what I said.'

Odo stood upright. 'A truce?'

'As I said...'

Now I felt as if my belly was going to split. I was on the floor before I knew I had hit it, I was holding myself tight, the pain ripped through me, spinning around and around. I could feel it moving, twisting up, lifting its head and slapping its tail against my insides. I let out a long, low roar; I felt hands on me, I do not know whose, and voices in my ears.

'Robert?'

'Hold him up.'

'He's swallowing his tongue.'

'Catch his legs!'

I could not control my legs. They were running though I was on my back on the floor, my eyes were closed but I saw a straight road in front of me, and I was being chased. I had to escape from dangerous men, I could not wait. If I waited, I would die. I could not allow anyone to hold me back.

The pain grew, it moved closer to my heart, I tried to force it back with breath, but it fed on my breath, so I did exactly what it wanted me to do. It took me and tried to suffocate me; my arms went rigid but my legs would not stop thrashing. I could feel them going, I wished they would stop but I had no control.

I opened my eyes and saw Ermenburga's face staring into mine. I felt a cold hand reach up from the pain and tickle my mind, a voice whispered, What's the matter, Robert? Cat got your tongue?

'Robert?'

Cat got your tongue?

I opened my mouth.

'Robert?' Now Turold's face was close to mine, it was pale and worried.

'What sort of cat would it be, Robert?'

The pain burst out of my belly and covered my heart. It took my heart and held it in its cold hands, and weighed it. I could feel my heart going up and down, I felt sick, I could not hold my head up, my eyes closed, I saw lights the size of towns, horsemen on hills and ships sailing across the sea. Birds flew, wolves hunted, I opened my eyes again and all I saw was darkness. I was blind, I heard voices, I felt hands, salt filled my mouth and then I forgot. I forgot who I was, where I was and why; my body shouted at my mind and my mind had no strength. I closed my eyes, there were no lights there and then no feeling at all.

21

I do not know how long I slept. A day, a week, two weeks. I did not ask. I did not care. I was not hungry. I did not drink. Three weeks, a month. I lay in Rainald's cot, I lay in the air of his death, and Martha sat by me.

I had suffered a paralysis of my body. It had attacked quickly and completely. It saw me vulnerable, it was sharp and light, exactly like a blade, unexpected and in you.

Mostly I knew nothing. I saw nothing, heard nothing and felt nothing, but there were times when my darkness was filled with movement, light and action. Sometimes I would see action, but silence would be on the scene. So I would be witness to the massacre of innocents, and I could see women and children as they died screaming, but I could not hear their screams. Their mouths were open, their murderers were yelling, flames licked the walls of buildings and horses shied at the slaughter; all in silence, and the silence slowed the action. So now I was watching a dagger pierce a woman's side, and as her hands went up to the blade, as she cried for help, as I could not take my closed eyes from the scene, I heard nothing. I was not deaf, I could hear myself breathing, but the rest of the world was dumb, the world was living as I live.

Once, I was aware of movement around my cot. I was awake but could not open my eyes. I wanted to but my lids refused to move. There was the sound of rustling habits, stools scraping across the floor and a rank, green smell in the air. This smell grew, it moved towards me, I heard a voice and it was Ermenburga's. She said, 'Has he woken?'

'No,' said Martha.

'Sister Ethel?'

'Yes?'

'Sister Ethel,' said Ermenburga, 'has prepared a poultice for his head. Something of her own recipe that has, in the past, proved valuable. She will apply it now, and you must watch her carefully. She will leave enough for tomorrow and the next day, and return the day after with a fresh mix.'

'A poultice?' said Martha.

'Yes,' said Ethel.

Oh God I remember sister Ethel. Her potions and poultices, made from the vilest herbs she could grow, were hot, evil smelling and rarely did good. The fact that they had done some good once was enough to sustain the faith the house had in her; I heard her shuffle to the cot, and the smell of the poultice stung my nostrils.

I felt Martha's hand on mine, I felt it squeeze, then it let go and the smell was over me. I could hear the smell, it was screaming down at me, telling me it would do no good. It would not release me from my paralysis, I was trapped and there was nowhere I was going. It was steaming, sister Ethel leant over me, I felt her presence, the poultice was on my forehead.

It was useless, it burnt me, but I could not move. I could not raise my hands, I was defenceless.

'There,' I heard her say.

'Will it help?' said Martha.

Her voice was like a bell in the desert, a bell at sea, a bell with a perfect note. The note will never change, it will never pretend to be something it is not. It will never pretend to be a choir, it will never pretend to be flutes, it will never try to sound more than one note. It is a truth that cannot be denied, it is this one note. Its clapper is a voice, its metal is flesh, everyone understands it. It does not ring unless it means something, it is loved and it is feared.

Poultice.

Bells.

Fear.

'My poultices,' said Ethel, 'are known far and wide.'

'I know,' said Martha, 'but do they do any good?'

I could feel Ethel as she controlled herself. Her poultices had relieved many illnesses. Many people would not be alive if it were not for her poultices. Her poultices were the result of a lifetime's study. 'My poultices,' she said, 'are the best medicine he could wish for.'

I heard Martha sniff.

I wanted to throw up, but my stomach was empty. My throat gagged, I felt it grab my mouth but it could not hold on.

'Poultices,' said Ethel, 'are undervalued. Even the well can benefit from a poultice. I spread steamed bran and oak leaves on my legs, and am the more sprightly for it.'

'Are you?' Martha was polite.

'How old do you think I am?'

'Forty-five?'

'How did you know?'

'I guessed.'

Martha.

I could see her in front of me, but I could not open my eyes. I could see fields of flowers and fields of feathers. My pigeons flew by me, the poultice stank on my head, as if animals had shat there, and I was not allowed to move.

Snow covered the world and I was walking through it. Although I could hear voices – sometimes Turold's, sometimes Ermenburga's, sometimes Martha's – I was alone. I was on a journey but I did not know where I was going. I had been given a letter and been promised a guide at the edge of the forest. The forest lay along the bottom of a valley. The valley was below me, the snow crunched beneath me, a cold sun hung in the sky. There were no birds, no tracks but mine, the smell of wood smoke hung in the air.

I crossed a field and came to a wall. The letter was tucked in my belt. When I lifted my leg to climb the wall, it dug into my stomach. A hand came from above and lifted me over.

Rainald was alive, he was standing in front of me. He had shaved, his hair was cut, he was holding a Bible to his chest and wearing a smile on his face. There was no doubt in his eyes, no doubt at all, and his arms were strong.

'Come on,' he said, 'I am your guide.'

Where are we going?

'To fetch your voice.'

Where is it?

'In a woman.'

In a woman?

'Yes. I will show you where she is, but it is your job to take your voice from her. Do you think you can do that?'

I do not know. What will I have to do?

'I do not know,' said Rainald. 'Do not ask me about women.'

The snow was cold, but I was not. The sun was cold, but the sun was hot. I knew I was in dead Rainald's cot, I knew I could not move, but I was walking beside him, full of belief and trust.

Rainald showed me nothing, the snow melted, I was with Turold, and we were talking about the embroidery. Here were the

171

ships and here was the sea, here was the wind filling the sails, and the patient horses. Here is the landing on English soil. Turold wants me to tell him where a tree should go.

I do not think the scenes need trees. I do not think he needs to stitch any trees before the horsemen leave Hastings; then there should be three. Two big ones with a small one in the middle.

I think he has been thinking this too. He nods at me, and as a reward, tells me where to find my voice. It is in my stomach.

I want to tell him that Rainald says it is in a woman, but Rainald is dead, how could he have told me? Then I know I am not talking to Turold anyway, he is in my head, I am tired though I have done nothing but lie down for a week, two weeks, a month? Two months? I am lost inside, I cannot feel my body, I am nothing but these thoughts, and this smell. This smell is a new poultice from sister Ethel. This one, I think, will make me want to eat. She says that if I want to eat, I will have to sit up. I will have to open my eyes, I will have to open my mouth and move my arms. One thing will lead to another, I am closer to recovery than anyone thinks.

I think I have a red patch on my forehead, I think my nose will stop working. Turold put his finger on it, I opened my mouth to speak, he put his finger to my lips.

'Ssh,' he said. 'Don't try.'

I am not trying.

I was not dreaming anything, I was awake, but my eyes were closed. I could not open them, but I could smell. Martha was at the cot, we were alone, there was the smell of flowers in the air.

I heard bubbling, then I felt my hand taken from my stomach, my fingers were spread and laid on a pigeon.

A breast.

A pigeon.

Martha had brought one of my birds to see me. It knew who I was. I recognised it as the hen with red on her wings. She is small and delicate, with bones like needles and healthy eyes. I would hold her, I would like to keep her beside me, and teach her things I have learnt. A pigeon is pure and trusting, she flies for miles but returns to me.

I felt Martha's breath on my face. She whispered, 'I love you,' and kissed my cheek. 'I brought her because I love you.'

Why can't I move?

'The poultices will heal you. You have more colour than you used to.'

Do I?

'Hold her.' She put the bird on my chest and folded my hands over her wings. The bird's beak touched my lips, I forced them apart and tried to poke my tongue out.

'Robert?'

What?

'Robert!'

I closed my lips.

'Do you want a drink?'

I tried to shake my head, but I was too tired. I was too tired in Rainald's old cot, I had been drained and now, as I lay as dead as a living thing can be, I prayed for the old monk's strength, and I wished to work again.

Martha came to me one night, and stood by the window. She held her arms behind her back, and stared down at the empty yard. I put my arms around her and kissed her.

She kissed back, deeply, ran her fingers from my neck and down my back, spread them and pulled me towards her. Her body was warm, a soft breeze blew, she said, 'I need you.'

'I need you more than you need me,' I said.

'Show me how much that is,' she said.

I stood away from her, untied her belt and slipped her dress off. She let it drop, stepped over it and undid me. I took deep breaths, took her hands and led her to a bed that stood in the lodging.

The bed was bigger than the lodging, but I did not wonder how. It was spread with red covers, furs and strips of white linen. Bolsters were piled at one end. I led Martha, laid her down and I lay next to her.

'Whose bed is this?' she said.

'I don't know,' I said.

'Is it ours?'

'It could be.'

'It's too big for us.'

'How can that be?' I said.

I took her head in one hand and a breast in the other. The free breast sat on her chest. She raised one leg and rubbed it against mine, touched my lips with the tips of her fingers and said, 'I love your voice.'

'It's the one I was born with,' I said.

'When were you born?'

'I don't know.'

I am looking down at Martha. She is waiting for me, and I cannot wait for her, but every time she closes her eyes and pushes towards me, I lose sight of her. She slips away from me, she opens her eyes and wants to know why I am doing nothing.

I am talking. 'What do you want me to do?'

'Fuck me.'

'How can I?'

'Do you need to be shown?'

'No,' I said, 'but I need to know.'

'Know what?'

'Why,' I said, 'are you so old?'

'I'm younger than you!'

'And why do you lie to me?'

'Robert?'

Her face was covered in lines, her body was shrunk and wrinkled, and her legs were throbbing with dark, thick veins.

When I looked away, she took my chin and turned my face back to her.

'Robert?'

I can hear her voice, but I cannot see her lips move. The cot I am lying in is not the bed I thought it was, and the feeling that is growing in my body is the colour of milk. My eyes are shut, my eyes are open; open or shut, what I can see does not change.

'Robert?'

She lifts my arms and holds my shoulders. She shakes me, I can smell her breath. It smells of flowers, it smells of grass, it smells of cooking.

'Please,' she said.

I opened my mouth, but I could not speak.

'Robert?'

I heard a dog barking in the yard, and birds on the roof. A month? Two months?

'Can you hear me?'

I can hear you.

'Ethel's here. She wants to give you a fresh poultice.'

How many poultices has she given me?

'Are you going to lie flat?'

No. I am going to open my eyes.

'Robert?'

I opened my eyes.

Martha, Ermenburga and Ethel were looking down at me. The light in the lodging was blinding. I put my hand to my chin and felt the hairs I had grown there. I looked at the steaming bowl of herbs Ethel was holding. She held up a muslin and began to pack it; I pushed myself upright and shook my head.

'Robert?' Martha sat beside me.

I was tired and weak. I needed rest.

'Do you feel better?'

I swallowed and nodded.

'Do you want some water?'

I nodded.

She passed me a bottle but I was too weak to hold it; she put it to my lips and let me drink.

Water is, to a man who had not drunk for weeks, a kiss. I held a mouthful and rinsed it around my teeth. Ethel tied her muslin and moved towards me. I held my hand up. She wanted to put the poultice on my head. I shook my head and did not stop shaking it until she had backed away. Ermenburga nodded at her but did not say anything. Martha smiled at me. It is a difficult life, made more difficult by our minds, and our minds play dangerous games with us.

When I could walk, Martha took me to the city walls, and we sat on barrels to watch the execution of Earl Waltheof, traitor. The son of Earl Siward of Northumbria, he had been trusted by William, but this trust had been repaid with rebellion. This rebellion led the Earl to prison and then, as the spring faded into summer, and sunlight hurt my eyes, to St Giles Hill, beyond the city walls.

We had a good view. Crowds had gathered around a scaffold that stood on top of the hill. Stalls had been set up; some sold drink, others sold bread, others sold crucifixes. Pennants flew from poles, soldiers guarded the scaffold. Their armour glinted in the sunshine, their pikes were sharp and pointed, the sound of the crowd drifted across the fields to where we were. Children played, women stood in groups and wagged their fingers at each other.

Poor Waltheof. He was a weak man, he was drawn to rebellion reluctantly. All he wanted to do was manage his estates, love his wife and have ten children. He was a small man, he looked hungry, he had eaten his last meal and now he was led from his cell, through the streets. Behind and below us, we could hear the crowd chattering as he passed. There was some sympathy for him, there was some derision and some grief.

'It's a nice day for it,' said Martha.

I am sure Waltheof is pleased about that. I expect he is glad it is not raining.

Martha tipped her head to catch the sun on her face as the city gates opened and the condemned, his escort and the crowd poured out.

Here; I can lean over the walls and see the Earl. He was a brave man but stupid. He never believed the sentence, but now he saw the scaffold, he saw the crowd waiting and he saw the sun. He held his head up and walked manfully. Soldiers kept the followers in order, dogs barked, and above us, wood pigeons flew over the fields and swooped down to the forest.

'Could a man live without his head?' said Martha.

No.

'They can live without arms and legs, why not their head?'

I think Martha knows she is being foolish. I think she likes the sound of her own voice. I like the sound of her voice, as I liked the sound of my own voice. I heard my own voice, I know I was talking, but I could not fuck Martha. I am worried about this, I am very hungry, I have a bottle of water. I want to faint but my body will not let me.

Does Waltheof want to faint? He looks sturdy, walking up the hill. The crowd parted to let him pass; as he reached the scaffold he stopped, his guard stopped, and he stared at the sky.

As he stared, so the guard turned to look, then the priest, then the executioner and then the crowd. Soon everyone was looking at the sky, but only Waltheof could see anything. His eyes were clear, he was an example, his confession had been true. He had been afraid, but he was brave now. He saw the gates of heaven and he saw the angels of God, buzzing at the foot of stairs that led from St Giles Hill.

He climbed the scaffold, the priest muttered, the crowd stilled in anticipation, the executioner held a sword. He weighed it in his hands. Waltheof did not take his eyes off the sky. He stared and stared, the sun was hot, flies buzzed around my head.

The colours of the world were very bright, I had forgotten how bright. They were more like colours in a dream than colours in a dream can be. Waltheof, the scaffold, the hill, the crowds and the sword were from a dream, but I was awake, I could look down, scratch my leg and know that that was all I was doing. Martha smiled at me and then, as the executioner took the first swipe, she said, 'Disgusting.'

The executioner had taken the side of Waltheof's head off and embedded his sword in the rebel's shoulder. The rebel was not dead. He screamed in agony, the executioner put his foot on his back, pulled the sword out and aimed again.

The priest fainted, the crowd stood back, the executioner succeeded with the second blow. Waltheof's head flew off his shoulders, rolled to the edge of the scaffold and teetered there. Blood fountained from the dead man's neck, a groan ran through the crowd, the pennants cracked in the breeze and the head dropped off the scaffold. It fell on the grass and lay there. Martha looked away, I looked at her, the sky was deep blue and cloudless.

22

When I returned to the workshop, Turold was burning for the work, he was working day and night, he had blocked all other thought, but he put his arms around me and held me tight. I do not think I have grown at all. He is as big as he always was. His head is full of ideas, he handed me a needle and some green wool and said, 'Could you thread this?'

You never forget how to thread a needle.

I took it, licked the wool, twisted and threaded it. Turold smiled at me. His beard was thicker than it had ever been, but his teeth still showed through it. They were friendly teeth, they were stained and eighteen were missing.

I ran my finger over the figure of Rainald carrying a sack of corn and followed the horses to the invasion fleet.

The crossing was dangerous. William had prayed for a kind wind; when it came his army embarked with great haste. Many of Turold's faces are worried. They do not know if the wind will hold, they do not know the strength of the army they will face, some are sick and some fear the depths.

In the middle of the night, in the middle of the sea, William's ship lost touch with the rest of the fleet. A lantern burnt at his mast-head, but it could not be seen. Here, following William's ship, are two smaller ships with pointing men. The Duke, his faith in the wind complete, took a place at the bow, spread some bread and meat, and ate. He was relaxed, never more in the Hand of God. His claim was right, supported by relics, sanctioned by the wind. Turold has stitched him after his meal, standing in the bow to admonish the faithless and faint-hearted.

'Do you like the work?'

Do I like the work?

'We have been busy.'

Turold wants to know if I like the work. I shrugged.

He laughed. 'I missed your shrug.'

I missed you, you bastard.

'You do not do much, but you do me good.'

What do you mean?

'What do you mean?' Ermenburga came from behind a frame, wagging her finger. She thought Turold was cruel. Turold can be stupid, he can forget himself, but he is never cruel.

'I do not mean it,' he said, and he messed my hair. His hands are so big, I forgot how big. And he sews these faces, he gives a horse a calm expression, or an excited one.

Ermenburga touched me. 'We prayed for you,' she said, and she pointed to the sisters. They stopped work and looked at me. 'We missed you.'

I felt a lump in my throat.

All the sisters were smiling. From where I stood, their smiles stretched along the hanging, across the workshop to an open window. They were like a row of flowers beside a path, pleased to feel the sun. I was wanted, I was prayed for and wished health. I was chosen and I was blessed; I turned away and sat on a bench, sniffed into my sleeves and prayed for my voice. I wanted it more than ever, I wanted to dream again, and I wanted to shout. I opened my mouth, spit came out, I could feel the sisters looking at me.

The horses are unloaded and the army advances on Hastings. Here comes a lamb for the slaughter, and here is Turold's cow. He sketched this cow in place of a man, he stitched it and gave it a knowing look and a leap of joy. He likes cows, he likes horses, he was going to give the lamb a look of horror, but he let it stare blankly at the axe about to fall.

The axe.

Oh Lord, listen to me.

Bishop Odo.

Bishop Odo is clean, he has lost weight, but he has lost none of his habits. He is winking at the sisters, he is twirling his hair around his fingers, and now he is rubbing his left ankle with his right foot. He cannot stop doing this, he stands next to Turold. He looks tired, he looks worried. What he sees cheers him, and when he sees me he says, 'Robert! Back to work?' He still talks to me as if I was a fool, he turns back to the work and studies himself.

He is pictured twice within two spans, the first time saying grace before the Hastings feast, the second time in conference with William and Robert.

In the first scene, he wears a serene, confident face; he is studied by William, regarded with confidence. The table is spread with the Lord's blessings, Odo remembered the day. It was warm, it was their day. The army was prepared, the horses were strong, the archers were practising.

In the second scene, Odo is advising William while Robert lends an ear. The Duke is listening carefully, impressed by the Bishop's understanding of the terrain, the enemy's strength, the Norman army's weaknesses.

The Norman army had few weaknesses, the day — Odo remembered — was as good a day as he had known. Now he was reduced, now he could not relax, now he did not know who he should be. Warrior or bishop? Patron or schemer? Schemer and patron? And bishop? Philosopher? He wanted a sign, he had to be shown that he could be the man he had been, he did not have to live with nothing but the comfort of what he had done. The hanging reminded him, it nudged him, he did not wink once as he stared at his own faces. He touched them, one with his left hand, the other with his right. Then he whispered, 'You are the cleverest man, Turold. For all the insults, you are the most cunning man.'

'I am pleased,' said Turold.

'I am pleased.'

'We have worked hard.'

'I know.'

The two men leant towards each other. Bishop Odo nodded slowly, rubbed his left ankle with his right foot and sighed. The hiss of the sisters' needles could have come from bees, dandelion seeds blew into the workshop and floated in the air.

Odo traced his finger back to his face at the feast, and gazed into his own eyes. They were full of grace, his face concealed nothing. He was trusted and would be trusted again. William would understand that he only wanted to prove his loyalty through the hanging, not seeking preferment by it. He was a satisfied bishop, he was humble but proud to serve. William admires him at the feast; Odo put his arm on Turold's shoulder and said, 'Thank you.'

'My Lord...'

'Your faces are alive…' He fingered William's, then moved to the left, said '…and…' and then his face dropped.

'And?' said Turold.

'This!' Odo took a step back, then a step forward and peered closely at the scene. 'Who is this?'

Turold peered closely too, as if he did not know what the Bishop was talking about, then folded his hands and said, "This man?'

'Yes!'

'Ah…'

'Turold!'

'My Lord?'

'Who is it?'

'I think…'

'Tell me!'

'You will…'

Odo stamped his foot. 'Turold!'

'Me.'

'You?' Odo's face was blue at the edges.

'Yes.'

'I think…' Odo took a deep breath.

'It was suggested to me…'

'Suggested to you?' Odo's voice was up again, he started to pull his hair. 'Someone suggested that you place yourself here…' he jabbed a finger at the hanging, '…next to the King, with your elbow in his face, a bowl of wine in your hand, drinking while I say the grace!' His face was popping, stitches were being dropped, Ermenburga sat in her chair, but she did not move. She had lost weight.

'My Lord, I…'

"What is it about you?' Odo stepped on his own foot and winced. 'One moment you prove your worth, the next you remind me that your worth is nothing compared to your foolishness.' He took a deep breath, wiped his brow and looked at me. He winked at me. Lord. 'And who? Who can insist on this…' he pointed at Turold's image, 'knowing I cannot refuse its inclusion?'

'You will be…'

'And do not say the King. His enemies leave him no time to consider you or the hanging.'

'The King's problems are not…'

'Who?'

'If I say, will…'

'Turold!' I think Odo's face will burst. His nose is glowing like a coal, his cheeks are out like a toad's. 'Who?'

'It's difficult for me…'

Now Odo had Turold by the throat and he screamed, 'Who?' in his face. They tumbled towards the wall, slammed against it, Ermenburga jumped out of her chair and Turold yelled, 'The Queen!'

This stopped Odo like a rabbit shot. His hands went limp and his cheeks went down. Turold stepped away from him, the Bishop stared into his eyes, said, 'Matilda?' and looked away.

'She…'

'How many times has she visited?' Odo's voice was quiet again, and tired.

'Four times.'

'Four times?' Odo slapped his forehead.

'She wants me to design some hangings, and came to see if this work pleased her.'

'And it did?'

'My Lord…'

'And this pleasure led her to persuade you that your presence at a feast you never attended, your face, drinking…' Odo took a deep breath, and held his chest. I put my hand over my own heart, but it was safe.

'As she told me, it is her way…'

'Her way of what?'

'Her way,' said Turold, 'of pleasing the King.'

'Pleasing the King? What sort of…'

'She did not explain why it would please him, but she said it would. I thought it improper to press her. She has a great appreciation of the arts, and is a formidable woman.'

'You noticed?'

'I would not like to anger her.'

Odo smiled now. 'Why not?'

'As I said, she…'

'Do not tell me,' said Odo, and now he walked away from Turold and stood at the workshop door. He took a slow, deep breath, sniffed the air, kicked his right ankle with his left foot and said to no one, 'Battle was less trouble than this.' He sighed. 'Battle is less trouble than this.'

Turold took a step towards him but Ermenburga caught his eye and shook her head. A duck flew over the precinct yard, then another and another. The weather was warm, the rivers were cool, and all along their banks, shady places offered sanctuary.

Martha and I walked into the forest and followed the path to Rainald's hollow. The trees were alive with birds, sunlight dropped in pools around us, I was strong and healthy. I was eating well, drinking more beer every day, and sleeping less. As Turold was burning with the work, so I was; living the scenes, understanding the men, preparing horses for battle. I was excited, as if I was going into battle myself. I held Martha around her waist, and she was happy.

'Once,' she said, 'we thought you were going to die. Ermenburga was going to call the priest, but Ethel knew you would recover.'

Ethel.

I made a face.

'She is wiser than you think. And kinder. Her remedies work.'

They stink.

'And you should be grateful for them.'

I know. I smiled. It is bad for you but it does you good. I did not stop smiling. I smiled all the way to the hollow.

The hollow never lost Rainald's scent, it never lost a feeling of peace he threw over it. This feeling was not touched by his death, it hung like the roof of a tent over us. I sat on the bank with my feet in the brook, Martha walked upstream, searching for pebbles in the water.

She tucked her skirt into her belt and waded slowly, bending down to look, moving on, bending again and whistling through her teeth when she found a pebble she liked. It was white, flecked with pink spots. She polished it on her sleeve, held it up to the light and put it in a bag.

'Where do stones come from?' she said.

I have no idea.

'Do they come from heaven?'

I doubt that anything on earth comes from heaven. I do not think heaven's gates allow anything to leave; they only open to allow entry. They can be as wide as the sky or as narrow as the eye of a needle; stones are stones, and there is no mystery about them. They lie in the bottoms of streams, they lie in fields, they sit in walls, they do not ask questions. They might breathe, but who cares if they do? They cannot see and they cannot hear; they do not care.

'They are so perfect.' She found another, popped it in her mouth, rolled it around with her tongue, dropped it into her hand and tossed it to me. I caught it and held it to my eye.

It was grey, but a jagged line of glass ran through it. I could see light through it. It sparkled, it was warm and some of Martha's spit covered it. 'Here's another,' she said, and waded back to where I was. 'A blue one.'

Turold would like a blue one.

'Shall I give it to Turold?'

I nodded.

'Then I will.' She sat next to me, I turned to face her, kissed her, put my hands on her shoulders and pushed her back so we lay in the hollow together; the trees spread over us and the brook burbled below.

She closed her eyes, spread her arms and wiggled her fingers. Her neck was shining, her hair lay upon the grass, her skirt was tucked into her belt. I put one hand on her leg and stroked her cheek with the other. Her leg was wet. I began to dry it with my sleeve.

'Robert?' she whispered.

I did not stop drying.

'What are you doing?'

Answer your own questions. I did behind her knees.

She opened her eyes and looked at me. They were brighter than any blue stone could be, and brighter than the sky.

I want you.

'Please,' she said, 'not today.'

Why not?

'I can't.'

Who told you?

'But I promise,' she said.

What?

'I mean it.'

I do not understand what you mean. I am confused by people, I think Rainald had a good idea. His hollow is perfect in the summer, but it needs to be protected from winter. He is gone but we are here; she put her arms around my neck and kissed my mouth. Birds sang in the trees, her tongue was warm and tiny. She passed a pebble from her mouth to mine. I put it in my cheek, and held it there.

Turold and Ermenburga stood on the wall and watched a fire burning on the edge of the forest. Soldiers were there, cooking a pig. A ring of women surrounded them, and some children played around a tree. The night was warm and soft, like a sea of black feathers.

The two did not touch, they did not speak, they were relaxed. They could have been brother and sister, they could have remembered things they did together years ago. What were they like as children? I do not know.

Do I care? I do not want to ask myself questions. I should ask my pigeons questions. They know answers.

They are quiet in the night, sitting on their perch in the loft. I sat by them and listened. Silence is full of noise that has not reached it, as any mouth waits to speak. The night is dark before the day, I did not feel tired.

One of the hens bubbled, that started the rest off. They moved along their perch until the one closest to me could rub her head against my cheek. I kissed her, she did not kiss me. The loft smells sour and the loft smells sweet. I am here and there, beyond the walls, the soldiers sit down with the women and eat the pig. The children are lying down, dogs circle, the fire is low and in the trees beyond, owls begin to call.

Three trees — two big ones with a small one in the middle — close the scenes of the feast, the conference, the fortification of Hastings, news of Harold and the burning of one house. More men fight and more men stand doing nothing but work on the fortifications. The news of Harold is received by William with relief, the woman holds her son's hand and asks the firers why they are burning her house. What has she done? If they left her in peace, she would leave them in peace. Anyone can live next to anyone else. She understood that William's claim was just. She was a believer. Relics are relics. Leave me alone. Burn in hell, witch.

Before the gates of Hastings, William stands, dressed for battle. His groom has brought his Spanish stallion. Harold's men are close, the three trees bend like dancers and here, the soldiers went out of Hastings and came to the battle against King Harold.

23

On the hottest day of summer, the Queen visited the workshop. We were sweating, the windows and doors were open wide, Turold said he would cut his hair and beard. I did not believe him.

The Queen came with her Ladies, she left them outside. Ermenburga welcomed her and pointed the way.

Turold stood and bowed, the sisters let their needles hang and folded their hands on their laps.

'No,' said the Queen. 'Continue.'

Matilda.

'Have you seen finer work?' said Ermenburga. 'Work with more life?'

'Never. You are a master, Turold.'

Turold bent towards the Queen, she stared up at him and smiled. Her tiny face was transformed by that smile. Her eyes lit up, none of her teeth were missing, dimples appeared in her cheeks.

'I look forward to seeing your designs for me, but,' and she held her hand up and dropped the note of her voice, 'Bishop Odo's hanging must be finished first. I do not want to interrupt you.'

Turold bowed again, his hair hung over his eyes.

'I do not,' she said.

'Thank you for your understanding,' he said.

'It takes little effort to understand,' she said, and then she wiped her brow, turned to Ermenburga and said, 'It takes more effort to keep cool...'

Heat.

Horse.

Matilda.

She came to me and said, 'Robert?'

I nodded.

'I have heard about you.' Her eyes were kind. She was no taller than me, but she seemed to be. A dusting of William's power covered her, she walked upright, her head thrown back. Her crown was made of gold and studded with precious stones. Some hair hung down from its sides. 'Are you better?' she said.

I nodded.

'I think you were very ill.'

'He is better now,' said Ermenburga.

Yes I am. I nodded.

The Queen put her hand on my head. My scalp tingled, she took her hand away and said, 'I am glad.'

So am I.

'We missed him.'

'I am sure you did,' said the Queen, and then she walked to inspect the image of her husband asking the knight Vital for news of Harold's army. The King holds his mace in the crook of his right hand, and points with the left; the Queen stood on tiptoe to stare, and gently touched William's face.

Turold stood behind her, took a step forward and for a moment I thought he was going to lift her up, so she could see better.

'Vital?' she said.

'He is included at Bishop Odo's insistence. He promised the knight, in return for some favour.'

'Some favour?'

'So I was told.'

'Why is it always favours?' The Queen's voice dropped another note. Her face hardened and her mouth lost its lips. 'Does the man know the meaning of anything else?'

'That is not for me to say.'

'But for you to know?' The Queen grew, Turold shrank, he could not resist her. Her gaze was spun like a spider's web, her voice could stun dogs.

'I cannot lie,' he said.

'I know...'

'Bishop Odo is a worried man. He feels his power is slipping, his ambitions will never be realised. He has great ambition, but it has become becalmed. He does not want to reach beyond his means, not while he is so close. But being close worries him; he is not close enough, maybe.'

'The closer you get to your ambition, the more dangerous ambition becomes.' The Queen stroked her chin and squinted at Turold. 'Do you think?'

'Yes...'

'The King finds this every day. He has never been more powerful, but he has never had more enemies.'

At the mention of the King, Turold tugged his beard. He wanted news of his scene, he grew agitated by the gap in the design, but the look in Matilda's eyes warned him. She threaded her fingers together and cracked her knuckles. I jumped at the sound, she took Ermenburga's arm, said, 'It is too hot today, isn't it?' and led the way to the precinct yard.

I should remember dates, but I cannot. I cannot remember what month it is, though I never forget a day. It was a Tuesday and there were wasps. It was warm, I had a drink, Martha had a loaf.

When a wasp flies, what does it see? I have killed wasps and looked at their heads. They have huge eyes. They can look around corners without moving their heads. If you swallow one and it stings you inside, you die quickly. Your wind pipe swells up and you cannot breathe. They are such small things and all they do is steal honey. God's creation, and Martha is God's creation too. From her head to her feet her skin is white and she has no spots or scars. In Rainald's hollow, she loses her shyness, she lay with her head on my chest, took the belt from her skirt and hung it from a bush.

'People...' she said.

What about people?

'...are talking about us.'

Let them.

'But what do they know?'

Nothing.

'Nothing. They are fools.' She looked at me. 'But we know, don't we?'

I nodded. Yes we do.

'We will show them.'

Show them what?

She untied her shirt and let it fall open, so I could look down at her breasts, put my hands on them, lean my head towards them and kiss them. She closed her eyes, whispered 'You show me,' and fumbled for my ties.

I tie double knots; I sat up and undid them myself, pulled my tunic over my head, tossed it over the bush, she did the same, we put our arms around each other, rolled into the middle of the hollow, the grass was warm, wood pigeons flew up and fluttered around, the brook was running slowly, it had not rained for weeks.

'Robert?'

Yes?

'Are you ready?'

What does that feel like?

'You are big.'

I am desperate.

'Does it hurt?'

No.

'It looks so...'

I kissed her mouth, straightened her back, spread her legs and lay between them. Her eyes widened, she sucked air from me, dug her fingernails into my back and blew in my ear.

It is sweet. It is sweeter than honey, bigger than the sky, brighter than the sun and longer than years. With Martha it burns me, she is full of instinct, she does not know any short-cuts, and does not want to. She is quick and then she is slow, she is light and twists, there is the grass and there is the sky. Here are clouds and there are insects, crawling away. Creation is moving, it never stops. There are arrows in my heart and I am in her, over and over. The table is piled up, the table is swept; my bottle is propped against a stone, and her loaf is in her bag. The meaning of it, as she moves beneath me and I run my fingers down her back, is plain but hidden for a day; the day dies every minute, but not with sadness. It knows it is born again, it does not worry. Pieces of it can be held and here, in my hand, is Martha's bush.

The hair is soft as down on a pigeon's neck, and curls in waves. The skin beneath is white, the lips appear as a closed sleeve, moist and warm. When I traced my finger around its edge, she let out a gasp, then a longer, full moan. It has a heart in it, it beats quickly, it feels and wants me. She pushed it at me, it allowed me in. There was a promise in the air, and the smell of fish.

I do not need a voice. This thought came to me, sat at my feet and watched me move. It did not say anything, it did not move, it kept still. It had no body and it had no smell. It was part of me, it was as pure as what we were doing, and the sounds we made in the grass. Martha was never going to give me a voice. She would give me a hundred other things, she would move me sideways, forwards and change the way I walked, but she could not change the way I talked. No one talks like me, and that is how it was meant to be. Now I am part of another person, and she has enough voice for two. The hollow is warm, I cannot hear the brook, she has my hair in her hands, and pushes my head between her breasts. She has her legs around my waist, she rolls me on my back. I stare at the sky, I close my eyes and the sky does not disappear. It is painted on the inside of my lids, weeping clouds. I can put my hands up and scrape my fingernails across it, and pull its nerves. It is smaller than we are, and moves slower. It cannot have my joy or change its face. There are jewels on the floor and jewels for you, and jewels in the seas of morning dew. I do not think I knew Martha. She kept a part of herself hidden, even when she showed me all I thought she could. Her legs were smooth and her belly was lying on mine.

'Robert?'

What?

'Do you love me?'

Yes.

'I love you.'

I love you.

She closed her eyes and laid her head on my shoulder. I held her around the waist and pushed in. 'Go on,' she said.

I was growing from the inside out. There was no pain at all, no warning and no sin. From the hollow to the sky and back again, in the wing of a wood pigeon flying from the forest to the stream; the forest was quiet for us; its voice is something no one who hears it can forget.

I dreamt I had a voice, but lost it. When it came, when I said, 'Listen to me,' to Turold, I could not think of anything else to say, so I took it from my mouth and carried it to a cliff.

I held my voice in my hands. It was made of blue air. Below me, waves broke along the shore, sea birds circled overhead and a cold wind blew inland. I was alone, but someone was whispering in my ear.

'Get rid of it,' said the whisper.

My voice looked at me and said, 'How long have you wanted me?'

All my life.

'You do not need it. You are better off without it.'

'No you are not.'

'Even if you had it, no one would listen to you.'

'They would.'

'Believe me,' said the whisper.

'No,' said my voice, 'believe me.'

The sea birds cried as they circled.

'Listen to them,' said the whisper.

'Do not listen to them.'

'They have voices...'

'They are birds. You are a man.'

I am a man.

'Bird, man, woman.' The whisper coughed. 'What is the difference?'

'The difference is plain,' said my voice.

Who do I believe? My voice is warm but does not know anything. The whisper is wise.

'In one way, it is, but not in the most important way.'

'And what,' said my voice, 'is the most important way?'

'The way you cannot see.'

'And that is the way you can see, is it?'

'Yes.'

My voice laughed now, but as it did, a bird swooped down and picked it up in its beak, and carried it to a cliff ledge. It laid my voice at the edge of its nest, turned it over and stuck its bill into the softest part. I opened my mouth, my voice screamed, the bird tore it apart and fed pieces to its chicks. The chicks had birds' bodies but human faces; the bird that killed my voice had a bird's face and a bird's body. It was a black-backed gull and it could smile, all the way from my cot to the floor, where I was lying when Turold tripped over me on his way to the workshop.

Ermenburga dozed in the workshop, Turold looked at her with a needle in one hand and his other hand resting on the hanging. I was growing. The top of my head was level with his shoulders. I held the wool box on my lap and watched a man give news to King Harold about Duke William's army. The man is panicking, Harold cannot believe the news. The English army have marched from the north, the Normans have rested, feasted and they ride horses.

As Ermenburga dozed, she made bubbling sounds, like a pigeon. Turold put his hand over her head but did not touch her. I put my fingers to my nose and smelt them.

Ermenburga woke slowly, opened her eyes, smiled at Turold, looked at his hand and whispered, 'What are you doing?'

'Nothing.' He looked blameless, a boy caught at the bakery door.

'The sisters never do nothing. Why do you?'

'When I say I am doing nothing,' said Turold, 'I do not mean it...'

'You are deceiving me?'

'No, I am thinking.'

'And the sisters do not need to think?'

'I did not say that.'

'I think about...'

'I know,' said Ermenburga, and she put a finger to her lips, 'what you think about.' She turned her head away from him. 'Forgive me. I was playing...'

'I was playing too.'

I was sniffing my fingers.

'Do you forgive me?'

'There is nothing to forgive.'

'You are...' said Ermenburga, and then she stopped. She held her breath and put her hand over her mouth. I do not know what she was thinking, I do not know what he wanted to say. There was a bridge in the air between them, I could see it and so could they. The bridge was guarded by archer angels and pots of fire. I do not know what this meant, I was thinking about something else. All I know is what I heard and saw. Some weeks, nothing happened, then a week was full of incident. A week would pass and the work progressed as the story it told had done, and the work did not allow any interruptions. As the work grew, it grew itself senses, and these senses gave themselves the power of understanding. The understanding meant nothing at all, but that did not matter, for it was only a story.

Ermenburga sat, Turold went back to work. He put out his hand for wool, I had it ready, I looked straight in his eyes and he said to me, 'What is different about you, Robert?'

I am growing.

'You are taller, but that is not what I mean.' He looked me up and down, he shook his head and stitched into William's face. 'Your face has changed,' he said.

How long?

Weeks.

I am thinking about Martha.

'And you work harder.'

I want to do the best I can. I do not want you to think I am useless.

'Are the sisters putting something in your soup?'

I shook my head.

'Sisters?' He called to them, but they would not look up. Some smiled but the rest stared at their work.

They will not answer.

'The dumb lead the dumb,' said Turold, 'or do the dumb lead the dumb?'

I forget.

Once we started, we did not stop. Martha and I fucked on Sundays, we fucked in the lodging and behind a barrel. In daylight in the woods, in the dark in the woods, we were the beast with two backs in fields, and flat on top of each other in the yard behind the bakery. We fucked on a hill with sheep watching, and in an orchard of apple trees. Bees flew over our heads and flies bothered our creases, the grass was long, a leaf drifted down and landed on my head.

I had her in a barn, we returned to Rainald's hollow and went like rabbits. The more I fucked the more I could, the more she had me the more she wanted me. At twilight beneath the city walls, beneath a cart, beneath a blanket. She bit my neck and I nipped hers, she licked my stomach and laid hers on my face. Her skin was warm as breath, it felt like breath, I sucked it into my mouth and circled it with my tongue.

In an empty watchtower, we sat afterwards with our backs against the walls. When wood pigeons flew over, she said, 'How are your birds?'

I feel guilty about them. I fly them but I do not give them the attention I should. I shut them in at night, but I think I will leave their door open.

I shrugged.

She put her hand on my thigh and squeezed. 'You do not carry them as much as you used to.'

I do not need to.

'Why not?'

I looked at her. She is simple and bright. She notices things, she wants to know about the world. She has been covered by the King's cloak, she is loved. I put my hands on her breasts, held them there and then opened them, as if I was releasing them. I stared into the sky, as if I was watching their flight. They moved slowly, and disappeared into the trees. 'Robert,' she said.

Martha.

I feel the world inside. It is giving itself a body. It is giving itself legs, it will wear shoes. I want you now, I want you every day, in every place and every way.

William points the way, and then, across twenty spans of the hanging, mounted knights gather speed as they charge the English. Some carry gonfalons, others spears. The horses canter, archers aim, the horses break into a gallop and here, in a brave stand, the English knights defend themselves.

In the border, two birds lie on their sides and the first of the dead is stitched: a soldier on his back, a spear stuck in his throat. The noise of the battle is in the linen, the thunder of the horses, the shouting and wailing of men, arrows and spears whistling through the air, shields clattering together.

With his gonfalon beside him, Harold repels attack with an axe. Headless bodies appear below him, Turold had his hair cut short. He said it would help him think, that his head liked to be cool.

Harold's axe is heavy. He holds it with both hands. His moustache is long and greasy, the axe falls on a horse's neck, the shield wall holds.

24

In late summer, Bishop Odo travelled to Kent. Trusting us to work, and believing a spy was a greater pleasure for Turold than a worry, he did not leave one; he did not misjudge, and returned to Winchester in autumn, refreshed by an inspection of his estates, reassured by them and fresh sea air. When I saw him in the workshop, he was content, he did not shake his head at the gap between the palace at Rouen and the horse, he clapped Turold on the back and laughed. He had lost weight, his cheeks did not puff when he spoke. 'As usual,' he said, 'you and the sisters produce the best work.'

'We try.'

'And you succeed! You succeed, Turold, and you please me.' He stared at the image of the knight Vital and scratched his balls. 'I think,' he said quietly, 'that I allowed the hanging to worry me, and that was a mistake. It is your job to worry about it, and my job to worry about other affairs. I see that now...'

'I never worry about it, but I...'

'It is difficult for me to separate my wider concerns from the interest other people have shown in your work, but I must.'

'I think...'

'Thinking again?'

'I think you know what I think.'

'I think I do.'

Odo looked at me, looked away then looked again. He narrowed his eyes and said, 'Robert?'

I took a step towards him.

'It is Robert, isn't it?'

'Yes,' said Turold.

'What has happened to you?'

'He has grown.'

'I can see that.' Odo shook his head, 'And something else...'

What?

'...something in your face, Robert.'

I do not know anything about my face. It means nothing to me. I do not care about the shape of my nose or the colour of my eyes. Martha has told me it is the face she wants, that is all I need to know. Martha's breasts are growing. Her hair is longer. Hair is growing on my chest. I shrugged at the Bishop, and he shrugged at me. 'I think,' he said, 'that you could tell a few secrets, couldn't you?'

I would not.

'He wouldn't, even if he could,' said Turold.

'Do you mean,' said Odo, 'there are secrets? Things you have kept from me?'

'Nothing is kept from you.'

'No?'

'No.'

'Not even the smallest thing?'

'There is nothing small about this work...'

'You know what I mean.'

'My Lord,' said Turold. 'If we are to finish I must...'

'You will finish.'

'But...'

'No buts but the King's scene, I think.'

'Do not remind me.'

Do not ask me if what I remember is fact. I do remember Odo's face, I do remember Turold saying that there were no secrets in the hanging, I know I felt released, but did not know what from. I had longer legs and a bigger head than when I arrived, I had carried pigeons with me, but now I had given them their freedom. Occasionally, they returned to the loft, but mostly they roosted in holes in the city walls.

'Why not?' said Odo.

'The space irritates me. I carry it in the back of my mind; as I finish one scene and move to the next, I know it's there, waiting for me.'

'And for me?'

'I would not know.'

'Have you ever wondered?'

'What?'

'What you would do if William failed to return.'

He will return.

'He will return. The Queen said...'

'The Queen?' Odo's face tensed. 'What did she say?'

'He has not forgotten me or the hanging. A sketch of his scene will arrive by messenger.'

'So your irritation will be eased...'

Turold turned to the work. 'However great the man, his design cannot do anything but intrude upon mine. It was not meant to be tinkered with. However...'

'However?' Odo's eyebrows were up, there was a smile on his face.

'As with Brother Lull's text, so with the King's scene.'

Odo laughed. 'You are comparing Lull with William?'

'No.' Turold took a threaded needle and stabbed the linen. 'Not as men...'

'William will be glad to know that...'

'...only in the sense that...'

'I know the sense...'

'...they both made a contribution.'

'It is a contribution now, is it?'

Although I have given my pigeons their freedom, I still leave corn for them. I spread it in the loft, on the cleaned floor beneath their perches. As they had flown, so a part of me flew; the empty space was filled by Martha.

We fucked in the pigeon loft, and while people made music beneath us. We fucked as the sun came up and as the moon

200

went down. The stars were out, the stars were in. Wind came and ripped leaves from the trees but we did not stop. I was tired but had the energy to carry on. I forgot my wishes, I spared myself and I spared Martha. She was there and I was there, we were there together, and after every fuck we arranged the next.

On your knees.

Queen Matilda, and she will not stand for nonsense today. She has heard from William, she catches Turold in conference with Bishop Odo, her Ladies are pale.

On your knees.

Odo goes pale. As the Queen enters the workshop, a blast of cold wind blows in, and leaves race across the floor. The sisters drop stitches, Turold leaves Odo.

Kiss the ring.

Listen to her skirts rustle.

The Queen has given birth to nine live children. She is deep in thought, and walks slowly. Turold bends towards her, she stares at him, her face is grave, then changed by a slight and knowing smile.

'Messengers have arrived,' she said, 'carrying this.' She held up her sleeve so he could see a roll of parchment there. He opened his mouth to speak, but she stopped him. 'No,' she said. 'Not here. It might upset someone.' She looked around Turold, towards Odo. The Bishop was holding his chin in his hand, hovering. He bowed at her look, she raised a hand, he took a step forward, she showed him her palm.

'His scene.'

'Yes.'

Turold took a deep breath.

'You are relieved?'

'Yes.' He looked at the Queen's sleeve, she put her hands behind her back and shook her head.

'I will send for you.' She looked at Odo, who took a step forward.

'I hope…'

'Bishop Odo!'

'My Lady.'

'You spend more time in Master Turold's workshop than you do at your offices.'

Odo did not know whether to shake his head, nod, smile or stare at his feet. He had a wink, twirled his hair and winked again.

'Bishop?' said the Queen. 'Are you all right?'

'Majesty; I was bitten by a bee yesterday,' he said, 'and have a rash.'

'A rash?' The Queen peered at him. 'Maybe one of my Ladies could provide you with some balm. I think Hilda is the one to ask.'

Odo bowed low, almost banging the top of her head with his nose. 'I thank you,' he said, 'for your concern,' through clenched teeth, 'but sister Ethel has already applied a balm of her own.'

'Sister Ethel?' said the Queen, 'I have heard of her.'

Turold opened his mouth to say something, but nothing came out. I stood by him. Above us, Harold's brothers died, the borders choked with bodies, weapons and shields.

'Her potions appear vile but seem to work.'

'If it smells bad,' said the Queen, 'then it must do you good. Is that true, Bishop?'

'I know no one who would argue otherwise.'

'But is it true?'

'My Lady,' said Odo, and he bent his head again. 'It is.'

'That's a comfort.'

'I feel much better today,' he said.

'Have you been ill?' said the Queen.

'The bite. It swelled to…'

'Oh yes,' said the Queen, and she held her hand up. 'Forgive me,' and then she turned, closed her sleeves and walked away.

On your knees.

The sisters licked their lips.

Odo took a deep breath.

Turold waited for the Queen to leave the workshop and cross the precinct yard, then he slapped his knees and laughed.

'A woman,' said Odo, 'should not be allowed to...' and then he stopped, turned away and kicked his left ankle with his right foot.

'Allowed to what?' said Turold.

Odo shook his head.

'My Lord?'

'Go back to your work!' Odo narrowed his eyes, put his chest out and pointed. 'Never forget,' he said, 'who I am.'

'How could I?'

'And who you are.'

'I am...' said Turold, but Odo was away from the workshop, crossing the precinct yard slowly and waiting at the gate for a moment, until he was sure he was safe.

Martha and I have fucked in the lodging, and as we were lying afterwards, she asked to see the hanging.

Tonight?

'Show me now.'

It is late.

'Show me.' She put her mouth to me, and licked me.

The moon is full, the workshop is cold, Turold is working by candle-light. The midnight bell has rung, he has not noticed it. He has a jug beside him, but has not touched it. His mind is concentrated, he works without knowing what is happening around him. The more he works so the more he wants to work. The story is driving him as a rider on a horse. The whip is on his back, spurs are in his sides, the road is clear. His fingers, his eyes and his mind joined at the gates of his invention, banged on them, refused to leave; he did not look up when I pushed the workshop door open, pulled Martha inside and led her to the first strip.

Here and there candles burnt in holders, and strips of moonlight broke through gaps in the walls and windows. The workshop was a dreamy place. The frames were invisible, so the hanging floated in the air. The light drifted, the flames guttered, breath rushed from Martha's mouth, she stood before the first scenes and bowed her head.

I stood next to her. She looked up and stared into Edward's eyes. She put her fingers up to Harold's dogs. She glanced at me, I nodded, she touched the hanging and shook her head.

As her fingers touched the wool, I felt a crack in the air. I know she did not feel it, and Turold was not disturbed, but it was there. It was as if threads were snapping all around me; I looked down the strips, but they had not moved. I looked above me. A bat dived towards my head, twisted over a candle and flew towards Turold. I watched its flight, I decided to keep bats. 'I've never seen anything like this,' said Martha.

There is nothing like it.

'Show me some you have done.'

I took her hand and led her to the boy in the border; I traced the outline of his body and the length of his slingshot. The stone misses the birds, who fly to a tree. She put her finger on mine and said, 'You did this?'

I nodded.

'He is you?'

Yes.

'And this is Turold.' She touched his image, then took her finger away, as if it had been burnt.

Yes.

She looked down the workshop. 'He doesn't mind us being here?'

I shook my head.

He sat at the last strip, sewing into the face of a fleeing English soldier. A circle of candles surrounded him, the bat flew into the light and out, the hiss of his needle, his face craned towards the work. His eyes were full of urgency, he threw a huge shadow on to the wall. This moved with the flames, Martha took my hand, her lips were pursed and her eyes were wide.

We walked slowly around the frames. She looked in a trance; her feet made no sound on the floor, she held her fingers to the hanging, but did not touch it. She traced the shapes of men and horses in the air, she shook her head at Harold at Bayeux, she smiled at the horses in the ships. Her face relaxed, she hunched her shoulders, she looked older than she was, when I put my face to her hair she did not notice.

I could hear her mind and I could hear mine. They were working together, her thoughts were slowed down by the art, mine sat on their back and whispered. The bat squeaked, it flew from the ships with wind in their sails to the slaughter of English soldiers to the quicksands of the Couesnon to its roost. It hung there for a moment then dived again, over our heads to a place in the dark by the door.

I concentrated on the word 'Martha', and put it in my belly. Tonight I was going to take air from a whistle, swallow it, make it grab the word and shoot it out of my mouth. Martha's hand was in mine, we reached the end of the fourth frame and I tripped over a bench.

'Who's there?' Turold's voice was tired. 'Robert?'

Martha snapped back from where she was with panic in her eyes; she grabbed my arm and hissed, 'Robert?'

I touched her cheek and shook my head. I walked around the frame and along to where he was working.

'Robert?'

I stood beside him.

He put his hand on my shoulder. 'What are you doing, creeping around?'

I smiled, put my hand over my heart and Martha came behind me.

'Ah...' he said, and he grinned. 'Nowhere else to go?'

I shook my head.

'Speak for him, Martha.'

She was afraid.

'Do not be afraid.'

'I am sorry,' she said. 'I wanted to see the hanging. Robert brought me.'

He held his needle in his hand. 'Did he?'

'Yes.'

'You like it?'

'Yes.'

'Good.'

I had the word in my belly, sitting on its own, and I had the note of the whistle in my head. The bat flew through the light again, a dog barked once, Turold's needle twinkled.

'Can you stitch?' he said.

'Me?'

'You.'

'Yes,' she said.

He gave the needle to her. 'Here,' he said, 'show me.'

'But…'

'No buts!' He stood up, picked her up and sat her on the bench. She stared at the figure of the fleeing soldier. He was waving an axe, running from the Norman horses as they crashed to the ground beneath the English ridge. 'Give him an eye.'

Martha held the needle between her fingers. She was shaking, she opened her mouth to say something, but nothing came out, so she jabbed at the soldier's face, pulled the wool through, took a deep breath and moved away.

'Again,' said Turold.

Martha did as she was told.

Here is the word and here, beginning softly but getting louder all the time, is the whistle. It is a low note, it could be the wind though a hole in the door. It could call a pigeon and it would catch a word. There is no trick to it, no skill that cannot be learnt. I am growing, and as I grow I learn.

'You could work here,' said Turold.

Here is the word.

'No, I don't think I could do as well as you or the sisters.'
She looked at me. 'Or Robert.'

'You could!' he said. 'If you wanted.'

The whistle is pure and round, like an apple. I could bite it,
I could hold it and tell you what colour it is.

'I could not leave the bakery. My father would not allow it.'

'Your father would change his mind at the sight of silver?'

Blue.

'I will ask him.'

'Do,' said Turold, and then he turned to me and said, 'Why
are you whistling?'

I whistled a moment longer, swallowed my breath, pushed
it into my belly and forced it on to the word. It covered the
word but did not stick. It rushed out again. Turold said, 'Are
you all right?'

I nodded. The word melted inside me.

'What are you doing?'

Nothing.

'I think you two are making each other old...'

What?

'...as you are supposed to.'

A second bat joined the first and they flew together, as if
attached by wool. The wool was light, they circled each other
and landed on the hanging, and crawled across the untouched
sketches of the death of Harold. They had mouse heads and
pigeon feet, leather wings and ears the size of leaves. 'My pets,'
said Turold, and then he took the needle from Martha, and
turned back to the hanging.

25

A solemn Lady came for Turold, and asked him to follow her
to the Queen. I followed too, across the precinct yard to the

gate, down the alley to the street, up the street to the market square, across the square to the palace.

Word had been left at the gate. The Lady knew the guard. As we passed, he whispered in her ear. She put her hand to her mouth and giggled behind it, then put on her solemn face again, led us to a small door, showed us inside and told us to wait.

As we sat on a bench by a window, Turold put his hand on my knee and said, 'What surprise has William got for us?'

I have no idea.

'Something to worry Odo?'

Could be.

'I think so,' he said, 'but I hope not. However far the Bishop goes, he'll only ever be William's half-brother. That gives him enough grief; I do not think he needs any more.'

Are you supporting him?

'He cannot help being who he is, no more than I can help who I am.'

Below us, the sound of marching soldiers cracked across a yard. It was a cold day, a hard wind blew from the east.

"We were all born by accident,' he said.

What accident? Turold speaks his thoughts without explaining them. He thinks we can read his mind, but we cannot.

'Master Turold?'

'Yes?' He stood up, brushed his tunic and smoothed his beard. Another Lady had come. Her dress was finer than the first's, and she carried a sheet of parchment. 'You may come with me now,' she said, and led the way.

We crossed the main hall to a small door in the wall that led to a flight of curved stairs. We climbed these to another floor, passed through a curtain and into a corridor.

The corridor was long and brightly lit, and filled with the smell of lavender. This smell was so strong that I put my hand to my nose and breathed through my mouth. Turold sniffed once, smiled at the Lady and waited for her.

Rooms led off the corridor. We walked the length of it, turned a corner at the end, the Lady put her hand up, we stopped, she knocked on a door and waited.

I heard the sound of rustling skirts and curtains being drawn. Turold wore a calm face, I wiped mine, the sound of feet echoed down from the floor above. The door opened, another blast of lavender blew up my nose, the Lady took one step into the room and said, 'Master Turold, your Majesty, and...' she looked at me '...his boy. I understand he accompanies his master wherever...'

'Yes, yes,' said the Queen, and she bustled from the window to where we were. 'We know Robert.'

'Majesty.'

'Thank you.'

The Lady bowed her head and bit her lip. She held her sheet of parchment tight. She did not like me and she did not like the Queen. She was as tense as a dead lady. 'My duties...' she said.

'Yes,' said the Queen, and she waved a hand. 'You may return to them.'

The Lady backed out of the room, the Queen watched her leave, the door closed, the Queen looked at it, shook her head and turned to Turold.

'Turold,' she said.

'Your Majesty.' He dipped and kissed the ring.

'And Robert...'

I was on one knee. She put her hand on my head.

'I have something for you.'

Turold was on his feet.

'But sit first.' She smiled, her eyes were moist and her hair hung down. It was black and shiny as a bat's, and reached to her waist.

We sat on low chairs, she sat on a high chair, so her eyes were level with his. His knees nearly touched his chin, he held his hands between his legs.

'Here,' she said, and she passed him a roll. 'In the King's hand, drawn on the banks of the Couesnon.'

He took the roll and said, 'The Couesnon flows through a scene in the hanging.'

'Yes.'

Turold unrolled the parchment, spread it on his knee and looked at it. He squinted, he scratched his head, he looked at the Queen, then back at the scene and said, 'What does it mean?'

The Queen smiled again. 'You have no idea?'

'None.'

The Queen rubbed her chin. 'Ælfgyva is not a name you know?'

'No, Majesty, it is not.'

'Never?'

Turold looked at me.

I shrugged.

'Ælfgyva,' he said, shaking his head. He passed the sketch to me. 'Never.'

The parchment was torn at the edges and stained with mud and rain drops. I smoothed it on my knee.

A tonsured man, dressed in tunic and cape, leans towards a woman who stands framed beneath a pillared gateway. His hand is held outstretched, and brushes her cheek. William's hand was not as skilled as Turold's, but he gave the man an expression of regret and the woman one of love, and here, over the gateway, the text 'Where a cleric and Ælfgyva part.'

'Who was she?' said Turold.

'She is,' said the Queen, 'a sister, in York now, I believe.'

'And the cleric?'

'Do you need to ask?'

'Bishop Odo?'

'I never replied…'

'And what have they to do with the hanging?'

'Another question?'

'Forgive me,' said Turold. 'I did not mean…'

'The King has his reasons.'

'I never…'

The Queen held her hand up. 'It is your job to complete the hanging, Turold.' Her voice was stern. 'And whatever his Majesty wants; that is his privilege.'

'Forgive me.'

'You are forgiven,' she said, and her voice lightened. She rubbed the corner of her right eye with the tips of her fingers. I could see a piece of grit stuck there. 'Take the sketch back to the workshop, stitch it in place and do not forget: you are working a scene designed by the King.'

He bowed, rolled the parchment and said, 'Your Majesty.'

She stood, we stood, the smell of lavender was strong. 'This is one chamber I wish you to consider,' she said, 'but later. I will call for you again.'

'I would be honoured.'

'I know,' said the Queen, and she banged on the door. The tense Lady opened it from the outside, we bowed and left.

Turold showed Ermenburga the King's sketch. 'What does it mean?'

'You do not know?'

'Would I ask if I did?'

She studied the sketch.

'Would I?'

She frowned and said, 'No,' impatiently. 'You would not.'

'So?'

'All I know is what I heard.'

'Is that all anyone knows?'

'Not if they were there. Not if they saw it happen.'

'Of course. But even then, the truth can twist.' He pointed to the hanging. The text read 'Here Bishop Odo holding a mace encourages the young men.' 'Odo told me that this is what he did, and he was there.'

'The Bishop's word is proved by others, and I think,' said Ermenburga, and she tapped his knee with the tip of one finger, 'you know that.'

He did.

Odo wears a quilted jacket over his hauberk, and the young squires, who believed that William had been killed, rallied. Eustace, the papal gonfalon in his left hand, pointed with his right to the Duke, who raised his helmet and showed his face. It is truth because Odo said it was, William agreed, the gonfalon breaks into the border, the young men resume their charge.

'I only know what I am told,' said Turold, 'and I know nothing about this.' He tapped the sketch. 'And if I am to translate it, I must know what it means.'

'Ha!' Ermenburga laughed. 'And what is translation?'

'Discovering what something means, and giving it a different voice.'

'Is it?'

'Yes?'

'So if you are to translate it, you must know what it means? What does that mean?'

'Abbess!'

I dropped a stitch.

'Master Turold?'

'Who is Ælfgyva?'

'She,' said Ermenburga, 'is a sister in...'

'York?'

'You know...'

'That is all I know.'

'Nothing more?'

'Please,' said Turold. 'How many more times?'

Ermenburga looked at him. I could not translate her eyes. 'It is said,' she said, 'that of the women Bishop Odo has known, she is the only one he regretted leaving.'

'Ælfgyva?'

'Yes.'

'When was this?'

She shrugged. 'A year after the conquest, maybe two...'

Turold tugged his beard. He regretted having it cut, there was not enough to pull. 'And it is common knowledge?'

'I do not know. Some people have heard the story, others have not. Common knowledge...'

'Did he love her?'

Now Ermenburga slipped on the first face I had seen her wear, the one in her cell, the stick-faced queen of Nunnaminster. She did not know about love between men and women. She knew about respect, she knew about companionship but she wore Christ's ring. The thought of Bishop Odo loving a woman, the idea of a woman loving him, disgusted her. She straightened her back and said, 'How should I know?'

'You did not hear?'

'No,' she said, 'I did not.'

'But their parting,' he said, 'to be reminded will upset him?'

'Maybe...'

'So why does William wish to include it?'

'Maybe he wishes to upset the Bishop.'

'He has no reason to...'

'He has every reason.'

'It makes no sense.'

'Why should the sense of it mean anything to you? It is your job to do the stitching, not...'

'I cannot,' said Turold, and he took the sketch from Ermenburga, 'do my job if I do not understand its meaning. To place a scene like this; it is a mystery to everyone but three people, and only one of them wants to be reminded of it. I think...'

'The King.'

'What?'

'The King is the one who wants to be reminded. I think you should understand that better than I do.'

'I expected...'

'What,' she said, 'did you expect?'

Turold stared at the sketch, he stared at the hanging, he stared at Ermenburga, then he stared into space. 'My job...' he said.

She touched his shoulder. 'Do it well.'

'Do I,' he whispered, 'ever do it any other way?'

On a cold day, as the last leaves were ripped from the trees and spots of rain blew from the forest, Martha said, 'I'm going to have a child.'

Oh Lord.

She looked at me. 'Your child.'

I put my arms around her and held her tight. She held me as if she was about to fall, she squeezed the breath from my body. 'Are you pleased?'

I nodded.

A child.

'What do you want?'

My voice.

'Boy or girl?'

I put my hand on her belly.

'Boy?'

I nodded.

'Girl?'

I nodded.

'Both?'

I nodded.

She laughed. 'You're greedy,' she said.

I am not.

She put her hand on mine and said, 'Your child.'

A father must have a voice. My voice is waiting for the child to be born. It will arrive with it.

'My father wants to see you,' she said. 'He is happier than I am.'

Martha has a happy face.

I lifted her tunic and kissed her paps. She put her hand to my head and held me there. I could feel her heart beat, and the blood as it ran through her body. I listened for the child's cry, I listened for the sound of its legs rubbing together, but I heard nothing. Martha was warm, warmer than ever, feeding two.

I wanted her. I laid her on the grass. The grass was damp, the top branches of the trees creaked in the wind. Her belly was no bigger, but I did not put any weight on it. We lay side by side, she wrapped her legs around my waist. As I was in her, her hair was in my mouth, as we moved, the rain became heavy. It rattled through the trees and dripped on us. It was cold but we were hot, there was no music in the air, but I heard music that had been there before. Whistles and flutes, drums; they played together and we played with them.

Bishop Odo brought news of William's defeat at Dol. He stumbled into the workshop, he did not know whether to be afraid or thank God. He knew the King had suffered heavy losses, he knew Philip of France had ranged against him, he knew the siege machines had failed, Dol was defended with more might and cunning than his spies had reported, William had retreated in panic, then disarray; now he was returning to England. His power was not diminished but it was not extended; he had learnt lessons, he needed peace and rest to reflect upon his mistakes.

Odo said, 'Some say the King is badly wounded. He is returning to die.'

'And others?'

'That he is not. Think the worst and hope for the best.'

'Yes?'

Odo jabbed the air with a finger, stuck it in his hair, twirled it and said, 'Yes. He is wounded, but not badly.'

'That is the truth?'

'That is what I hope...'

'Hope...' said Turold. He stabbed the linen and pulled the wool through. '...is good medicine. Ask Robert.'

'Why?'

'He hopes, don't you, Robert?'

I nodded.

'He is going to be a father...'

Odo looked at me and shook his head.

'Hope,' said Turold, 'is a poultice for the mind.'

'What are you talking about?'

Father.

Turold's mind was attached to the hanging as Odo's was to confusion. One only wanted to finish, the other did not know whether he was finished or beginning a new life, free of the shadow of his brother. Both ideas terrified him, he wished he could be away from Winchester. He would like a month in the forest, time to remind himself of his calling. God was his Lord, there was no other. He stared at the hanging, but he did not see it.

'Without hope,' said Turold, 'even the keenest ambition is doomed.'

'Ambition,' said Odo, 'is dangerous.'

'Have you said that before?'

'Maybe.'

'I thought so.'

'You agree?'

Turold did not know. He shook his head. 'Without ambition, the hanging would never have been stitched. It has its uses.'

Odo was not convinced. He turned away, passed the King's scene without noticing it, scratched his chin and narrowed his eyes, as if he was thinking about a serious problem. William's blood drained from his body and ran to the sea; it floated from Normandy to England and drifted on to the shore. He wanted the power the King might lose but he did not want it. He wanted to see William alive, he wanted to reassure him, he wanted the security that would come from the man's gratitude. He was afraid the madness he felt was born of his mind's betrayal. He had never wanted to be the man he knew William thought he was. He pushed the workshop door open and stood for a moment, staring at the sky. Rain clouds were rolling from the west; he drew his cloak around him and hunched his shoulders. I felt some pity for him there. He was lost, he kicked his left ankle with his right foot and the door slammed shut behind him.

26

Martha was ill. She could not walk without falling over, she sweated, her eyes faded. Her fingernails broke without reason and she could not hold things. She went to bed, I joined her mother at her side, and held my hand on her belly.

Her mother was a fat woman, her father was a fat man, there was flour in their hair and a light dusting on their faces.

They said nothing. They stared at Martha as though she was a stranger. Once a child, then a mother, here is the father. They stared at me as though I lived in the bakery, as if they had known me all their lives. Maybe, I thought, they stole Martha when she was a baby. How could two fat people have such a thin girl? Her real mother was searching for her. I could be her brother. Her father had died of a broken heart. I looked at her face.

Her eyes were ringed by shadows, her lips were covered with tiny cracks. I held a damp cloth, and dabbed her forehead. She was hot, she poked her tongue out and licked her lips. 'Robert,' she said.

Does it hurt?

'It hurts.'

Do not die, Martha.

'It hurts so much.' She put her hand on mine and squeezed it. Something was running through her body. I was scared.

Her father and mother said nothing. They knew they had lost her to me, I was the one she needed. I could fetch sister Ethel.

'Fetch sister Ethel.'

I fetched her.

She brought a bag of all the things she needed, sat on the cot, lifted Martha's dress and laid her hand on her belly. She tapped it gently, then laid her ear to it and listened. As she listened, she widened her eyes and counted quietly. Then she said, 'What do you feel?'

'Pain.'

'All over?'

'Just here.' She put her finger on her belly. She looked down, then she looked at me, and her eyes were full of tears.

'Have you eaten?'

'No.'

'You must.'

'I cannot…'

'Food will give you strength.' Ethel spoke quietly. I remember her voice. The softer it was the closer the poultice. She put her hand on her bag.

'…it will not stay down.'

'This,' said Ethel, 'will help you.'

Martha.

Ethel rummaged in her bag, pulled out a muslin, a bag of bran and a bag of herbs. 'Robert?' she said.

What?

'Boil some water, please.'

I looked at Martha and she looked at me. She nodded at me. Her face was drifting. I did not want to lose her.

'Robert?'

Going.

I stood with Martha's father while the water boiled. He said nothing. He had a voice but chose not to use it. When he moved, a cloud of flour followed him. I stared at the fire and he stared at a stack of loaves. A rat sat up and watched us, Ethel's murmuring voice carried to where we were. The world could have been on its side, bells could have rung, the hills could have been full of lost sheep. Time flies, innocence dies and trees crack in the cold wind.

Bishop Odo left for the coast, to meet the King. He left in a hurry. He was pale and could not decide which horse to ride. First he wanted a black, then a piebald, then a brown mare.

I watched him go. I was on the wall. I had sat with Martha, I had stitched with Turold, I had listened to the wind in the forest and said a prayer for Rainald. He had grown a beard like mist and had believed in doubt. He had died in the day, in his cot. Martha lay in her cot, Ethel's yellow poultice sat on her belly. She would not stop sweating, she could not speak. Her hands shrunk on her arms, and the bones in her neck showed. Her breathing sounded like rain rattling on a roof.

Odo's men were patient with him. As he ranted about the black horse, and then the piebald, they stood in small groups and picked their noses. They said, 'He is mad.'

'Look out.'

'Where?'

Odo was trying to mount the brown mare. When he put his leg over her back she took a step forward; he grabbed the reins and tried to pull her back, but she took another step. 'Whoa!' he called, she shied to one side and he slipped off the mounting block.

There was sleet in the air, and the wind whistled through gaps in the walls. I hunched my shoulders. The taller I grew the colder I felt.

Odo mounted at the third attempt, then his men mounted and gathered around him. He held the reins in one hand, twirled his hair with the other and looked over his shoulder, towards where I was standing. I almost waved at him, but I stopped myself.

Four English soldiers attempted to stop the attacking Norman knights, but they rode their horses through the defences, and killed Harold.

The first soldier lies dead, killed by a spear through his heart. He has not had time to unsheath his sword. His face is dull and his eyes are closed. He was tired before the battle began.

The second soldier, his shield stuck with arrows, prepares to throw his spear, the third soldier has just thrown his. It is flying towards an angry Norman on an angry horse, but misses.

The fourth soldier has an arrow in his eye. He is trying to pull it out. The point is in his brain, the Norman rides past him, and with a single blow, kills Harold.

Harold dies slowly. He cannot believe what has happened. He had been caught between Edward and William, a King's touch and a Duke's relics. He had been caught between William and Harold Hardrada. He had forced the march from the north and fought Hastings without Edwin or Morcar. The wind had never favoured him. His men were brave, they believed in his right to rule but they die, their armour is taken from their bodies, and their swords gathered up.

Harold dies slowly. He drops his axe. His mouth splits his face, his one eye is closed and his hands lie by his side, as if prepared for the shroud.

Harold dead in the hanging. As Odo rode to the coast, Turold moved to the gap between the palace at Rouen and the horse, and began to stitch the pillared gateway that frames Ælfgyva. The only gate of its kind in the hanging, he stole its style from a page in the abbey Bible. The pillars twist and grow beasts' heads. The beasts wear collars around their necks, and flash their tongues.

Here a cleric and Ælfgyva part.

I fed the wool.

Bishop Odo rode through the sleet to the coast, and his men rode with him. He camped the night in the forest and rode again at daybreak, and waited ten days at Bosham. The wind was too strong for a crossing, he spent more time in the town church than anyone imagined he would. His men had been expecting days of drinking; he allowed them to do as they wished, but he was drawn to prayer and contemplation, harried by his mind into considering his purpose, and the reason for his ambition.

We moved Martha to a nunnery cell, where she would be warmer and closer to sister Ethel. Her father and I carried her on a pallet. She said nothing, he said nothing, Ethel walked beside us and said, 'Faith, men.'

Faith. Have faith and live, doubt and die. I had little faith but no doubt Martha would live. We covered her with skins and rugs, so all she showed was her face. I put my hand over it as we crossed the precinct yard and climbed the steps to her cell. I felt her breath in my palm, she opened her eyes, then closed them.

Her cot was raised and surrounded by curtains. A table had been set beside it, and a stool. There was a bowl on the table and strips of linen piled; the window was shuttered, and a curtain hung over the door. Candles burnt, the smell of Ethel's herbs hung in the air. There were no draughts.

'She will be comfortable here,' said Ethel.

Martha's father nodded.

I nodded.

Ethel looked at us as if we were two fools, sent from the bottom of the hill to the top, and we had always thought the top was the same height as the bottom.

'I know he is dumb,' she said to Martha's father, 'but I did not know you were.'

Martha's father shrugged.

I looked at him.

'Are you?' she said.

He shook his head.

Martha lay in the cot, the covers were piled over her. I sat beside her and dabbed her forehead. When she opened her eyes and smiled at me, Ethel said, 'We have moved you to St Mary's. You will be more comfortable here.'

'Talk is not comfortable,' said her father.

'What?'

Her father did not repeat what he had said.

'I will mix a poultice.'

Martha did not stop smiling at me.

Her father left.

Ethel went to a small room next to the cell, and stoked a fire.

'Get in with me,' said Martha.

I got into the cot. She was hot, she took my hand and put it on her belly. Her heart was beating fast and her breath smelt of rotting leaves.

'Can you feel it?' she said.

Yes.

'When I get well, we will have a cot like this.' She looked at the curtains and rubbed her chin on the covers.

Anything.

Martha had blue eyes. How blue were they? Were they as blue as the sky or as blue as the sea?'

'I am hot.'

Her hair was brown.

'Too hot.'

The smell of boiling bran came from the small room, and the sound of a spoon stirring.

'Do not leave me,' she said.

I will never be a moment away.

'I need you.'

Ethel pounded some herbs.

I put my fingers to my lips. Do not talk. She lifted her hand and touched my cheek. I kissed her.

'And love you,' she said.

'Out!' said Ethel.

Now?

'Go on,' said Martha.

I stayed with her until I was pulled out of the cot and chased to the door; I stood and watched until the curtains were drawn around the cot, and the smell of the poultice made me wish for fresh air.

Harold dies slowly. His army are either killed on the battlefield or chased from it.

As night falls, William and his army camp amongst the dead and dying. Smoke obscures the stars, the moon does not show. The relics' power is affirmed but heaven is closed. The wailing men, the stink of guts, a low moan of agony rumbles over the Normans. Here, a knight stands and hacks the head from a wounded Englishman's shoulders.

Piles of swords lie in the border, stacks of armour and a horse's head. I stitched a bird with an arrow through its heart, and the branches of the single tree the battle was fought beneath. The ground was firm for fighting, the horses were strong and here, tied to a post are five of them, drinking from a stream.

While the sisters stitched the carnage and the night, Turold worked on the King's scene. He made Bishop Odo young and slim, with an honest face and light hands. His right caresses Ælfgyva, he holds the other to his waist. He has small fingers, strong legs and wide hips. His cloak is held by a fancy clasp.

I sat next to him and fed the wool. His hair stood up in spikes, there was a bald patch in his beard. He scratched it and said, 'Ælfgyva.'

She is a small nun.

'I think she was young.'

She looks young.

'As young as Martha.' He sat back, let his needle hang and put his hand on my shoulder.

Martha, I am thinking.

'Do Ethel's potions relieve her pain?'

I do not know.

'Can she sit up?'

Yes.

'Could she stitch in bed?'

Yes.

'We need tassels. She could sew them.'

What tassels?

223

'Here.' Turold took his needle, stuck it in a scrap of linen and gave it to me. 'My gift to both of you. My sharpest needle. More useful than a ring.'

I held the wool box.

'And take all the wool you need.' He looked along the frame to where Ermenburga sat. She nodded at him and smiled at me. The bats watched us, rolled around each other in their hanging, but they heard nothing.

27

Martha at night and Martha in the day, Martha sitting up in her cot and then Martha lying down, asleep. Martha, with a name that calms weather, a face branded on my eyes and her voice in my ears. Martha with Turold's needle, Turold's needle on the stool beside her. My child, her child, Ethel's poultices and a bowl of soup.

Bishop Odo returned with William. They came to Winchester as night fell, the noise of their party could be heard an hour before they were seen. Footmen carried tapers, their flames shot the forest with light, the shadows they cast were taller than the trees, and climbed the city walls to where I stood.

Matilda stood at the gate. The King reined his horse when he saw her, dismounted, unbuckled his sword, passed it to his squire and walked the last hundred paces. When he stood before the Queen, before she had a chance to lift his ring, he touched her head, as if in blessing. They exchanged words, he reached into his tunic and pulled out a wrap. He gave this to her, she held it to her chest, bowed and stood to one side. He bowed, she took his arm and they entered the city together. I heard a ripple of voices as they passed through the gate and into the streets, and a pigeon flew over me.

One pigeon, one King, his Queen, his Bishop and a column of knights, squires, archers and footmen. There was no sign that the King was wounded, no limp in his walk, no bandages on his head, his arms moved freely. He adjusted his cloak as he walked, Matilda did not take her eyes off him, he leant towards her and said something. She nodded, a horn blew from the palace.

Odo followed, ten paces behind. He walked with a limp, he looked over his shoulder, he looked up to where I was standing, he twirled hair with his fingers and twitched his head. The noise of horses' hoofs and clattering armour filled the streets, shutters opened, heads poked out, children were sent back to bed.

'Trouble always returns to roost,' said Turold. He came to stand behind me, Ermenburga followed.

'"Although affliction cometh not forth of the dust,"' she said, '"neither doth trouble spring out of the ground."'

'You sound like Rainald.'

'"Man is born unto trouble, as the sparks fly upward."'

'The words of prophets, as I said to him, are not...'

'The book of Job,' she said, 'is not a work of prophecy.'

'No?'

'If you knew anything, Turold, you would...'

'If I knew anything?' He laughed. 'Can't you tell when I'm mocking you?'

'Do not try to hide your ignorance with pretence. You are too clever for that.'

'I am ignorant and clever?' he said. 'At the same time or every other day?'

Be quiet.

'Job,' she said. 'You should read it.'

'I have no time to read.'

'No one,' she said, 'knows who wrote it.'

'Knowing,' said Turold, 'who created a work of art has nothing to do with the work itself. It cannot change the way you look at it. How you appreciate it.'

Oh Lord.

'It should not but it does. Knowing a hanging was designed by you makes it worth inspection.'

'Does it?'

I turned around and stared at Turold. I had been happy to watch William and Odo return. I did not want to listen to them argue. I wagged my finger at him, spread my arms, pointed below and cupped my hands over my ears.

'Robert?' he said.

Sometimes, you speak because you have nothing better to do.

'How is Martha?'

Martha, at night and in the day, Martha sitting up in bed and then lying down asleep. Martha, with a name that charms wild dogs, a face branded on my eyes and her voice in my ears. My child, her child, her thinning body, Ethel's poultices and a bowl of soup sitting on a table.

As the sisters stitched William's haranguing of his army and the march on London, Bishop Odo came to the workshop. He knew. He had already prayed for forgiveness.

He was quiet now, and had lost weight. He looked as though he had not slept for a week, his arms hung by his side as he walked along the strips, and here he stopped and stood in front of the King's scene.

I pitied him. As he studied the scene, he shrank, he sank at the knees, he did not fidget.

He raised his hand, spread his fingers and held them over the work, but he did not touch it. A tired breath climbed from his belly to his mouth. He cocked his head to one side, then the other, then moved closer.

Turold left the Norman army — William had ordered them to limit the pillage — and went to the Bishop. He coughed in his approach, and scuffed his feet on the floor. Odo did not look up. His eyes were fixed upon Ælfgyva's face, her forgiving hands and her tiny feet. Her beautiful eyes and her lovely smile. And he was so young and slim, with an honest face and a light touch. His cloak is the finest in the hanging, his tonsure shines like ice.

'Master Turold,' he whispered.

'My Lord.'

'Master Turold...'

I picked my sleeve and said a prayer for Martha.

'...this is what we have been waiting to see.'

'The King...'

Odo held up his hand. 'No,' he whispered. 'I do not want to hear.' He squinted at the beasts' heads. 'I never want to hear.'

'I tried,' said Turold, 'to do justice to his sketch.'

'Do you have it?'

Turold took it from his sleeve and gave it to the Bishop, who unrolled it, studied it and said, 'This text...'

'Yes?'

'Here...' he swallowed, '...a cleric and Ælfgyva part.'

'It is what the King wants.'

'Please,' said Odo, and now he gripped Turold's arm. His eyes were wide. 'Please do not say they part.'

'Why not?'

Odo did not answer.

'Bishop?'

'Please?'

'The King will not like it.'

'I am patron and I ask you, please.' He sniffed.

'The King...'

'The King knows the truth, and so do I, but to be shown parting — I would rather us shown in greeting...'

'I cannot change the pose.'

'I am not asking you to. Just the word.' Odo reached up and now he touched the hanging.

'The word?'

'Turold.'

'It would be easy...'

'Please?'

Turold looked away, tugged his beard, looked back and said, 'I will have a lapse of memory.'

Odo nodded. His face was calm, with faith at its edges. 'If I was to be delivered a reminder, this is the way I would choose...' He brushed Ælfgyva's face and turned towards us. 'I am reminded but I never forgot. But he knows,' he whispered, 'or thinks he knows. He thinks this scene will be a slap; he thinks I will regret knowing Ælfgyva. He wishes to ruin my ambition, but in truth...' he turned back to the scene and laid the palms of his hands over the figures '...this is a caress.'

You do not need a voice to say a prayer. I have a short prayer for Martha, and I repeat it twenty times a day. God hears me, He sees her in her cot, and watches Ethel as she prepares her poultices.

'I am glad,' said Turold.

'And so am I,' said Odo. He looked at us again. He held my eyes for a moment, then Turold's. He rubbed the tips of his fingers together, then smelt them. 'Are you surprised?'

'I did not know what to expect, apart from surprise. So the surprise is no surprise at all.'

'What?'

'I am resigned,' said Turold.

'Then we are resigned together,' said Odo, and now he put his hand on my master's shoulder. 'You to me and I to the truth.'

'And what is that?'

'My truth?'

'Yes.'

Odo patted Turold's shoulder, turned to the hanging and touched Ælfgyva's face again. 'To be reminded...' he said.

'I...'

'...to be reminded like this; I know I made more mistakes than I should have. All the way from there to here, and you. And Robert, and the Abbess. And William. He is above flattery and favour.' He sniffed. 'I smelt him today, and he smelt of fire.'

He does smell of fire. He smells of flesh and cold metal, sharp edges and horse.

'And the Queen smelt of fire too.'

The hanging ends with the coronation of King William. He sits enthroned, his face is big and grave. To his left, Geoffrey of Coutances holds his hands in prayer; to his right, Alfred of York looks nervous.

Ermenburga came to me while Turold stitched the King's eyes, and she said, 'Come with me.'

Me?

'Now.'

Why?

'I need him,' said Turold.

'Martha needs him more.' Ermenburga looked at him and shook her head.

I am gone, out of the workshop, across the precinct yard, up the steps to her cell. There is a smell I do not recognise, and the sound of sobbing.

'Wait!' Ermenburga was behind me.

My head is pounding heavy music, heavy words and dead prayers, all together, all filling my ears.

The smell is coming from under the door. I tried to open it.

'It's bolted!'

Why?

'Knock twice.'

I knocked twice. I waited for a moment, Ermenburga caught up with me, the bolt was drawn and the door opened.

The curtains had been taken from around the cot, and piled by the window. Martha lay flat, two sisters were standing over her, I saw her face between them.

Is she dead?

'I am sorry,' said Ethel. She came from her small room and took my arm. 'I could do nothing.'

What happened?

'She has lost her child…'

The child?

'…and blood. But she is a strong girl. Very strong.'

Will she die?

'I think,' said Ethel, 'with God's help and our prayers, she will live.'

And your poultices.

'I will change her poultice tonight.'

Please.

'I think she would like you to sit with her.'

The two nuns moved away from the bed, Ethel pushed me gently in the back, and I went to Martha.

She looked as though the blood had been drained from her body, her hair was wet, her lips were dry. I kissed them and licked them. She whispered, 'Robert.' I touched her cheek. It was freezing. I took a rug and pulled it up to her chin. I sat down, held her hand and listened to the nuns in the small room. They were washing pails and towels, murmuring prayers.

'She died inside me,' she said. 'I could not feed her.'

I put a finger to her lips.

'No,' she said, 'I can talk. Please.'

Talk to me.

'I wanted to but could not. All the time I was wishing and praying, but my body was saying no. I tried to make it understand, but it refused to listen.' She coughed. 'My mind is not strong enough.' She lifted her hand and pointed to the small room. 'Nor was my body.'

You are strong enough for two.

'I am sorry.'

I know jealousy and ambition are lost before they are found, and nothing can check them, but great men do not. This makes them great.

I have seen small men confuse themselves with jealousy and ambition, but they do not understand why they are confused, and that makes them small. We are small people, we must prove that great men are who they are.

Martha's child, the size of a hand, was swilled away by the sisters. The cell smelt sick. Martha's hand was cold, the veins in her arms throbbed, and a fucking, fucking dog barked outside.

Christ! You have put me here, You gave me the choice but You gave me no choice at all. A voice would give me the choice; a dumb, bastard throat gives me no chance. I bleed with spit and my head breeds more words, more garble than anyone with a voice could. The hanging is poison, the hanging is linen, stitched with wool. The hanging can be rolled up and carried on a man's head. Its threads breathe but they have no voice. The text speaks but it has no voice. It is enough. No more.

Ethel came from her room and stood next to me. She held a steaming pot, the two sisters muttered to each other. The mutter is from a voice's bad side, its scheming head. I kissed Martha again and her mouth broke on mine. Ethel put her hand on my head, I stood up, Ethel moved to the cot and the two sisters showed me to the door.

28

There is no one like Turold. I have seen him in every way, but I do not know him. He swings from one thing to another; skill and foolishness, cunning and anger, resignation and ambition, I can never tell. I know Odo, the warrior Bishop of Bayeux, ordained at nineteen, father of a dozen bastards. At Hastings he rallied the young men in their panic, now he prefers the attention of martyrs. He intends to retreat for two months, to contemplate God's will. He has forgiven Turold, forgiven the King and forgotten Ermenburga.

Martha bathes in front of the bakery ovens; her breasts are like apples, swollen by a wet season. I will protect her when I am not with her, as William protects us.

His clothes are magnificent, his face is grave, his hair is the colour of rust. He is with Matilda, his men and her Ladies are absent, the hanging has been removed from the frames and hung around the walls of the workshop.

The weather is freezing. A cold wind blew.

Bathing.

Rust.

Turold and I stood with the King and Queen, and Bishop Odo. Ermenburga and Martha sat in a corner by the stove, the sisters stood in a line along the far wall.

'When you stand back,' said William, 'and see the hanging as one piece, there is no doubt...' he nodded '...the ships sail, the horses charge.'

'And the borders,' said Matilda. 'Your animals are so lively.'

'The apprentices,' said Turold, 'learnt their arts.'

'I will have them,' she said.

'They would be honoured...'

'Would they show me their favourites?'

Turold beckoned the apprentices. When they bowed, they disappeared into their habits. They appeared again and Edith, the oldest, took her to the lion that welcomes the other beasts to his lair. A monkey introduces the beasts. Edith said, 'These were stitched by Isabel, our youngest.'

'Isabel?'

'Yes.'

'Where is she?'

Isabel stepped forward and fell to her knees.

'Your animals are charming.' Cough. 'You will work for me.'

'M...'

'Please, child. Stand.'

Edith helped Isabel to her feet. 'Majesty,' she said, but she could not look at the Queen's eyes.

'Good.'

Isabel bowed again, Edith stopped her before she touched the floor with her nose.

'And your sisters will join you.'

'Majesty.'

'Show me more.'

Wolves lick their paws to silence their stalking.

The Raven, the Fox and the Cheese.

The Cow, the Sheep and the Goat hunt with the Lion.

Ploughing, sowing, harrowing. Boy with a sling-shot.

Bear-baiting.

Camels.

Peacocks.

Fire-drakes.

Griffons.

Pards.

Quails.

William, Bishop Odo and Turold made their own inspection. The King was slow and thoughtful, Odo was quiet. He had the air of a man home from a tiring journey. He had thought he would never see home again, he had rejected it, but now he has seen it he is glad. It did not give him a burning head or dreams of any kind. He walked with his hands behind his back, his hair was shorn, he wore fresh clothes. He looked at Turold and thanked God.

Turold was anxious to explain subtleties an untutored eye would miss. 'Here,' he said, 'the English horses are hog-maned.'

'I noticed,' said William.

'And only Harold wears spurs.'

The King leant towards the hanging, squinted at Harold and nodded his head.

This scene — Harold riding with hawks to Bosham — was begun as I first held Martha's breasts. I left Turold and sat with her and Ermenburga. I held my hands over the stove. When they were warm, I put them to Martha's cheeks. She put her hands on mine and smiled through them. 'Speak to me,' she said.

I am.

233

'Speak to me.'

I moved towards her and put my lips to her ear and whistled a low, quiet note.

'No,' she whispered. 'Speak.'

Listen.

'I want to hear you say my name.'

I have tried. I have carried your name from my head to my belly and tried to catch it with my breath.

'Martha,' she said.

Martha.

'Martha?' said Ermenburga.

'You would have a beautiful voice.'

Ermenburga looked at me and shook her head. The girl in her and the girl in me.

'Robert?'

Talk is not comfortable.

'I love you.'

Do not say anything else.

'Do you love me?'

I nodded.

On the far side of the workshop, William had his hand on Bishop Odo's shoulder, and was talking in his ear. Turold was standing back, squinting at a horse's head.

Matilda, surrounded by sisters, stood to admire the eels and fish that swim in the River Couesnon.

A gust of wind blew across the precinct yard and forced a window shutter. The draught blew through the workshop and disturbed the hanging. It rippled in waves along the wall, so the action appeared to move backwards, undoing itself. I jumped up and closed the shutter. The hanging settled again. Turold put his hand up and called, 'Thank you, Robert.'

'Yes,' said the King, and he looked at me. 'Thank you.' I bowed and then he bowed to me, in Winchester, before the people who knew me and Odo's hanging, and the bats hung asleep in the eaves.

From the forest and the hills to the town; one of my pigeons returned. She sat on the window ledge and watched me. I put my hand out, offered a finger, she fluffed her feathers and squeaked. She was the one with red on her wings.

Martha joined me at the window. As she did, the pigeon started, spread her wings and hopped off the ledge. She flew over the yard, turned and rose over the walls of Nunnaminster. Below us, Martha's father carried a bag of flour from his store to the bakery. At the door, he looked up to our room. We backed away from the window and fell on to Turold's cot.

'Will you go back to him?' she said.

No.

'Do you miss home?'

No.

'Would you rather stay with me?'

Yes.

I work for the nuns of Nunnaminster. I am the only man with the freedom of the nunnery. Women treat me as their boy, they give me familiar names and believe, because I do not speak their language, that the names make sense. I understand what they are talking about, but do not believe it. I live close to God but never feel His presence; the nun's God is elusive, He walks barefoot on air, and never speaks.

Turold promised word from home, but it has not come. He is working designs for the Queen, his workshop in Bayeux is not as large or light as Winchester's, but he needs home. I have a home here. It is a small room, with a small window. It smells of flour and straw, and is too high in the house for rats.

Turold had promised one thing and Odo had promised trouble, but the Bishop is a different man now, and in retreat, in Rouen. His room is small, with a small window, a crucifix on the wall and a benched desk. He wears a monk's habit, his ambition is not dead, but sleeping. His hanging decorates his hall, but the hall is locked, no one sees it. Sunlight does not fade the wool, and the linen will be as fresh as the day it was drawn from Ermenburga's stock.

Linen.
  Forest.
  Walls.
  Pigeon.
Distance is only miles, and as the sun rises, so there is no real distance between men and women, only faithless acts. I can speak but I cannot talk.
  'I do not have to work today,' said Martha.
  Why not?
  'And I have some cheese.'
  I can smell it.
  'Do you want some?'
  Yes.
  'How much?'
  A lot.
  'Bread?'
  No.
Martha cut me some cheese. It smelt of old water. A pigeon came to the window and sat on the ledge to watch us. It was nesting weather.

Made in the USA
Monee, IL
14 April 2021

65759672R00142